Time Tells

By Jan Woodhouse

New Generation **Publishing**

Acknowledgements

Many thanks to the various people who have
encouraged me in writing this novel.

Thanks especially to:-

Anne Woodbridge, for proofreading and for her
alertness to inconsistencies.

Karen Godfrey of The Literary Consultancy for her
comments on my first, embryonic draft.

William Armstrong (former Norfolk Coroner), Ami
Roberts of Sussex Police, and Anthony Deacon of
Norfolk Police, for taking the time and trouble to
answer my questions and clarify where I had gone
astray. Any errors that have slipped through the net in
spite of this help are my own.

Notes

North Walsham exists, but there is no Willowherb Close in the town, and no nearby village called Dartingham. All the characters are fictional.

One

The last thing I wanted to concern myself with was another death – even, or especially, if I'd never actually known the person who died.

Sarah's suicide earlier in the year was still uneasy in my mind, lodged there like a DVD that had become stuck and refused to be ejected. I would sometimes see her – or her ghost – out of the corner of my eye when shopping at the supermarket. Or hurrying past the window of my favourite coffee shop. Or she would appear in my office, the way she used to, edgy, torn between hesitancy and impatience.

Oliver refused to talk about her. More accurately, since she'd died, he'd hardly spoken to me at all about anything besides work. Our relationship was as stone-cold dead as Sarah's body should have been, except that she kept coming back to haunt me, tripping my conscience with a sense of guilt which, if not totally misplaced, was wildly disproportionate.

She'd even appeared in a recent dream, looking like she did when we were friends some twenty years ago – a gawky teenager in school uniform a size too large. Several inches taller than me, she'd put her hands on my shoulders and hunched down, so that her face was right up close to mine. I could feel her breath, like the fluttering of a moth. I could smell it, musty, like an old woman's breath. She was saying, 'You need to know what really happened. The truth.'

Two

As it happened, I'd been trying to talk to my mother about Sarah that Sunday. Just before we were interrupted by one of those before-and-after moments, and everything veered off on a different course.

We'd been eating roast pork with apple sauce, followed by apple pie. It was September, and someone had given her a bag of fallen Bramleys.

After the initial shock of Sarah's suicide, I hadn't had a lot to say about it. What was there to say? When her name was mentioned at work, I'd kept my head down. When other staff took time out to go to her funeral, I'd stayed in the office. But as the weeks and months moved on, there were questions I wanted answered. Questions that, like a niggling recurrent headache, hovered on the edge of my consciousness, however much I tried to pretend they weren't there.

So I asked my mother whether it had worried her at all when I stopped being Sarah's friend. Surely she must have wondered about it. Sarah had been in and out of our house, almost one of the family, for all those years. Hadn't it been rather selfish and uncaring of me to cut her off like that?

I expected her to exonerate me by saying something like 'We all do some selfish things when we're young' or 'Things change, we all have to move on.' Instead, she pursed her lips the way she used to do when I was a child, pestering her with questions she hadn't worked out how to answer. She muttered that it was a long time ago, which wasn't very helpful. And then she said, 'Anyhow, she did alright for herself, didn't she? She had a good job. We'll never know why she decided to do what she did. It was all very sad, but it's best to let sleeping dogs lie.'

I knew now, of course, that Sarah's mother had suffered from depression. I also knew that her father had been run over by a taxi while Sarah was at university, and soon after that her mother had sold their house and moved up north. Mum had told me all that a long while ago, when she still worked as a dental receptionist, soaking up the local gossip.

I wasn't ready to change the conversation. I thought those particular dogs had slept for long enough. I hadn't told my mother about Sarah's relationship with Oliver. I hadn't even told her about my own relationship with Oliver. She'd long stopped quizzing me about my love life, or lack of it. Suddenly, I wanted to confide in her, like I did when I was a teenager on my first dates, and she was the best mum in the world, always ready with hot chocolate and a hug when I felt like being a child again.

Whether I would actually have opened up to her just then – and, if so, how the conversation would have progressed – I'll never know. Because that was the moment when the blue lights of an ambulance came strobing through the living-room window.

***

'*That's* a rare beast,' was all Mum said, at first. She'd recently become involved in some sort of Save The Ambulance campaign. A bit like Save The Whale.

But then her curiosity kicked in. There weren't all that many emergencies, right there, in my mother's quiet little close.

She jumped up from the dinner table, and was about to go out in her slippers and make herself useful. I jumped up too, and put a restraining hand on her arm. 'It's an ambulance, Mum. Those guys do know what they're doing.'

She dithered. 'They might need some help.'

'They won't. And all you'll do is look like one of those horrible voyeurs. Like those people who gawp at traffic accidents.'

'I suppose.'

'Sit down. Finish your glass of wine.'

But that was one thing she couldn't do. She stood conspicuously at the window. She doesn't like net curtains, thinks they're old-fashioned and fuddy-duddy. It's something we have in common, although personally I prefer venetian blinds to the fish-tank effect.

'They've gone into Lizzie's house,' she informed me. 'She's such a nice woman. A bit unconventional. I used to see her at the surgery, once in a blue moon. Brenda's told me she's an artist, paints and makes things. I don't think she ever sells anything.'

And then, as we watched to see what would happen next, whether someone would come out on a stretcher, a police car pulled up behind the ambulance, followed a short while later by a second, everything tracked by my mother's commentary.

'Oh dear, all those police, it doesn't look good, does it? Whatever's going on in there? Do you know, I was only talking to Lizzie the other day, in the marketplace, and she seemed fine, full of beans. She was buying flowers, I seem to remember. She had one of those shopping trolleys, doesn't drive, she always walks everywhere. She has a grandson living there with her, Justin, he's grown-up now of course, probably in his twenties. It's actually her stepdaughter's son. Her *step* grandson, it would be. I don't think *he* drives either. You never see a car in front of the house unless there's somebody visiting. Oh dear, I wonder what it's all about.'

She was jigging from one foot to another, joined by Micky the spaniel, woken by her sudden restlessness. I must admit, I was slightly curious myself, but I remained seated at the table. I could watch everything she was seeing without being quite so obvious about it. I twiddled my empty wine glass. The bottle on the table was still half full, but I resisted pouring another glass because soon I'd be driving back to Norwich. I poked my finger around in the crumbs of my apple pie, and licked it. Nothing seemed to be happening, not visibly at least, and I went to the kitchen to make a coffee. By the time I returned, she'd finally decided to tear herself away from the window. She'd picked up her wine glass and was sitting in one of the armchairs, making sure she still had a view outside. I curled up on the sofa, careful not to spill coffee on the patchwork cushion covers. I picked up the Sunday supplement from the coffee table and leafed through it, glancing at the fashion pictures, while keeping one eye alert to whatever was happening across the road.

At last, the paramedics – a man and a woman – emerged from the house, and we watched as they drove the ambulance round the loop of the close, before disappearing from view. 'At least they're not taking anyone anywhere. I wonder why the police are still there, though.'

'Seems a bit dodgy,' I offered.

'I suppose it doesn't have to be Lizzie, does it? It could be Justin, of course. I've seen *him* come home the worse for wear a few times.'

She wriggled forward to the edge of her chair as another car, unmarked, pulled up outside the house, and a rather portly man went inside.

There was a strange hush in the close, different from the normal quietness. Micky was back in his reclining pose in his favourite corner. There was nothing to see, and after a while she said, 'I suppose we might as well start tidying up.'

I helped her clear the table. She put the roasting tin to soak, and we set about loading the dishwasher. Trivial conversation seemed inappropriate, and I don't think we'd ever been so silent.

We could still see what – if anything – was going on over the road from the kitchen window. A further car turned up. Two men disappeared into the house. '*Whatever's* going on in there,' my mother commented. It wasn't a question and I had nothing to add.

***

I'd been having afternoon lunch with my mother almost every Sunday since my father died of cancer a year and a half ago. At first, she'd carried on living in our old house on the edge of the town. I hadn't wanted her to move. The house was still *ours*. Even though my two older brothers were long gone with families of their own. Even though, for nine years, I too had owned a house of my own, in the suburbs of Norwich – pretending, so it sometimes seemed, to be grown-up. So many childhood memories were rooted in that untidy old house in North Walsham that I couldn't imagine it being lived in by strangers. But she'd convinced me she needed to downsize, and so I'd helped her choose the characterless place she's living in now, within easy walking distance of her old address. She said she wanted to keep in touch with all her old friends. Rather weirdly, 'neighbours' and 'friends' mean much the same thing to my mother, though she's still working on this in Willowherb Close. It's early days.

***

10

There was a loud tap on the kitchen window, just as we were jamming the last dishes in the machine. Unsurprisingly, it was Brenda from next door.

'Oh, hello Melanie, I'm sorry to interrupt,' she said, when I opened the front door. As if she hadn't known I was there. She must of course have seen my little grey Fiat parked at the front. Probably about twenty years older than my mother, she was of that generation of women who always wore a pinafore around the house, as if to demonstrate they never stopped being busy. Sorry or not, she made her way, awkwardly, into the living-room. She was recovering from her second hip replacement.

'Do come in.' The invitation was redundant. 'We were just going to have a cup of tea.' First I knew of it. My mother grabbed Micky, who'd woken up again and was about to start attacking Brenda's crutches.

'I'll put the kettle on.' I'd been on the point of saying I didn't have time, I was about to be on my way, but then I thought it might be interesting to hear what Brenda's views were on the drama.

I fixed another mug of instant coffee for myself, and made proper tea in a teapot for my mother and Brenda. I found two cups and saucers, and a dish of white sugar lumps. I put some milk in a little jug and carried it all on a tray into the living room. Brenda was sitting on one of the high-backed dining chairs, easier for her to get up and down. I put the tray on the coffee table, and my mother raised herself from her armchair and poured out the tea. 'One sugar isn't it?' she asked Brenda, popping it in and stirring without waiting for an answer. She handed the cup to Brenda, took her own sugarless one, and sat herself down again. I helped myself to my mug of coffee and returned to the sofa.

11

Brenda blew on her tea, to help it cool. She waited a second or two, and I could see her lips moving, as she rehearsed her words. 'Well, what a to-do,'she said, finally.

My mother nodded, raised her cup to her lips, returned it to its saucer, nodded again.

With a little frown, Brenda sipped her tea, then continued talking, tea cup aslant. I held my breath, waiting for it to spill. 'You know, I did think it strange that I hadn't seen Lizzie leave the house all weekend. Not once, did I see her. She usually goes for a little walk to the shops, doesn't she? Breaks the day up for herself. Come to think of it, I hadn't seen Justin drifting in and out, either, like he usually does. I don't know what he does with his time, he hasn't got a job as far as I know, probably just makes it down to the pub, you can tell he's had a few when he comes back, though I've no idea where he gets his money from. But I hadn't seen either of them all weekend, and then this afternoon, just before all that palaver, I happened to see him walking up the garden path with his rucksack on his back, as if he'd been away somewhere. And then, a few minutes later . . . well, he must have rung 999 or something mustn't he?'

'Something awful must have happened. The ambulance, and then the police. Dreadful. Dreadful,' Mum repeated, having recovered her voice. 'I was just telling Melanie, I saw Lizzie at the market the other day, and she seemed right as rain. Not all that old, either.'

'The last person I saw going in the house was that *step*daughter of hers. Philippa. That would have been Friday. Friday morning. She always goes there on a Friday morning. I think she was in there about an hour or so, and then she got back in her car and drove away, like normal.'

'I wonder why the police, though. Why all those cars. Surely they don't suspect anything unnatural.'

'Strange things happen sometimes don't they? We don't really know our neighbours, do we? I always thought they were an odd family though.'

Despite the age gap between them, it struck me they sounded like elderly twins, one taking over where the other left off. It was obvious neither of them had any answers. I gulped down the last of my coffee. 'It's time I went home.'

When my mother was still living in the old house, I never used the word 'home' about my own place. I would have said, 'It's time I went back' or 'It's time I was off'. The old house had always been my home. In a locked-up part of my mind, it still was.

***

The phone rang early that evening. I'd just had a long bath, and was about to settle down in front of the TV. I knew it had to be my mother.

'I told you there was something odd going on,' she said, as if I needed convincing. 'Anyhow, a body's been carried out of the house, and it must have been Lizzie, because I saw Justin come outside and get into one of the police cars. They must have needed to get some information from him. One of the police was holding onto his arm, but I don't think there was any sort of struggle going on. He had his head down, looked a bit shaky, well he would be wouldn't he – coming home from wherever he'd been, and then going in there and finding whatever had happened to Lizzie. Poor woman. It's all very sad.'

***

13

I had another dream of Sarah that night. The grown-up Sarah. She was being pulled into an ambulance by two men, one at each side of her, holding onto her wrists. Another man was pushing her from behind. She was wriggling about, trying to escape. She looked terrified. I was watching her from an upstairs window, very high up, in a tall building. She looked up and saw me there. The window was open, and I was trying to shout something down to her, but there was no power in my voice, and it drifted away, like a leaf in the wind.

Three

I need to explain about Sarah. About how we were best friends, and then we weren't friends at all. And how she suddenly appeared in my life again, all those years later.

We started secondary school at the same time, and we were in the same class, but as we'd been to different primary schools we hadn't previously known each other. Although there were lots of girls I knew and could chat to, I didn't have a best friend at the time, because the parents of the girl I used to go around with – Leanne – were paying for her to go to a more prestigious school in Norwich. Sarah seemed rather isolated. I would see her wandering around on her own at lunchtimes, and I suppose I felt sorry for her. She was taller than most of the girls in the class, and she used to hunch in on herself, in an effort to be less conspicuous. One afternoon, after school, I saw her walking home from the school in the same direction as I was, and I caught up with her. She told me they'd only recently moved to North Walsham, having previously been living in Swaffham. I can't remember what else we talked about. I decided she needed befriending, and I started to take a short diversion in the mornings, as I walked to school, so that I could meet her at the run-down terraced house, with its overgrown front garden, where she lived with her parents. She told me she had no brothers or sisters. She was always waiting for me at the garden gate. I can only remember one time when she wasn't there waiting, when I knocked on the door and her mother answered and told me she wasn't well. Her mother was wearing a dressing gown, and the door only opened so far because it was on a chain. The house looked dark and secretive behind her.

Thinking about this now, maybe it was because everything in her family was so hidden, that Sarah was so obsessed with the truth. Personally, I always thought that truthfulness was a bit overrated, that it was more important for people to hear what they wanted to hear. From an early age, I've made up stories. Nothing major, just a few events here and there to embellish my life, make it sparkle a bit. Or sometimes just to smooth out the wrinkles.

This was a problem for Sarah. I remember one lunchtime at school, I'd been spinning a yarn to some of the other girls about how we'd met Madonna, and she'd invited us to the studio where she was recording. It was good being the centre of attention, seeing the envy in their eyes, until finally one of the girls said, 'Come off it, Melanie, I don't believe you, you're having us on,' and the others copied her, and they wandered off. I was left feeling a bit of an idiot, but I didn't care. Or anyhow, I pretended I didn't.

But all the while I was relishing my story-telling, Sarah had been shuffling her feet and growing more and more uncomfortable. And I'd been teasing her, exploiting her discomfort. Every so often I'd turned to her and said, 'Didn't we Sarah?' or 'Isn't that what happened, Sarah?' And, wanting to be loyal, or maybe just afraid to contradict me, she'd nodded and blushed.

The next morning, she thrust an envelope into my hand. She'd written: 'To Melanie, Private and Confidential' in her careful childish handwriting. I ripped it open, and read the note inside while Mr Beaney called the register. 'My Mum says that we go to Hell if we tell fibs. We can lie to other people but we can't lie to God. He knows everything, even our thoughts and our dreams. SO PLEASE DON'T TELL FIBS EVER AGAIN. I don't want you to go to Hell. Your Best Friend, Sarah.' I crumpled it up, and put it in my bag, with my exercise books. I was aware of the effort that must have gone into writing those words of warning, and how Sarah must have tormented herself about giving it to me.

And I did try not to tell any more stories, at least for a while. I talked to my brother. 'Jake, have you ever told people stuff that isn't exactly true?'

He shrugged. 'Probably.'

'Then you'll go to hell, like me.'

'Don't be daft,' he said, 'there's no such place.'

OK, if there was no such place, then it was Sarah's Mum who was telling lies, and she'd be the one going to hell. But then of course, if Jake was right, and there wasn't any such place, then none of us were going there, and it didn't matter much either way, whether I made things up or not. So I reasoned.

***

We hadn't been friends for all that long when I first invited Sarah to my house for tea. She didn't talk very much. I think she felt a bit overwhelmed by my brothers. After we'd finished eating, Joshua and Jake rushed off to do whatever they were doing. I stood, expecting her to follow me, and she said in a small voice could she please leave the table. I asked her afterwards, 'Is that what you have to do at home?' and she nodded and looked a bit embarrassed. She joined us for our family meals on many occasions after that, and gradually she started to relax.

One day I said to her, 'Can I come round to your place sometime?' and she stiffened and didn't say anything. But a few weeks later, she told me that I could come for tea on Sunday. I wasn't sure how it would be, with this strange mother who locked herself in her house with a chain, but I was more curious than apprehensive, so of course I said thank you very much, I'd love to.

***

Her mother had obviously made an effort in an old-fashioned way. The table was laid with plates of sandwiches and scones and a bowl of tinned fruit. Even so, it all felt rather strained and dismal, and there was a darkness overhanging the room. Instead of the random conversation bandied to and fro across our table at home, we sat in silence punctuated by stilted efforts to break it. Her father kept asking me boring questions, like what lessons did I most enjoy at school. I accidentally knocked my glass of orange squash with my elbow and it spilled over the tablecloth. Sarah's mother rushed out for a tea towel and mopped it up. She said it was all right, but the expression on her face told me it wasn't. I remember the house smelt rather damp and musty, and the wallpaper looked as if it had been there a very long time. There was no TV because, Sarah told me, her parents thought it an unnecessary evil. I began to understand why Sarah was so weird.

***

Surprisingly, though, we were friends right up until the year we were taking our GCSEs. I was never invited round to her house again, but almost every day she came to mine, gradually realising it was OK to come and knock on the door without waiting to be asked. My father never really talked to anyone who wasn't interested in wildlife photography or golf, but my mother always made a point of being talkative and friendly with Sarah. I'm ashamed to say I was the one who broke off the friendship.

It was after the school trip to Paris. Sarah had been a bit of a drag when we were there. She didn't want to socialise with the rest of us in the hotel in the evenings, she just wanted to spend her time sitting on her bed and drooling over the postcards she'd bought in art galleries. She never had much pocket money and I think she spent all the money she had on those postcards. One afternoon I was walking along the road with a girl called Sam, and a couple of others. Sam always seemed older and more sophisticated than the rest of us. Sarah was trailing behind.

'Sarah's boring,' Sam remarked. 'She's the most boring person I've ever known.'

'I know.' I felt guilty and almost fearful as I agreed with her.

'You don't *have* to go around with her. She's not your responsibility. Life's too short. Why go around with someone as boring as that when you could be having a good time? *You're* OK, we like you, but we're not going to be your friends if Sarah's part of the package.'

'I know,' I said again. 'I think I'm going to have to terminate the friendship.'

'Exterminate, exterminate,' Sam said, in the voice of a Dalek. We all laughed. I happened to turn round. Sarah was walking not very far behind us. She must have heard the conversation. I carried on walking with Sam and the others. I pretended I hadn't seen her. I felt knotted with guilt and a sense of disloyalty.

After we returned from France, Sarah and I continued to be friends for a while. Nothing had really changed. And then one morning, without planning anything, I suddenly decided not to meet her for the walk to school. I just didn't turn up at her house. She must have been waiting for me at the gate. She was late for registration, and I tried not to look at her as she walked in. And after that, we just pretty much stopped talking to each other. It was as simple as that.

***

If my mother asked me at that time why Sarah had suddenly stopped turning up at our door, I probably said I had no idea. I was a bit moody around then, and she always knew when to back off, to keep her distance.

After GCSEs, I left school and went to do a secretarial course in Norwich. I didn't consider university. I suppose I lacked ambition. Sarah went to the sixth form college in North Walsham. I used to see her around, hanging out with kids who dressed like Goths. Later she went to Newcastle, so I heard, and studied for an art degree.

***

It wasn't until many years later – in fact only a couple of years ago – that Sarah appeared in my life again. By now she was a freelance illustrator and, like Oliver, she started working part-time at the arts university as a course tutor. I believe they both started working there at around the same time. It was my job to photocopy the student assignments, prepare their tutorial lists and so on. Sarah would ask me, very sweetly and politely, to do these various tasks for her, and much as it irked me I couldn't refuse. I was the admin skivvy, it was what I was paid for.

She was still tall and thin, but now she wore clothes that flattered her. Slim tapered trousers and clingy jumpers, or fitted jackets and mid-calf skirts. Her former mousy hair was dyed chestnut, and she either

20

had it freely tumbling around her shoulders, or loosely pinned up.

I remember the first time she came into my office. It was one of the days when her hair was freely tumbling, like an advert for l'Oréal, and she was wearing tight jeans and a blazer. When she saw me, sitting there at the desk behind my computer, she did a double take, and her pale skin went even paler, but then she recovered and held out her hand. I took it, stiffly, conscious of the sweatiness of mine. It was hot in the office. The central heating was always turned on too soon. She said, 'It's good to see you again. How are you?' Her voice was deeper, and had lost that childish squeak that used to irritate me.

I told her I was fine. I'd already typed up her contract, so – unless it had been another Sarah Bannister – I did have the advantage of being prepared. I'd been dreading that moment. I said, 'It's been a long time.' I tried to say, 'You're looking good,' but the words stuck in my throat.

After that, we only ever talked about work. Sometimes I was asked to take the minutes at course meetings. As I sat there pounding the keys of my laptop, I noticed that, whenever she spoke, all the heads turned towards her, even the ones that were habitually jaded and bored. I could tell that people listened to what she was saying, took her seriously. I could tell, too, that they found her attractive. She'd evolved so completely from that mousy shadow she used to be at school. By contrast, I felt that I was still the schoolgirl, with no particular talent, sitting at my desk and being told what to do.

I suppose you could say that, without even trying, she'd had some sort of revenge. There was an element of justice in that.

Four

Since that Sunday afternoon in Willowherb Close, my mother had attached herself firmly to the grapevine. Needless to say, she kept me abreast of the latest news and developments with her frequent emails and phone calls.

It was suicide, she told me. An overdose. Dreadful. As Brenda had thought, Justin the *step* grandson was away all weekend. He'd gone to London on the Thursday to stay with friends and he'd come back Sunday afternoon. Poor young man, it must have been such a shock finding her like that. He wasn't there now, of course, he was probably staying with friends. It must have been bad for the stepdaughter, Philippa, too. How must she be feeling, knowing she was the last person to see Lizzie alive? Lizzie had seemed a bit distracted, apparently, but then she was often in a bit of a dream, Lizzie, it was the way she was. In a world of her own. No way Philippa could have guessed what was on her mind. There would have to be an inquest, of course, but they'd got what's known as an interim death certificate, that's what happens in this sort of situation, so the family could go ahead with the funeral. My mother was going, of course, taking Brenda and her crutches with her. They were Lizzie's neighbours, it was the least they could do, show their faces. If only she'd known Lizzie's intentions, she could have tried to help her. It might never have come to this.

I said, 'I don't suppose there's anything you could have done. She must have had it planned.'

Once again, Sarah flashed into my mind. When we were young, I was always the leader. Whatever I suggested, she used to agree to. It could have been that way again. I could have taken the lead, found an opportunity for us to talk. I could have said, 'I'm sorry about what happened.' And then she might have said, 'Don't worry about it, we've both grown up since then,' and we could have moved on. We wouldn't have been friends, the way we used to be, but we could at least have been two adults talking to each other. Not waiting till that awful conversation we finally had, not long before she died.

***

I wasn't sure that going to Lizzie's funeral was such a good idea for my mother. There'd been a run of funerals in our family. First my grandmother. Then Aunt Maureen, the older sister. Then my grandfather. And then my father. Yet another one would be bound to stir up memories. But I knew there'd be no point in trying to dissuade her.

'It was a *lovely* funeral,' she said, when she rang me afterwards, audibly sniffing. 'One of those humanist affairs. No religion. Though I must admit I do like a few hymns myself, something you can sing along with. It doesn't really matter whether you're religious or not, does it? But anyhow, they said some really nice things about Lizzie, and read this *lovely* poem, by an Indian person. Yes, it was a good funeral, even though there weren't a lot of people there. Mostly family. I don't think Lizzie had many friends. Anyhow, I'll tell you more about it Saturday.'

I couldn't see how there'd be that much more to tell. 'You mean Sunday.' It must have been a slip of the tongue. She wasn't normally the sort of person to confuse her days.

'No, Saturday. Oh, goodness, I hope you don't mind. I forgot to tell you. I had a little chat with Philippa, Lizzie's stepdaughter, after the funeral. I already knew her, of course. Not very well, but we did

23

know each other. I knew the whole family. They all used to come to the surgery, although Philippa was the only one who came regularly. Lizzie only came now and then, when she had a problem, and I don't think Justin did at all, not since he was a child.'

She'd worked at the dental surgery longer than anyone else, until her retirement a couple of years ago. You didn't need to look at the patients' files, you just asked my mother. The two dentists who'd first employed her had been replaced by younger ones. They'd been joined by another one, a woman. Other receptionists and dental nurses had come and gone. A new, more upmarket surgery had opened in the town, poaching some of their patients, and she'd been indignant about this, taking their desertion almost personally. Her job had been a big part of her life, as of course her marriage had been. But when she found herself with neither, she soon found lots of ways to fill her time. She made sure there was no space for moping around and feeling sorry for herself.

'So I asked Philippa if there was anything I could do to help, and she said well, yes, being as we know each other, and I'm Lizzie's neighbour – well, *was*, when she was still alive – maybe I could help with the house, sort out some of the wheat from the chaff, before the clearance people come along and take what's left. She said Lizzie had been a bit of a hoarder, not to mention all her paintings and so-called sculptures and so on. A lot of it would have to go into landfill, of course, but who knows, some of it might be worth saving. Well I wasn't sure at first, I didn't want to set my asthma off with all the dust that must be in there.'

She paused, and I could sense, down the line, her small shudder of distaste, before she continued. 'But I thought I could maybe give some of the stuff to that charity shop for Ugandans, in the town, and then there's always Barnardos. I'm sure the charities are more deserving than those *clearance* people, *they're* just in it for the money. And *you'd* know what to do about the paintings, wouldn't you? You work at the art college, you must know about that sort of thing. I hope you hadn't made any plans for Saturday?'

That last question was an afterthought.

'I work in administration. I haven't had an art education,' I pointed out.

'Even so, you've worked there a long time. You must know *something* about art.'

'I guess.' I was starting to become just a little bit interested. I'm not addicted to junk shops and flea markets, not like my friend Rachel, whose flat is full of so much bric-a-brac I don't know how she can breathe in it. I couldn't live like that. I'm a bit like my mother, too dust-averse. But nevertheless, I do like poking around once in a while, discovering the unexpected. And I was curious about Lizzie's art. She might have had a real talent, that had never been discovered. In my mind, I could see the write-up in the newspapers: *Elderly suicide stuns the art world with her collection of previously unseen paintings and sculptures.*

'And I think Philippa could do with a bit of moral support, not just the practical side of things. Bearing in mind she was there with Lizzie before, you know, before that awful *thing* happened. She was in a dreadful state at the funeral, Philippa was. She tried to say a few words about Lizzie, but then she broke down and wasn't able to finish. Not like the other daughter, Kate, Lizzie's *real* daughter. *She* had her feelings under control, Kate did. In fact she seemed almost detached from it all. A bit aloof. Maybe they weren't so close, she and her mother. She doesn't live round here, she lives in Brighton, I think that's what Brenda told me. She did give a very nice little speech though, and then in the middle of it she put her hand to her belly and I suddenly realised she was pregnant. Just the early stages. I couldn't help wondering whether Lizzie had known. I suppose she must have done. It seems a strange thing to do, doesn't it, kill yourself when there's a new baby on the way. A new grandchild. You'd think she'd have been looking forward to it.'

I thought of all the photos my mother has in every room of her house, mostly of my brothers' children in their various stages of development. She doesn't see them anywhere near enough, of course. Neither my brothers nor their families. I know how much she'd love it for me to settle down here in Norfolk with someone and have a child or two, but I'm afraid she'll be waiting a long time. The men in my life have always been married already or not the marrying kind.

Five

Willowherb Close consists of a loop of terraced and semi-detached houses. The semi-detached houses are on one side, the terraces of four on the other. Lizzie had lived at the end of one of the terraces. Her front garden distinguished itself by being untidier than the rest. The lawn, dotted with dandelions, needed mowing, and the flowers in the borders seemed to be losing out in their ratio with weeds. A straggly rose bush had shed most of its petals. Beside the front door was a pot containing a faded brown box plant that had probably once been cone-shaped. Next to it, rather bizarrely, stood a bronze-coloured sculpture of a woman in a flowing dress. It wasn't the sort of thing you'd pick up in a garden centre, so I guessed it was one of Lizzie's creations. If this was typical of her art, then it probably wasn't worth the effort of discovering any more of it.

My mother, carrying a pile of black bin bags, opened the door with a key on a Bart Simpson key-ring. 'Philippa won't be coming,' she informed me. 'She's got a migraine. Her husband dropped the key off this morning.'

So the agenda had changed. It wasn't about *helping* Philippa, moral support, all that. We were doing the whole job.

'I can smell cat.' That was the first thing that struck me, before I started to identify some of the other smells. Stale food. Turpentine. And, unmistakeably, tobacco and weed, which was probably residual from the grandson, Justin. The *step* grandson, as everyone insisted upon saying.

'There were two of them. I think Cats Protection took them away. I'd have had them myself if it wasn't for my allergy. And I'm not sure how Micky would

27

have taken to them.' She scooped up some of the neglected mail that was already littering the carpet in the small hallway. 'Let's have a quick look through, see if there's anything important.' Amongst the correspondence addressed to some anonymous occupier, and the North Walsham Times, and the leaflet advertising the latest prices at Lidl, there was one small white envelope addressed to Mrs Lizzie Brown, and a brown window envelope addressed to Mr Justin Morgan. 'I'd better give these to Philippa.' She stuffed the letters into her bulging handbag, and put the junk mail in one of the bin bags.

If Lizzie had left any washing-up, somebody must have already come in and cleared it. The sink was empty. The mixer tap was dripping, and I turned it off. I can't stand the sound of a dripping tap. Plates and mugs and a Pyrex dish had been left to drain. More than a few blind eyes had been cast over the cooker: it was encrusted with grease and spillages, and a burned pan lay abandoned on the hob. The cupboard doors were smeared with residues of food and greasy fingers. There was a small hinged table, with its leaves folded down. A stray tea towel that looked as if it hadn't been washed for months was draped over the back of one of the chairs stacked at the sides of the table.

'Philippa did warn me it wasn't very salubrious. The husband left eleven years ago. Went off to live with some young teacher he met at work, Pakistani I believe, not English anyway. That must have been the beginning of the end for Lizzie. Both daughters had grown up and moved out by then. She wasn't used to living on her own.'

Neither was my mother. She would have known what this felt like. My father would never have left her, of course, if he hadn't died. Even so she would have felt abandoned, in that big house, where we'd once been such a happy family.

'It must have been good for her, when the grandson moved in. A bit of company,' she added.

I tried to imagine this house of Lizzie's being a regular family home, like ours had been. Husband going off to work in the mornings. The two daughters sitting at the kitchen table to eat their sugar puffs. There were no cereal packets on the table now, just a few empty wine bottles, a portable CD player and a pile of CDs. Lizzie must have liked her music while she cooked. I flicked through them. Billie Holliday, Nina Simone, Bob Dylan, Joni Mitchell, Leonard Cohen. Some recent stuff, names I recognised but didn't really know. I put them all in my bag. If nobody claimed them, I'd keep them myself, for the trouble of coming here.

The fridge had been emptied, and smelt of sour milk, but in the food cupboard next to it were a battered packet of cornflakes, screw-top jars with different sorts of rice and dried pasta, tins of chopped tomatoes and various varieties of beans. 'I'll take all this lot to the food bank,' my mother said. 'Well maybe not the cornflakes, they're probably stale.'

We moved on to the living-room. To call it chaos was an understatement. Sofa and armchairs in a beige fabric, faded and stained, under piles of books, magazines and newspapers. Table cluttered with various artefacts: a goldfish bowl filled with marbles and buttons and shells; empty wine bottles, thickly textured with wax dripped from candles; an old wicker basket loaded with pine cones; mouldy oranges in a chipped ceramic bowl. Pictures hung randomly from a dado rail: portraits of a young girl in various stages of growing; a charcoal drawing of a nude, crouching. Lots more pictures were stacked on the floor:

geometric landscapes, abstracts, more portraits. Talented or not, Lizzie had certainly been prolific.

I reminded myself of my role. I was supposed to be casting a critical eye over all this, deciding what, if anything, was worth rescuing. I felt seriously ill-equipped. 'I'll take a few of these back with me and ask someone to come and have a look at them. Someone who knows more than I do.' It would at least give me an excuse to contact Oliver. To try to break through the invisible wall that had come between us since Sarah's death.

As for the sculptures, many unfinished, my instincts told me they weren't worth the hassle of saving, even if we had somewhere to store them. Random approximations of birds and beasts jostled for space around women swathed in sculptured dresses, similar to the one by the front door. Heaps of lace and net and other remnants lay tumbled around the carpet. It was impossible to avoid treading on stuff. Somehow, there was space for a small TV on a stand, and another CD player was wedged on a shelf between tubes of paint and jars of brushes. My mother found her way to the table and put the mouldy oranges into her bin bag. For once lost for words, she seemed overwhelmed and bemused by it all.

I was feeling pretty much the same. I sat on the sofa, the only space that was reasonably clear. It was facing the TV. I thought of Lizzie sitting there on her own, or maybe occasionally with Justin, watching whatever it was they watched. There was an ash-tray full of butts on top of one of the piles of magazines, and underneath it the television listings extracted from a recent Observer Review. Where did Kate and her husband sit when they came all the way from Brighton to visit? Or did they hover outside while Lizzie put on her coat, then whisk her off in their car for lunch at a country pub?

Partly submerged in the crevice between the cushion and the arm of the sofa was a fat ring-bound book, its cover decorated with scribbles and doodles. It was Lizzie's sketchbook. Without asking myself why, I put it in my bag, along with the CDs.

My mother was starting to gather herself together, do what she'd come for. She was picking up books, looking at the titles, putting them in one of her bags. Books were her territory, her comfort zone. 'I'll take these to that Break shop, they have a whole room downstairs for books,' she was saying.

I was only half listening. I needed a pee. There didn't appear to be a downstairs toilet, so I went upstairs.

More of Lizzie's paintings were propped around the landing, frames thick with dust. They'd been there a long while, even longer than the ones downstairs. Works of art or not, they would have to stay where they were.

The bathroom was directly opposite the stairs, and the door was open. I flushed the toilet to see whether the water had been turned off. It hadn't. I should have remembered, of course, the dripping tap in the kitchen. I hovered over the seat so that my bottom wouldn't touch where anyone else would have sat.

Like the kitchen, like everywhere else in the house, the bathroom was in need of a makeover. Even so, I had the feeling this was one of the few rooms, if not the only one, that Lizzie had attempted to keep clean. There was limescale around the taps, and a permanent stain in the bath, but the wash-basin had obviously had a squirt of cleaner, and I imagined Lizzie scrubbing the rim of the toilet with the brush. The grandson would probably never have thought to do it. Most men don't, only the fastidious ones, like Oliver. On the window-ledge, Body Shop shower gel jostled with aftershave, mascara and lipstick with Sure spray deodorant for men. I was rather surprised that Lizzie had used make-up. A lilac-coloured towel, in need of a wash, hung over the side of the bath. I peeped in the laundry basket. It was empty. If Lizzie had left any dirty underclothes behind, somebody had disposed of them.

There were three bedroom doors leading off from the landing; two of them had been left half open.

I peeped in at the typical small third bedroom. Pink and cloying, it was like a mini museum of childhood, so reminiscent of my own childhood bedroom it was cringe-making. The single bed was piled high with dolls and teddy bears; the shelves were filled with books, some of which I recognised from my own young days, books that everybody read at that time. The Lion, the Witch and the Wardrobe, and a couple of Roald Dahl's. Others were obviously older, possibly Lizzie's, from *her* early days. The Girls Book of Ballet. The Girls Crystal Annual. Little Women, a similar edition to one that had been my mother's school prize. Jigsaws, boxed games, old school exercise books were piled high on the floor, along with a tower of vinyl LPs. The one on the top, Complete Madness, I remembered from my own collection. An early poster of Madonna – I recognised that too – was taped to the door of the wardrobe. I opened it carefully, expecting the contents to spill out. It was stuffed with the clothes and shoes of a young girl, and then a teenager: a palimpsest of growing up. I guessed it had belonged to Kate, the younger daughter. The room was almost a shrine to this *real* daughter, who according to my mother had made an aloof and unemotional appearance at the funeral. Why wasn't *she* here, helping to clear the house? And then I recalled that she was pregnant, so

32

maybe it wouldn't have been so good for her, humping stuff around, inhaling all the dust.

I returned to the landing.

I pushed the other door that was ajar. This room, I decided, would most likely have been Justin's, and years before it may well have been Philippa's.

***

The room was surprisingly empty. Not the emptiness of a room that had been stripped bare. More an emptiness that had been there all along, as if the occupant hadn't needed to own a lot, or stamp his presence on the space. The pillowcase and quilt on the single bed looked unwashed for months. Bare walls were painted dusky red over crinkly wallpaper. There were the lingering scents of tobacco and weed that I'd noticed when we entered the house. Nothing littered the beige carpet, dotted with splashes of spilled coffee and possibly beer, except for an old Sainsbury's till receipt.

I looked in the bedside cabinet. Just a few old music magazines and a paperback novel.

I looked in the chest of drawers. Some tatty old T-shirts, boxer shorts, socks.

I looked in the wardrobe.

And I stepped back, blinked, and looked again, in disbelief.

It must have been overspill from Lizzie's wardrobe – but what an overspill. Vintage dresses, the sort that could possibly sell on the web for a lot of money. Going-out party dresses. Flouncy, lacy, chiffony, silky. Not the sort of dresses I would have imagined belonging to a woman in her sixties. Their scent filled my nostrils: a decadent muskiness, mixed with sweat. There was almost a warmth rising from the dresses, as if they'd been recently worn. A warmth that gave me an inexplicable shiver.

I shut the wardrobe door, feeling slightly guilty, as if I'd seen something I shouldn't. A side to Lizzie I wasn't supposed to know about.

**

I retreated to the landing. By now, it was all starting to feel a bit like Goldilocks and the Three Bears. The first bedroom was too yucky, the second too weird. Just the third one remained. The room with the shut door.

It must have been the room where Lizzie had died.

Holding my breath, I opened the door.

I'm not sure what I was expecting but it wasn't this – nothingness. All evidence disposed of. No smell, apart from a faint mustiness. No sense of death, but no sense, either, of a lot of life. The room had been left tidy. Two small neat piles of paperback novels remained on the bedside cabinet. A couple of sweaters hung over the back of a chair. Assorted slippers and plimsolls rested in a pile underneath it.

The bed had been stripped down to the double mattress. Try as I might, I couldn't summon an image of Lizzie lying there, waiting to die, nor imagine how she'd felt; whether she'd remained calm, or panicked and struggled.

I shivered again, thinking not of Lizzie but of Sarah.

I opened the double wardrobe. No surprises in this one: a predictable assortment of jeans, many of them paint-spattered, a few nondescript skirts, several unremarkable coats and jackets. A large holdall was scrunched at the bottom of the wardrobe, under some old shoes and boots. I extricated it.

I returned to the other bedroom and, in a sort of trance, I took the dresses out of the wardrobe – there were four of them – folded them carefully and put them in the holdall. For some reason, I didn't want to mention this particular find to my mother.

Quietly, I took the holdall downstairs, slipped outside, and put it in the boot of my car.

Six

I rejoined my mother in the house, feeling guilty that I hadn't been helping as much as I should have done. While I'd been prowling around upstairs, she'd overcome her reluctance to sort out the contents of the living room. Much of it, she decided, was destined for landfill. 'It's often better for somebody like me to do this sort of thing. Somebody who's not related to the family. It's so easy to be sentimental about stuff.' She sounded a bit choked, and again I thought she shouldn't have involved herself in this, that it was bound to revive memories of sifting through my father's golf clubs and photographic memorabilia. She'd hung on to a lot of it at first, but we'd had to let it go when she moved to Willowherb Close.

I said, 'There are some lovely old schoolgirl books upstairs.' The prospect seemed to cheer her, renewed her dwindling energy. I helped her finish the job downstairs. I still felt angry with Philippa for not doing her share of the work. I wasn't entirely convinced by the migraine attack.

***

Mission more or less accomplished, we sat drinking a well-earned coffee in my mother's kitchen. Four of Lizzie's paintings – two of the cubist-inspired landscapes, a portrait of a prepubescent child with orange hair, and an abstract in which slivers of fabric and paper were interwoven with daubs of paint – lay in my car boot, hopefully to be assessed by Oliver. I'd also chucked in a couple of portfolios. All the rest of the paintings we'd taken the trouble to rescue were now stacked in my mother's integral garage, along with the books, most of the CDs, various kitchen utensils, and

36

the teddy bears and dolls. She could now look forward to contacting her favourite charities. She seemed exhausted, depleted. We must have walked miles between us, lugging all the stuff from one side of the close to the other. All that was left would be up to the clearance company, to deal with as they thought fit.

'You might as well stay the night,' she suggested. 'You'll be here for lunch tomorrow.' It was supposed to be a statement rather than a question, but I sensed the hidden question-mark. She always tried so hard not to show how much she needed me.

I nodded, yes I'd be there for Sunday lunch, as usual. 'It's tempting,' I said, meaning to stay overnight. And it was: the idea of a cosy night with Mum in front of the TV, and then to tuck myself up in the spare bedroom. 'Only I've promised to go out with Rachel.'

Rachel was about the only friend I had at present who – like me – was what we called 'between relationships'. In younger days, there was always a small crowd of us to go partying, eating out, binge-drinking, whatever took our fancy. But as we grew older, one after another slipped out of the circle. I could have phoned Rachel, cancelled the evening, but I thought of her miserably washing off her make-up, settling down in her pyjamas amongst all her bric-a-brac, resigned to a night on her own watching crap TV, and I knew I owed her better than this.

Sometimes I had the unwelcome sense I was becoming like my mother, unable to say no to people, always swinging from one obligation to another.

I gulped down my coffee, muttered 'see you tomorrow', and went out to my car.

That was when I saw Justin.

Seven

He was walking up the path towards Lizzie's house, a rucksack slung over his right shoulder. I called out 'Excuse me' and then, when he didn't respond, 'Justin'. He still didn't hear me, and I realised his ears were plugged with earphones. I ran across the road and intercepted him before he could unlock the front door. He unplugged his ears, and looked at me quizzically.

'Excuse me,' I said again, 'you must be Justin?'

He nodded tentatively, gave a little frown.

'I've just been in there. I thought I should let you know. In the house. With my mother. Sorting stuff out. Philippa asked us to. At least, she asked my mother. I came along to help. She may have told you.' I was conscious of speaking in that disjointed staccato. The short sprint across the road had left me slightly breathless, or maybe it was the awkwardness of the situation.

He shook his head. 'No, she didn't tell me. She said something about some clearance people coming Monday, that if I wanted anything I'd better grab it first. Actually I came to pick up some CDs.'

Bloody CDs. No thought about coming to give a hand. Turning up when all the hard work was already done. Though, if he hadn't known we were going to be there, my bad temper was unjustified.

'I've got a few of them here.' I opened my bag, to show him. He shrugged, without looking. 'The rest are in my mother's garage with all the other stuff. Number sixteen. If you go there now she'll open it up for you.'

He shrugged again. 'It doesn't really matter. I just thought, while I was in the town. Actually I'm about to get a train back to Norwich. '

'I'm just about to drive into Norwich myself. Do you want a lift?' I don't know why I offered. I still felt

38

angry with him. My arms were aching from carrying all those paintings and books.

'That'd be great. Thanks.'

Tall and gangly, he sidestepped into the passenger seat, and stuffed his rucksack between his legs.

'It might be better if you push the seat back a bit.'

'Cheers.'

We drove in silence for the first few minutes. I couldn't think of anything to say without seeming to probe, or sounding put-upon, or both. And I didn't want to talk about the weather. As we waited for the lights to change at the junction where the by-pass crosses Norwich Road, it was Justin who broke the silence. 'It must have been bad in there. Lizzie and I, we weren't exactly house-proud.' The way he referred to Lizzie, it was almost as if she was his wife, or his girlfriend.

'Lizzie was your grandmother, wasn't she?' I knew she was, of course, it was just something to say.

'My *step* grandmother.' Like everyone else, he emphasised the *step*. For some reason, this seemed important to people. 'When I was a child I used to call her Aunty Lizzie. Then when I grew older it was just Lizzie. She never really seemed like a grandmother.' I was surprised, and rather touched, by the sudden confidence.

'It must have been a really big shock. Finding her there like that.'

I heard him take a deep breath, in and out. 'It was a shock, yes. It was . . . not something I ever expected.'

My irritability had subsided, and I sensed it might be good for him to talk. I'm the sort of person people tend to open up to. At work, the students always seem to come to me with their problems. And my friends all gravitate my way when their love lives aren't working out. 'I take it she hadn't given you any clues?'

'Nothing at all. When I left on the Thursday morning, to go and catch my train, I said goodbye, see you Sunday, and she told me to have a good weekend. You know, the usual stuff, that you say to people. She seemed fine. No different from how she always was.'

'Maybe she was good at covering up her feelings. Some people are.'

'Maybe.'

It was time to change the subject. 'So now you're living in Norwich?'

'Sort of.' He paused for a few seconds. 'I'm staying with friends. It's not ideal. My mate's OK about me being there, it's just his missus. They've got a new baby, you know how it is, three's company, four's a crowd.'

'I take it you don't want to hang out at your parents' place for a while? Does that seem retrogressive?'

'Sort of,' he said again. 'My mother . . . well, frankly, I think she'd rather I kept my distance. I'm a bit of an embarrassment to her. Never came up to her expectations. And besides, she lives way out in the sticks, which isn't the best place for me. Makes it hard to nip out for a quick drink with the lads.'

I could see his point.

'I'm looking for a place of my own, it's just that being unemployed, it's not so easy.' There was something beaten about him. Rather like a stray cat.

'Mm, I can imagine.' I really knew nothing about how it was to be unemployed, at least not from experience. It sometimes struck me how protected and straightforward my own life had been. I'd worked at the same job for the past fifteen years, since shortly after my twenty second birthday. I'd lived with my parents till I was twenty eight and then, with a bit of help from the bank of mum and dad, I was able to put down a deposit for my own little house. Everything had been smooth-running and uncomplicated. It sometimes crossed my mind that the trail of unhappy love affairs had been my way of injecting a few spikes of drama into my life. In reality, the worst thing that had happened to me so far had been the death of my father.

Justin didn't seem to have anything more to say on the subject. I considered putting on a CD, before the silence became uncomfortable, but before I could do so he asked me, 'What about you? You live in Norwich?'

'Mm. This side of Norwich. Sprowston. I've got a little Victorian terraced.'

'You work, presumably?'

'At the arts university.'

'You're a teacher?'

'Course administrator. It's an OK place to work. I like the atmosphere, the buzz, the students milling around. It's a bit hectic at the moment, start of the academic year and everything. Quite stressful, in a way, but I enjoy it.'

I've often thought how much I'd hate not to have a job. I can't imagine how I'd fill the time. I've never been the sort of person to enjoy being on my own for long, never had any burning hobbies or interests.

'Are you looking for anything in particular? I mean jobwise.'

'Not really. I'd like to earn money making music. But that's what we all say, don't we? I don't have illusions it's ever going to happen. I *have* worked. I've stacked shelves at Sainsbury's. I've worked behind the bar at the Kings Arms. I was working at Cromer Crab Company till they started laying everyone off. It's not that I'm workshy, but if I'm honest I find it hard to get my enthusiasm up when it comes to interviews. It all feels so false. I feel like saying, get real, it's just a job. I'll work hard and do whatever I need to do, but it's just

41

a job. I can't pretend to get excited about it. I guess that shows in my body language.'

'Did you train for anything in particular? After you left school?'

'I did the first year of a media studies course, then I dropped out. It wasn't a good time for me just then. But I doubt it would have got me a job. Everybody was doing media studies, weren't they, it didn't have a lot of currency.'

'I'm sorry, you must think I'm interrogating you.'

He shrugged. 'No. It doesn't feel like that.' There was another silence. 'What tunes have you got?' He bent forward and flicked through the CDs that were rattling around at the front of the car. 'Let's have some Amy Winehouse. Something cheerful.' That was presumably his attempt at a joke.

As we listened to the first track, Rehab, I managed to stop myself saying something banal about what a loss, such talent. It felt better to stop talking, just let the music fill the space. Eventually I asked him where he wanted to be dropped off. He said the train station would be good, if it wasn't out of my way. His friends lived just up the road from there.

I turned left at the roundabout, and then, instead of taking the next turn right into Sprowston Road, as I normally did, I continued to Gurney Road, through Mousehold Heath. That particular approach to the city showed Norwich at its most panoramic, the cathedral spire ahead of us. I almost said something middle-aged about the view. I turned into Riverside Road, and pulled up in the station forecourt.

Justin had already unfastened his seat belt, and was twisting round to open the door, as if he couldn't wait to escape. But the whisper of an idea had been floating about in my head. It was a crazy one, and probably ill-conceived.

I put my left hand on his arm, to slow him down, and turned off the ignition. 'As it happens, I'm looking for a tenant,' I lied. 'I had a friend sharing the house with me, and then she left to go and live with her boyfriend.' That part was true, except that Ellie had moved out five years ago. 'I just wondered . . . you said you were looking for a place?'

He turned towards me, eyebrows raised, gave one of his little shrugs. They seemed to be a mannerism rather than signifying off-handedness, as I'd thought at first.

'I mean, it's just a thought. It's only a room, everything else is shared, so you're probably looking for a bit more privacy. Anyway . . .' I had a pen in my pocket, a habit I've developed from work, needing to take notes on the go. I looked in my bag for something to write on, and finally tore a corner of a page from Lizzie's sketch book. 'This is my number. My name's Melanie by the way. Have a think about it, there's no particular rush. '

'I *will* think about it. Definitely. Thanks. And thanks for the lift.'

***

He slid out, and I watched him in the mirror as he walked round the back of the car and strode diagonally across the forecourt. I wondered what was passing through his mind. That offer of a room had taken *me* by surprise.

I swallowed an aftertaste of embarrassment, and wiped my sticky hands on my jeans. As he walked away – a skinny young man I hardly knew – I decided it was reassuringly improbable I'd see or hear from him again.

Eight

Two days later, I was sitting on a stool in the student bar, having a lunchtime chat with Kathleen. She's in her fifties, and she's worked at the university forever, long before it had aspirations to be called a university. Much longer, even, than I have.

I hadn't yet spoken to Oliver about Lizzie's paintings. It had seemed a good idea when I was talking to my mother. Now I wasn't so sure.

I sensed a shadow behind me before he put his hands firmly on my shoulders. I knew it had to be Oliver, and a shiver rippled through me. It seemed we might be talking to each other again. I turned around, met his eyes. 'Can I get you a drink?' he asked me.

'I'm fine at the moment, thanks.' I held up my almost full half pint glass, and smiled in a way that was supposed to say I was genuinely fine, not being huffy.

He moved away to order one for himself, and a couple of minutes later he was joined by Angie, another of the part-time tutors. Only recently appointed, blonde and pretty, she looked more like a young student than a tutor. I continued talking to Kathleen while I watched him out of the corner of my eye. I could see him focused on Angie, face close to hers, intent at first, listening, and then laughing at something she'd said, and I felt that familiar stab of jealousy. I was conscious of Kathleen looking at me in the way that women look at someone who they think has made a fool of herself for far too long. I didn't care. Deep down, I still believed – or at least I hoped – that there'd been something special between me and Oliver. And that we might be able to pick up the pieces.

***

Until a few months ago, things had been as good as they'd get. We'd been eating out together, sleeping together, visiting exhibitions together. We'd even had a short holiday in Paris. I knew Oliver's reputation, and I never expected to be the only woman in his life. As time went on, of course, I'd felt less and less inclined to share him. That's the way it is with love. You think you're cool and unpossessive, but as time goes on something primal kicks in and you start wishing for a good old-fashioned commitment. And I certainly wasn't happy to be sharing him with Sarah. Plain, gawky Sarah, who'd grown up to be no longer plain and gawky.

Now, watching him flirt with Angie, I made up my mind. If Sarah's suicide had driven him away from me, then Lizzie's more recent suicide could be the catalyst to bring us back together. I would phone him that evening. Although he was a practising photographer, he had a degree in fine art, so he was well qualified to cast a professional eye over Lizzie's paintings.

***

And I did phone.

But not straight away. A bit of preparation was needed. Or was it prevarication?

I took my work clothes off and had a shower. I slipped into joggers and a sweatshirt. I did a few stretches and touch-toes, and tried to remember a short sequence we'd learned in a dance fitness class I no longer went to. I poured myself a glass of red wine, and drank it while I cooked an omelette. Half-way through the omelette, which was burned at the edges, I decided I wasn't hungry and scraped the remains into the pedal-bin. I poured another glass of wine. I drank this one more quickly.

I looked at Lizzie's paintings that I'd propped against the wall of my living-room. Would Oliver guess they were just an excuse for making contact? Probably. But at least he needed to think they were worth the effort of being assessed.

That abstract collage looked rather like the effort of a sixth-form student. The portrait of the girl maybe had something going for it, a sort of boldness. I wasn't sure about the landscapes.

I wasn't sure about anything.

I needed Oliver. And never had a phone call been so hard to make. I poured a third glass of wine and took it upstairs to my bedroom. I needed something to do, something unrelated.

The vintage dresses that I'd taken from Lizzie's house were still in the old holdall I'd pushed under my bed on Saturday evening. I hadn't found time yet to take them out and look at them more closely. Suddenly they seemed to be calling for my attention. Or was it that I wanted something from *them*? A message, perhaps, or a secret. I took them out and lay them on top of the quilt. They still held that musky scent.

One was blue silk, patterned with white roses. Another was grey, full-skirted, with a cream-flowered print. There was an underskirt of white netting, and under that a white satiny lining. The waist was clinched with a shiny black band. The third was pale pink, a lacy bodice and a gathered chiffon skirt over a pastel pink lining. The last was navy blue, with a red floral print, and felt like cotton. There were small grey buttons down the front of the bodice, small square pockets on the chest. The skirt was gathered with loose pleats.

I stroked them, tentatively at first, feeling the textures. All that silk and chiffon. As a child, I'd loved dressing up. I'd enjoyed being in the school plays, pretending. And sometimes, for a treat, my mother had taken me to the Theatre Royal in Norwich. Ballet, drama, musicals. Just her and me, my father wasn't interested, and neither were my brothers. It was something we shared, something magical. A world where stories came to life even more than from the pages of a book. I used to hold my breath until the curtain went up, and from that moment I'd be transfixed. And, as with a good book, I wanted the stories never to end. I hated it when the curtain rose for the last time, and all the cast came out on stage, while the audience clapped. I didn't want to see the good person holding hands with the bad one, to show they were really friends all along, that it was only make-believe. I'd felt safe and secure in that make-believe world, where good and bad are separate entities rather than two sides of a coin, and goodness always triumphs over evil.

I picked up the navy blue dress and held it in front of me. I stood in front of my full-length mirror and did a few little dance steps. The colour suited me, the red flowers matched the red tints in my dark hair. I was thinking how I'd love to wear it out with Oliver because of the way he always noticed when I was wearing something new or different. It always made me feel good when he looked me up and down and nodded appreciatively. The thought of this gave me the final shot of courage I was needing.

I put the dress on top of the others on my bed. I drained my glass, and took it downstairs. The little pile of CDs I'd taken from Lizzie's kitchen now stacked next to my CD player, waiting to be played. Call me a throwback, but I still prefer CDs to downloads. They feel more real. More physical. I chose Billie Holliday, knowing that Oliver was a fan. I put it in the CD player and pressed 'play'. I turned the volume up so he would hear it over the phone, poured myself another glass of wine, and without further hesitation I dialled Oliver's landline.

He answered straight away. That was a good sign. If Oliver didn't feel like picking up the phone he didn't pick it up. 'Melanie,' he said, reading my name on his screen. Saying it as if it was a lovely surprise to hear from me. 'How are you?'

'I'm fine, thanks. What about you?'

'I'm OK. Not bad. Not bad.'

'I wanted to ask you a favour. I've been helping my mother sort out some stuff belonging to a neighbour who died.' I avoided saying 'committed suicide', which would have made him think of Sarah. 'A woman, in her sixties. She had this whole lifetime's work of paintings and sculptures and stuff in her house. You'd never believe how much stuff. So we stashed the paintings in my mother's garage, because we didn't know what else to do with them, and now we're wondering whether they're any good, whether anybody might want to buy them. So I brought a few of them home with me, and I was wondering if you could drop by sometime and let me know what you think.'

It all came out in a garbled rush, but at least it was out. I took a deep breath and held it, waiting for his response.

'OK,' he said, not sounding at all reluctant. 'When would you like me to come?'

'Whenever. When you've got time.'

'Like now? No time like the present, is there? Expect me in the time it takes.' He seemed to be laughing to himself. I wasn't prepared for it to be so easy. He must have been at a loose end, or feeling lustful. Or maybe – who knows? – he'd actually been missing me.

48

Of course, he knew I'd be there on my own. He knew I would have been continually checking my phone these past months, desperate to hear from him again. That was the arrogance of him.

He'd already rung off.

I ran downstairs to the kitchen, and scraped and scrubbed the frying pan I'd used to cook my omelette. I dried it with paper towels rather than leave it to drain. I washed the plate and cutlery, and my cereal bowl from the morning, and dried those too. I put everything away. I knew how Oliver hated an untidy kitchen. I filled the kettle and switched it on in readiness for coffee.

The Billie Holliday CD was still playing. It was one of those compilations that seem to go on forever. She was singing Fine and Mellow. About love being like a faucet. An appropriate soundtrack to my relationship with Oliver. Off and on. Sadly, he'd always been the one with his hand on the faucet.

I was singing along. A few glasses of wine do wonders for the voice.

And then he knocked, much sooner than I expected.

***

I live in one of those Victorian terraces where the front door opens from the living-room straight on to the pavement. I opened it, and he was standing there, in his immaculate jeans and leather jacket. He was carrying a bottle of wine. He didn't wait to be invited, just walked in as if there'd never been a break in our relationship. He put the bottle on the coffee table, then turned and pulled me up towards him. I could smell wine on his breath, matching my own, and the animal scent of leather. 'Did you drive here?' I was worried he might have been drinking too much. He could be a bit careless sometimes.

'I called a cab.' His tongue was in my mouth, the way I remembered it, firm and sure of its way around. His breath tasted faintly of garlic, mixed with the wine. His hand was up the back of my sweatshirt, his fingers moving around my spine. Then, with characteristic abruptness, he pushed me away. 'OK, I'd better do what I'm here for.' He took off his jacket and laid it over the back of one of the armchairs.

He'd always liked to play cat and mouse. Tease me. Make me want something all the more. Reluctantly, I turned my attention to the paintings. 'These are just the tip of the iceberg.'

I'd stacked them one behind the other, but he separated them, placed them around the room so he could stand back and look at them individually, like the professional he was. I turned the volume down on the CD player so he could concentrate.

'OK . . . they're not as dreadful as I thought they might have been.' When he finally spoke, I felt a surge of relief, almost as if the paintings had been my own. 'That collage is pretty tacky, but this one . . . the portrait, the young girl. It reminds me a bit of Alice Neel, it has that loose, slightly unfinished quality. Yes, I rather like it. And the two seascapes, well they're derivative of course, but people buy that sort of stuff. Do you know whether she ever sold any?'

'I don't think so. I think she just liked painting, she wasn't interested in the commercial side of things.' I was feeling pleased with myself, that my own assessment of the paintings had been roughly the same as his.

'It might be worth having a sale, maybe hiring a hall somewhere. It wouldn't be a waste of time. Are there any relatives who might want to take this on?'

'I don't think they're interested. Though they'd probably be interested in the money, if any of them were sold.'

'Well obviously you and your mother would be entitled to commission, if you took this on. I'd price them at around a couple of hundred. Anything less and no one would take them seriously. Anything more and nobody'd want to put their hands in their pockets. It might be worth trying to get some of them into a gallery. It depends on how much time you have, how much you want to get involved.'

I hadn't thought ahead that far. I hadn't thought any further than getting Oliver back inside my house.

'Anyhow, enough of this talk about paintings. Where's your corkscrew?'

I fetched one from the kitchen and handed it to Oliver. 'You've remembered I like Rioja.' I was already a bit wobbly from the wine I'd been drinking earlier.

'It just happened to be what I had lying around at home. No, actually I *had* remembered.' He poured us each a glass. He turned to me, looked me up and down, nodded. 'It's good to see you. You're looking well.'

He hugged me to him again, and this time he pulled off my sweatshirt, unfastened my bra. I loosened his shirt, unbuttoned it, ran my fingers through the hairs on his chest. I undid the clasp on his belt, and put my hand inside his jeans, finding my way around, the way we remember how to play an old tune on the piano. He moved away from me, then took my hand and led me up the pine stairs to my bedroom. I was bare to my waist, still wearing my joggers. His jeans were loose around his waist. The bedroom door was already open.

He stopped when he saw the vintage dresses laid across the bed. In my hurry to tidy up downstairs, I'd forgotten I'd left them there. 'What are those?'

'Something else I picked up from Lizzie's house. The old woman who died. I thought they were rather beautiful. '

I felt him turn rigid. He let go of my hand as if it was a dead rat.

'I'll put them away,' I said, quickly gathering up the dresses and bundling them onto a chair. Unsure of my next move, I crouched uncertainly on top of the bed, still in my joggers, chin on my knees. I didn't know what was going on, why he was suddenly backing away from me. So I just waited. Any minute now, I told myself, he'd be right there next to me, we'd be warm and close again, finding our way back into each other's bodies. Everything would be fine.

He continued to stand, looking downwards, fiddling with the one shirt button that was still fastened, as if trying to make up his mind what to do next. He did this for a ridiculous amount of time. At last he bent towards me and ruffled my hair.

'Sorry, Melanie, this isn't going to work.'

I felt like a child who'd been given an ice lolly and then had it taken away. I knew I wouldn't get it back before it melted.

I hesitated between tears and anger, chose anger.

'Oliver,' I said, 'I don't know what your problem is, but I don't like the way you're messing my head about.'

'I'm sorry.'

He *was* sorry, I could tell, but it felt like one of those times when I was very young, those times when I knew I'd done something wrong but I didn't know what or why or how to make it better.

I stood up, feeling vulnerable and exposed, my breasts still bare. 'Do you want a coffee or something? More wine?'

'No. No thanks.' He tucked his shirt back into his jeans. I opened a drawer and took out a T-shirt, pulling it quickly over my head.

'I'm sorry,' he said again.

He went downstairs, and I followed him. He put his leather jacket back on. At the doorway, he cupped my chin with his fingers and kissed me lightly on the lips. He ran his forefinger across my cheekbone, frowned in a regretful way, and then he left. I watched him take out his mobile as he strode down the road, presumably ringing a cab to take him home.

**

The CD had finally ended.

He was so mean, he gonna drive me away. Isn't that what Billie Holliday had been singing? Well now he had. Once and for all. I'd had enough of his moodiness, his unpredictability.

I picked up the glass of wine I'd started drinking before we rushed upstairs, but I no longer felt in the mood for wine. I put the cork back in the bottle. I took the two almost-full glasses to the kitchen and emptied them down the sink. I re-boiled the kettle and made myself a coffee.

I was just trying to make up my mind whether to turn on the TV or to have an early night and sleep everything off, when the telephone rang. At first I thought – hoped – it might be Oliver ringing to apologise. I was disappointed to see a question mark on the screen – probably someone cold-calling – and I almost didn't answer, but something mechanical in me picked up the handset and I muttered 'hello'.

'Is that Melanie?' I didn't recognise the voice, but it didn't sound like somebody wanting to sell me something. There was none of that 'How are you today?' routine. As if they cared. I didn't answer. But then the caller said, 'It's Justin. You gave me a lift on Saturday.'

'Oh hi Justin.' I made an effort to sound friendly, but I knew my voice sounded slurry with alcohol and suppressed tears.

'About that room you offered . . . I was wondering . . .'

Yes, I reminded myself. I *had* offered. I made an effort to overcome the slurring. 'Would you like to come and see it sometime?'

'How soon could I move in? That's if you're still willing to have me.'

This was all a bit too sudden. But it had been a strange evening, and I didn't have the energy to find some excuse to delay, or even to put him off altogether.

'Of course I am. Anytime really. I'd need to clean it up a bit. How soon do you want to move?'

'As soon as possible, if that's possible.' He must have sensed that I was stalling, hesitating. 'The atmosphere's getting a bit tense here. The baby's crying all the time, and what with Rita, that's the mother, having post natal depression – well, you know how things are with a young baby, it's not a good time for them. Like I said in the car, they've got enough to worry about without me getting in the way. But look, if you're not sure about me moving in, that's fine. I'll start looking for somewhere else.'

'No, really, I said you could move in.' I wished I had that glass of wine in front of me, the one I'd poured down the sink. Not because I needed it, but for the feel of the glass in my hand. 'What about tomorrow evening? Have you got a lot of stuff?'

'Not a lot. Just a couple of bags and my guitar.'

'Shall I can pick you up at the station, where I dropped you off at the weekend? '

I offer lifts like other people hand out cups of tea. It took me five years and as many tests before I was able to drive. I know all about not driving.

I calculated: I'd be home by six o'clock, I'd need a bit of time to sort out the room, I wasn't up to doing it this evening. 'Can you be there for half past seven?'

'Sure. That's amazing. Thanks a lot. I'll be there at half past seven. Thanks.'

***

The wine was still sloshing around my bloodstream, and I hoped I hadn't made a decision I was going to spend the next few months regretting. And then I told myself that, even if sharing a bathroom and kitchen with someone became a nightmare, it would at least help take my mind off Oliver. He'd been controlling my emotions for long enough.

Right now though, I needed an early night. I returned to my bedroom, saw the heap of dresses on the chair. My intention had been to hang them in the spare bedroom, but if the room was going to be Justin's I'd have to find a space for them in my own wardrobe. Luckily I'd recently taken quite a bit of stuff to recycling, and there were a few coat hangers floating around, not doing anything.

I hung the dresses one by one, first the navy blue one, then the others. They didn't seem quite so beautiful and magical now. I was conscious once again of the musty, musky smell of them, lightly mingled with sweat, and hoped it wouldn't spread to the rest of my clothes.

Nine

And now I suppose I should explain how it was for me with Oliver. How our relationship came about.

My friend Ellie was always reading books about psychology – not the heavy, professional stuff, but those lightweight ones geared to ordinary people who wanted to improve the quality of their lives – and she used to tell me I had a fear of intimacy. That was why I was always falling for men who had a commitment phobia, she said. The ones I would never end up living with.

Oliver, of course, came into this category.

I longed and lusted for him from the moment he first appeared in the office; from the moment his long, immaculate fingers flicked through the sheets of paperwork on my desk as he leaned over me, and I inhaled the leathery scent of his coat and the heat of his breath. I guessed he was in his late forties or early fifties, and he exuded confidence, experience, and a strong sense of his own worth. I heard rumours that he had an ex-wife somewhere in the background, that he was a bit of a womaniser, but I wasn't deterred. I wanted him. And, as they say, where there's a will.

So I made sure that on the days he taught at the university – it happened to be Wednesdays and Fridays – I was up earlier in the morning and made more of an effort than normal with make-up and clothes. I found out that he often went to the Playhouse for lunch, so one day I persuaded Kathleen and another colleague, Hazel, to go there with me. Our lunch break was nearly over when he came walking in, on his own. Hazel had already stood up and put her jacket on, and Kathleen was wriggling about, ready to go. I said, 'You two go on, I'll catch you up in a minute or two.' I'd been putting in some unpaid overtime, I was entitled to a longer lunch break.

***

He didn't notice me at first, as he made his way to the bar, but then he took a quick look round to see whether there was anyone there he recognised, and I threw him one of my full-on smiles, the ones I used to practise in the mirror when I was a teenager. He saw my empty glass and asked me what I was drinking, and I thought I'd better not have another beer as I had to go back to work, so I said a diet coke please. He sat where Kathleen had been sitting, pint of beer in front of him, and I can't remember much of what we talked about, except that he asked me how long I'd been working at the college and, in order to make myself sound more interesting, I spun some yarn about how I'd had ballet lessons as a child (that part was true) and that I was going to train to be a dancer, only I was injured in a car accident and had to change my career plan. That last part had happened to someone I used to know at school, only in her case she'd switched from dancing to nursing. After half an hour he looked at his watch and said he had to go and give some tutorials. We walked back to the college together, and I could tell that he'd started to become attracted to me.

***

It was some weeks later, when we'd been out together quite a few times, that I realised he was involved with Sarah. I was window-shopping in Norwich city centre one Saturday, when I saw the two of them walk out of the arcade, hand in hand. They didn't see me, they were too wrapped up in each other. She was talking about something, looking intense, gesturing with her hands. He was listening and nodding, smiling, in that way that makes you feel so special. Just as he did with me.

It felt like an ice-cold axe had cut me in two.

I raised the issue the next time we went for a meal in our favourite pasta restaurant. We'd drunk half our bottle of white wine and shared a dish of olives while we were waiting for our meals to arrive. We'd been talking about something inconsequential, I can't remember what. Eventually the food turned up – we'd both ordered linguini with seafood – and then, with my fork hovering, I said, 'I saw you out at the weekend. With Sarah Bannister.'

He frowned. 'Sarah,' he repeated, as if he had to think about it. 'Yes, that's right.'

'I didn't know you saw each other, outside of work.'

'We've known each other a long time.'

'How long's that?'

'A long time.'

'Before you were both working at the university? Or since?'

'Before, as it happens.' I could see he was annoyed at my questions.

'I was just curious.' I was still holding my first forkful of pasta, as if my arm had frozen halfway to my mouth. 'Are you in a relationship with her?'

'It depends what you mean by a relationship.'

'Do you have a commitment to her? More than to me?'

'Leave this alone, Melanie. You know I'm a no-strings sort of person. I've never pretended otherwise. To you or anyone else.'

But I couldn't let it go. 'You must have believed in commitment once. When you were younger. When you were married. '

'Let's say, once bitten twice shy.'

The waitress who'd served our meal came up and asked, in an Eastern European accent, if everything was alright. 'Everything's fine,' I snapped at her.

'Can we leave this now? Can we start to enjoy our meal?'

I put my fork down. 'I just need to know whereabouts I am in your top ten. I suppose I am at least in your top ten?'

'If you're going to carry on like this, I'm going. This is not my idea of a relaxing evening.'

I could see he was really angry now. I could see the muscles in his face starting to twitch, the coldness in his eyes. I was about to apologise, to try and recover the evening, when he opened his wallet, took out some notes, and dumped them on the table. Before I could say anything, he stood and strode out of the restaurant.

I was left there staring at two full dishes of pasta and a half-empty bottle of wine. I felt as though everyone was watching me, although that was probably just my self-centredness. No doubt they were more concerned with their own evening, and what they wanted from it. I was aware of other people's conversations bouncing back from the low ceiling, a medley of voices. The waitress was busy taking orders, but finally I managed to catch her eye. She came over and I asked to settle the bill. The uneaten meals must have told their own story. We never went back to that restaurant.

***

So I hardened myself to the knowledge that I was sharing Oliver with my old school friend. And probably other women too. It wasn't the best of situations, but – emotionally dependent as I'd become by now – it was something I would just have to live with.

I don't know whether Sarah knew about my own relationship with Oliver, not at that time. Our conversations were limited to work, and I doubt very much that Oliver would have spoken to her about me. But there was one occasion when I made sure that she *did* know, and it was a very short while before she died.

It was just after the Easter break. Oliver and I had taken a spur-of-the-moment long weekend in Paris. Apart from the weather, which wasn't exactly brilliant, our time there was all I could have dreamed of. We over-indulged in food, wine, art, and each other. We had wonderful sex, as much as we wanted, mornings, afternoons and nights, and we spent a lot of time just sitting in cafés, watching the life of Paris go by, as we chatted randomly or just relaxed. We were a couple.

Naturally, as soon as we came back home, we became separate people again: me on my own in my house, with Oliver at the end of the phone if he bothered to answer. Sometimes warm, lifting my spirits, at other times evasive and distant. Even so, I tried to cling to the magic that Paris had been. I wanted to believe that those consecutive days of being together had cemented something between us. And I wanted everybody to know. I was tired of being secretive.

***

I was hard at work on my computer when Sarah came into the office. I was already entrenched in piles of paperwork, but it was Sarah's first day back for the new term. It was a Tuesday. She worked there on Tuesdays and Fridays. She was more casually dressed than usual, in jeans and a blouse, her hair tied back from her face. She looked rather pale and tired. Without looking at me, she asked whether I'd had a good break. 'Really, really good,' I told her. 'Oliver and I went to Paris, he was showing me some of his favourite haunts. What about you?'

Sarah sucked her upper lip with her lower one, a habit I recognised from her much younger days. 'Not great, actually. Unfortunately my mother's got cancer and I went to spend a bit of time with her. She's on her own now, living in Yorkshire, where she grew up. I don't think she'll be around much longer.'

'Oh God, I'm so sorry.' It was the first time we'd exchanged any personal news with each other since school days, and it had to be like that. I remembered the figure in her dressing-gown, peering over the chain at the front door. The person flapping around with a tea towel, after I'd spilled my orange squash at the table. On both occasions her mother had seemed an unhappy person, uncomfortable with life. And now she was dying.

***

Following that conversation with Sarah, it occurred to me that maybe the Paris vacation had been more impromptu for me than for Oliver. That it may have been planned for Oliver and Sarah, only Sarah had decided to go and visit her dying mother, and Oliver had taken me as a substitute. Without, of course, telling Sarah.

And I have a feeling that Sarah relayed our conversation to Oliver. The Paris magic faded around then. Oliver started to restrict his contact with me to the office, and I was spending most of my evenings with a bottle of wine in front of the TV, or curled up under the duvet.

It was just a few weeks after that brief conversation I had with Sarah that she shocked us all with her suicide.

Ten

The spare bedroom was practically ready and waiting for a new tenant. I ran the hoover round superficially, checked the wardrobe and drawers were empty, opened the window to let in some air. Then I drove to the station forecourt, to pick up Justin. Now that I was committed to this, I no longer had any feelings one way or another, it was just something that had to be done. Like clearing Lizzie's house. For some reason, I was finding myself burdened with an obligation to this family I hadn't previously known. But then, I was my mother's daughter. Needing to look after people seemed to be part and parcel of our genes.

Once Justin had parked his bags and guitar in what was now his room, I showed him the kitchen (leading off from the little square dining room) and the bathroom (an extension behind the kitchen). When I was looking for a house to buy, I found that lots of the Victorian terraced houses similar to mine had their bathroom upstairs, converted from what had been the third bedroom in former times. Those were the days when people would have had a tin bath in front of the fire, and used the toilet in the back-yard. However, I made sure when I chose my house that there was a bathroom extension downstairs. I didn't want people traipsing through my bedroom whenever they needed a pee.

Having given him a tour of the house, which must have taken the whole of five minutes, we sat down in the front room and discussed basics. First of all, we agreed on the rent, which of course would be paid for by housing benefit until Justin found a job. That was the easy bit.

'OK,' I said. Now for the difficult part. Working out how I was going to share my space. How we'd be able to live alongside each other. I was conscious that I was twiddling my right ear lobe, a habit of mine. I clasped my hands together in front of me, like people sometimes do when they're learning how to speak in public. 'There are just a few things we need to sort out. Housekeeping stuff. Do you smoke?' I began.

He shrugged. 'Sometimes. I'm trying to give up.'

'It's hard isn't it. I gave up a year ago. Well mostly. I still lapse from time to time. But what I was going to say was, don't worry, this isn't a smoke-free zone, I don't have a problem with you smoking in the house as long as you don't chain smoke. I don't want the place to stink of tobacco. You can share the washing machine and the dishwasher. There's always plenty of space in the fridge. I don't like the place to be a tip, but I'm not obsessively house-proud. You're welcome to watch TV, as long as we don't clash. I'm quite flexible, I'm sure we'll work things out as we go along. If there's anything you're not happy about, just let me know, and I'll do the same.'

I gathered my breath, hoping I'd got the tone about right. All day I'd been rehearsing that little speech in my head. It probably sounded as though I'd read it all from my notes.

He gave his little shrug, and smiled. 'I can't promise I'll be the perfect tenant, but I'll do my best. I know I'm some guy you've only just met. Thanks for taking a risk with me.'

He almost seemed to be laughing at me. He appeared more relaxed, more mature somehow, than he'd seemed in the car, when I'd given him a lift from North Walsham, just those few days ago. He was probably slightly older than I'd thought at first, perhaps early thirties rather than late twenties. Not all that much younger than me. For some reason, this threw me a bit. Changed the balance between us.

I nodded, forced a smile in return. I needed a drink, needed to unwind. I needed to eat. Who was going to go first in the kitchen? He'd already put some stuff in the fridge, so he must have been planning to cook. He'd also put a bottle of wine in the kitchen. I wondered if he intended sharing it.

He must have read my mind. 'Have you eaten yet?'

'No, I was just thinking . . .'

'I'm not proposing to be your resident cook, but as it's our first night, do you fancy a stir fry?'

'You're thinking of doing one?'

'That's the general idea. Do you eat prawns?'

'Love them.'

'OK. It's going to be some sort of approximate Thai concoction. One of my staples. Can I pour you a glass of wine?'

'Even better. But first I'm going to have to change out of these work clothes.'

***

By the time I came downstairs, showered and wearing a long jumper over my leggings, there were knives and forks on the table, the wine bottle had been opened, a glass was already poured out for me, and exotic and unfamiliar cooking smells were sizzling from the kitchen. I picked up the glass and took a gulp. I realised how hungry I was. I sat down and fiddled with my glass, trying to make the wine last longer than five minutes. It was the first time I'd had a man cook for me in my own home.

Justin brought in the plates and joined me at the table. He was wearing a T-shirt with his jeans, and I noticed how skinny his arms were.

I held up my glass. 'Here's to my new lodger.'

'To my lovely landlady.' He seemed to be flirting with me a bit, which surprised me. He hadn't seemed the flirty type.

'This is good,' I said, tucking in to the food. He smiled, pleased with himself. 'Do you do a lot of cooking?' I asked him.

'I suppose it's my way of trying to be useful in other people's houses. I enjoy cooking. Lizzie did too, and the kitchen was her territory, so I didn't get to do so much then.'

I noted, as I had before, how he seemed to refer to Lizzie as if she was a friend, or partner, rather than a grandmother. 'You must miss her.'

'Mm.'

I shouldn't have said that. Not just then. It was a time for being cheerful.

'I'm afraid I'm the world's laziest, when it comes to cooking. It's mostly pizzas out of a box, or ready meals from the supermarket.'

'I did notice there wasn't a lot in your fridge.'

'My excuse is I work all week.' Something else I shouldn't have said, rubbing his nose in the fact that he didn't have a job. 'And when I'm home I just want to get the eating done and then slob out in front of the telly. I can't be dealing with all that vegetable chopping.'

He laughed. He had a nice way of laughing, warm and somehow appreciative. He laughed with his eyes as well as his voice.

'And every Sunday I go and eat with my mother. It's a ritual. Ever since my father died last year.'

'I'm sorry.'

'And Saturdays just *go*, somehow.'

'Have you . . . ?' He stopped in his tracks.

'Were you going to ask me if I had a boyfriend? The answer's no. Not currently. What about you, do you have someone special?'

'Likewise. Nobody at present.'

'Are you gay? I thought I'd better ask, before I made the wrong assumption.'

'Do I look it?' he laughed.

'People don't, do they? I once had this massive crush on somebody for about six months before I realised.'

'A while ago I went around with a girl for five years, that's the longest I've been with somebody. Then she went out with someone else and died in a car crash.'

'How awful.'

'You're probably thinking I put a jinx on people.'

'I'm not the luckiest person to be around, either. Maybe we'll, you know, cancel out each other's jinxes.' I poured more wine into our glasses. 'If we finish this, there's another half bottle in the kitchen, needs using up.' Was it only one evening ago that Oliver had been here, stirring up all that emotion? Already it was starting to feel like something that happened in another life.

***

With Justin around, I found myself being careful not to leave my underclothes on the bathroom floor after I'd showered, and worrying that my tampon might not have flushed down the toilet. He seemed to be out of the house quite a lot when I was in, and I had the sense he was giving me space. I guess he'd had plenty of experience of living in other people's houses, keeping out of their way when he needed to. For me, it was rather more difficult. Apart from Ellie, I'd always lived on my own, or with my parents and brothers. And Ellie and I had been friends since the secretarial course, where we'd first met. We were used to each other. She knew all about my irritable bowel syndrome and my PMT. I knew about her tendency to bulimia. Whereas Justin and I had barely started to tickle the surface of knowing each other.

So the week went by, and he didn't offer to cook for us again, and I hardly saw him. He didn't turn on the TV, although I reminded him it was fine if he did. From time to time I heard him playing his guitar in his room. On the Friday, when I came home from work, I found he'd left me a note on the table saying he'd be in North Walsham till Sunday, that he'd be staying a couple of nights with some friends. On the Sunday, I drove to my mother's, as normal.

I was running slightly late that Sunday. I'd spent Saturday afternoon and evening with some married friends who were celebrating their son's first birthday. Any excuse for a party, and the child was too young to mind sharing his special day with a houseful of noisy grown-ups. This meant I had to catch up with my laundry and household chores on the Sunday morning, already shrunk to barely a couple of hours after catching up on sleep. Justin still wasn't back, so I'd had the house to myself.

I hadn't yet told my mother about my new lodger. To be honest, I was rather dreading the moment. Despite her devotion to charitable causes, I knew she wouldn't be too thrilled that her daughter was sharing her house with a young man who was almost a stranger.

As soon as I let myself in through her front door, I sensed she had something on her mind. She was much less talkative than usual, and there was a stiffness about her that boded ill. I helped her carry the various dishes to the table. I sat in my usual place, took a mouthful of roast lamb. 'I've had someone round to look at those paintings of Lizzie's, like I said I would. He likes the portrait, and the seascapes. He reckons they might sell for about two hundred pounds, if somebody felt like organising a show.' I carefully avoided mentioning Oliver's name, as if that made him less real. I still shook with anger every time I remembered how he'd made me feel. It would have been better if I never had to see him again, but unfortunately that was impossible unless I changed my job.

'Oh yes, the paintings.' She couldn't have forgotten about them taking up more than half of her garage space. 'Philippa came round on Thursday, to pick up the key.' I glanced out of the window. There was already a FOR SALE sign outside what used to be Lizzie's house. They hadn't wasted much time. I hadn't noticed it as I'd driven into the close.

'Well I hope she was grateful for all the hard work we did.'

'Not exactly. Oh, she thanked me for the trouble I'd taken. So I told her my daughter had helped me a lot with it too. And then she said: "Oh, by the way, what's your daughter playing at?" I looked at her blankly, I had no idea what she was talking about. And she said: "All that snooping around the house, uninvited, and not content with that she's now ensnared my son. No doubt encouraging him to tell her all sorts of nonsense about our family." Well I was flabbergasted. I was fuming. "Do you mind," I said to her, "my daughter worked damned hard helping me sort out the stuff in that house for you. If you were so concerned about people snooping you should have done the job yourself, or got one of your family to do it. Such as your own son, for example. My daughter, who you've just insulted, was kind enough to give him a lift, by the way, even though he had the nerve to turn up after all the work had been done. I suppose that's what you mean by *ensnaring* him. And by the way," I said, "if those pictures aren't gone from my garage in a couple of weeks, I'm going to get the Oxfam people to take them." And then she said: "You don't *know*, do you? About Justin." So I said, "I don't know what?" And that was when she told me that he's actually there in your *house* with you. Is that *true*? It can't *possibly* be true.'

I put down my knife and fork. I knew this was going to be difficult. 'Yes, Justin *has* moved in, as a matter of fact. He's renting the front bedroom. I was going to tell you this afternoon, over lunch. I didn't expect anybody to get there first.'

'I can't believe it. You don't even *know* him. Whatever *possessed* you?'

'I actually thought it seemed quite a good idea. I mean, he hasn't exactly got a home any more, has he?' I inclined my head in the direction of the house that was up for sale. 'He told me where he was staying was a bit overcrowded, new baby and so on, mother with post-natal depression, and I'd been thinking for ages about getting another lodger, so it seemed like a good way forward for both of us. He seems an OK person, by the way, even if his mother sounds like an arsehole. And he *was* your neighbour. Not just somebody sitting in the street, asking for change.'

She finally took a mouthful of food, chewed, swallowed, sighed. That sigh reminded me of how she sometimes was when I was young and kept forgetting to do my homework. She really didn't want to have to nag me about it, BUT. 'You always *were* too impulsive with people. You always chose some strange friends. How do you know you can trust him?'

'I don't. I don't *know* I can. But I like to give people the benefit of the doubt. Like I thought *you* usually did.'

'You saw the state of that house.'

'The state of that house was down to Lizzie. You know that. You liked Lizzie. You told me she was a nice woman, remember.'

'You always were a stubborn little thing.'

***

Justin had returned during my absence. He'd apparently cooked and eaten by himself, and was loading the dishwasher. The kitchen smelt of curry spices. I felt illogically angry, seeing him there, acting as if everything was hunky-dory. My mother's words were still ringing in my head. 'I gather you told Philippa you were living here?'

'I mentioned it on the phone. I thought I'd give her the good news.'

'The good news? I don't think that was quite how she took it.'

'What do you mean?'

'I was going to tell *my* mother today, that I'd got a new lodger. Unfortunately Philippa pipped me to the post. And not in the nicest of ways. Apparently she thinks I've got you *ensnared*, that was the word she used, so I can dig out all your family secrets. As if I actually give a shit about your family.' That last bit was uncalled for, childish, but I was feeling like a child. That's what mothers can do to daughters, on a Sunday afternoon.

'Christ. Is that what she's been saying? I'm sorry.'

'It doesn't matter. Well, actually it does matter, but it wasn't your fault. I think what really upset my mother was that Philippa knew about you being here

71

before she did. She doesn't take well to being the last person to know things.'

'Even so, if that's what Philippa said to her, it's inexcusable. I can't . . . I was going to say I can't believe it, but actually I *can* believe it.' He gave his little shrug, and my own anger faded as I realised what he'd probably had to deal with over the years. 'I'll have a word with her.' I was a bit surprised, the way he echoed me and called his mother Philippa. I wondered whether he always did, or whether it was because he was talking to me, and I didn't know her.

'Don't worry, it's no big deal.' I was holding a bottle of wine. 'Overpriced plonk from the off-licence round the corner. I need a drink. Do you want to share it with me?'

It was a screw-top. I took the bottle and a couple of glasses into the living-room. He followed me. It was the first time we'd said more than half a dozen words to each other since the evening he'd moved in. He must have felt, as I did, that there was some damage to repair. I poured the wine, and then I curled up on the sofa, and he stretched out in one of the armchairs. We were both simulating being relaxed and comfortable. 'So, have you had a good weekend?' I asked him. The question sounded false and strained after what had been said before.

'Oh, the usual. What about yours?'

'Not bad. Yesterday I got rather drunk at a one-year-old's birthday party. Today I spent most of Sunday lunch trying to convince my mother that having a new lodger wasn't the worst idea of my life. I did remind her you'd been her neighbour. She usually likes neighbours.'

'I hope it wasn't. The worst idea of your life. I still can't get over Philippa saying what she did. Apart from anything else, she's the last person who should be worrying about family secrets. Seeing as she's already put most of her dirty linen on her website.'

'She's done what?'

'A couple of years ago, she got me to shoot a video of her, talking about her life. My media studies come in handy, once in a while. I'm not bad at videos. Anyhow, she comes on-screen talking about how she's managed to overcome all the problems of a lifetime and now here she is – bingo – this reinvented person. It was supposed to promote her therapy business. Or rather, her *practice*, that's what she calls it. Not business. I think the general message is supposed to be: If I can do it, you can do it too, and I can show you how. I don't know whether it's ever got her any clients. I was quite proud of the video, at the time, even though I thought she was being a bit self-indulgent. It's very *Philippa*, the essence of her, if you know what I mean. It's one of the few things I've done for her she's actually been pleased with.'

'So that's what she does? Therapy?'

'She says so. I don't think she has many clients. Possibly one or two a week on a good week. We're in a recession, aren't we? People don't have money for stuff like therapy these days, do they?'

'Can I see it? The video.'

'Do you really want to?'

I nodded. I wanted a glimpse of this person I still hadn't met, who'd accused me of snooping. Ensnaring.

'Is that your laptop down there?' He pointed to where I kept it, under the coffee table. I opened it up, and he came and sat next to me on the sofa, so we could both see the screen.

He was wearing jogging trousers and a loose cardigan with what appeared to be nothing underneath. I could see the light downy hairs on his chest. His plimsolls were untied, no socks. He smelt of soap, and he'd shaved the stubble that had been growing the wrong side of designer. He'd obviously spent time in the bathroom while I was out.

'Are you sure you want to see this?' he asked me again. I nodded.

He clicked on to Philippa's website, and launched the video.

Eleven

THE VIDEO

On the screen, a woman sits in an armchair in her living-room. There's an abstract print on the wall behind her, a vase of tulips on the coffee table in front of her. Her legs are crossed, her hands on the arms of her chair, and she has an enormous ring on the middle finger of her right hand. She is wearing a purple and black kaftan over black leggings. Her shoes, too, are purple. The camera zooms in to her head and shoulders. Her hair is a blonde frizzy mane, radiating from an off-centre parting. Around her neck, slightly askew, hangs a silver pendant in the shape of some sort of insect or sea creature. Her eyelashes are heavy with dark mascara, and her lips are a glossy red. She appears to have a touch of blusher on her cheeks. It's hard to guess her age, she isn't young, perhaps in her late forties. She gives a little nod to the camera, takes a visible deep breath, and starts to speak.

'I'm sharing my experience with you today because I want to show you how we can take control of our destiny. All of us. Every one of us. Nobody has to be a victim. Nobody needs to be buffeted by the winds of misfortune. Nobody needs to be, what you might call, unlucky.'

She closes her eyes for a moment, as if searching deep inside herself, trying to remember.

'I used to believe I was unlucky. I used to believe all sorts of things about myself. I thought I was ugly. I thought I was rather stupid and unintelligent. I thought I was unloved. Anything negative, you name it, I thought it. And the more I had those negative thoughts, the more they coloured my self-perception. I was drowning in negativity.'

She swallows, a little wave passes through her neck, and the pendant moves with it. Her eyes, under the thick and rather doll-like eyelashes, stare out from the screen.

'Well, as you can see, I changed. I reinvented myself. I changed my life by changing my perceptions of myself. I realised it was possible and I did it. You can do it too. But let me start by telling you about my life, about where I came from.

'I had quite an ordinary childhood. We had enough to eat. I had presents on my birthday. I had a younger brother and we used to play together, and we sometimes fought, like brothers and sisters do. Just normal, you might say. I daresay I had quite an innocent sort of childhood. I wasn't physically or sexually abused. Nothing particularly shocking happened to me. I didn't bother to think about whether I was happy or unhappy.'

She exhales a long sigh, before continuing.

'The troubles started when I became a teenager ... '

She looks at the camera, pauses for effect. Her face is replaced by a photo of a chubby schoolgirl in uniform. It is apparently the same person, but, instead of the sophisticated, stylish figure who has been talking, her teenage self looks awkward, self-conscious and unhappy.

The camera returns to the woman talking on the video. The woman with the blonde frizzy hair, eyes peering out under thick mascaraed eyelashes, glossy red lips.

'I'm going to share my story with you. We all have our stories. Some of you may consider you have worse stories than mine. Whatever our stories, we have to deal with them. Once we've dealt with them, we can choose whether to give them a happy ending or a sad one.'

She gives a little nod, inviting agreement.

'Sixteen is a bad age to be fat. Everything you want to wear is designed for thin people. And your friends moaning all the while about their absence of boobs doesn't help. You just keep seeing how good they look with their flat tummies and skinny thighs and you want to be like them. And then you eat chocolate and cream doughnuts to cheer yourself up. Get the picture? You may even see some of yourself in it.

'Well, that was me. I was the fat girl with skinny friends. I was the one the boys didn't bother chatting up if there was anyone else around. But there was one exception: a boy called Ricky. He was a few years older than me. I think he was nineteen when I first met him. He seemed really mature. He was one of the best-looking boys around, and I thought he couldn't possibly be interested in me, the fat girl, but he said he liked a girl with some meat on her. I started to regain a bit of confidence. But things were happening around me that I couldn't control.

'Bear with me, because I'm going to share some of these personal matters with you. I want you to know that I've had my problems, just as I'm sure that you have. We all have our problems, don't we? And once we acknowledge that, we can start to help one another.

'Around that time, my mum decided she was bored with my dad and went off to live with a woman. Her name was Marianne. They'd met at some women's group they both went to. So there I was, having to cope with adolescence, and being fat, and having my first boyfriend, and at the same time I was supposed to be swotting for my GCEs, and not only that but I had a mother who'd suddenly decided she was a lesbian.

'She didn't want me calling her 'mum' any more. I had to call her Sandra, she said it was more grown-up, that we were equals now, not mother and child. Well I

didn't feel very equal. Nobody actually listened to my point of view about anything. So, OK, I'll try to remember to call my mum Sandra from now on, when I'm talking to you.

'Sandra's girlfriend, Marianne, she did try to sit down and talk to me. She wasn't very old, nearer to my own age than Sandra's. She said I was welcome to live with her and Sandra, but I said thanks but no thanks, I was perfectly happy living with my dad. And I had my boyfriend. I had Ricky. Sandra didn't like Ricky, she never had, she took a dislike to him from the word go, so I knew he wouldn't be welcome in their little love-nest. Not that he'd want to visit. He said he found it repulsive, the idea of two women in bed together. Political correctness wasn't one of his strong points. Mine neither. That was something we had in common. We liked to call a spade a spade.

'As I mentioned earlier, I had a brother, his name was George, he was fifteen months younger than me, and nobody suggested he should go and live with Sandra and Marianne. There was this idea going around at the time – in what was known as the women's movement – that men were the enemy. Not just grown men, but also male children, as they used to call them. My mum, I mean Sandra, actually had a badge: THE FUTURE IS FEMALE. How daft was that?'

She shares a little mocking smile with her unknown audience.

There is a long pause, while she swallows, visibly, and switches to another key. Sad, subdued.

'Anyhow, he died. George, my younger brother. He died. It wasn't long after mum, Sandra, had left us. He was on the pillion of a friend's motorbike, an older friend who should have known better, and they crashed.'

78

Her eyes tear up, and the camera zooms in on them. She wipes the tears away with the back of her hand. Her lips pucker up. She takes a deep breath, regains control.

'We were all devastated of course. Even Marianne seemed upset. Maybe she felt guilty for saying he was the enemy. I thought this might make Sandra change her mind and come back and live with me and Dad again, but no such luck. No such bad luck, I should say. Dad and I were just fine on our own, we didn't need anybody else.

'And then Dad had to find somebody else, a woman called Lizzie. She moved in with us, this stranger, and Kate, her daughter. Kate was five years old at the time. I didn't want a little sister. I wanted my brother back.

'As soon as Dad got his divorce, he and Lizzie were married. He didn't waste much time. It wasn't that I actually disliked Lizzie, I just thought she was weird. She used to dress in dippy hippy skirts, and she baked bread and made jam, as if she was trying to be some sort of an earth mother. She wanted us all to be vegetarians, only Dad always put a stash of beefburgers in the freezer, so I used to give the nut roasts a miss and go and fry myself some burgers and chips. Lizzie hated the smell of the chip pan, so after a while she started cooking chicken. It was a compromise: I'd eat the veg as long as there was meat to go with them.

*'She used to spend lots of time with Kate, reading to her, doing all this arty-crafty stuff. She ignored **me** most of the time. Not that I made much effort talking to her, either. Like I say, we didn't hate each other, we just didn't have a lot to say to each other. I could see it got on her nerves, the way I used to sit on Ricky's lap watching TV, and I got fed up hearing her prattling away to Kate about birds and butterflies and so on.*

79

'Get the picture?'

Her eyes stare out from the screen, challenging.

'I was starting to feel like a fish out of water in my own home. As if I didn't belong. So I began to spend more and more time at Ricky's place. His mother was fat, fatter than me, and she cooked a lot of chips, and their telly was on all day long, whether anybody was watching or not. I put on more weight. Obese, they call it nowadays. I think I was looking for comfort ... '

Twelve

I found it hard to believe that this overbearing woman, with that mane of frizzy blonde hair, was Justin's mother. All that heavy make-up and ostentatious jewellery and clothes. She certainly had a presence. Once seen, never forgotten. Unlike her son, who you wouldn't really notice, who could quite easily disappear in a crowd.

I watched, repelled and fascinated at the same time, as she made her little speech about choices, about not being a victim. I listened as she talked of her ordinary childhood, how the troubles started when she was a teenager. And then I started to squirm inwardly as she plunged into the details of her life story, mentioning people by name. I couldn't believe that she was doing this. Their actual names. Sandra. Lizzie. Kate. Ricky. Justin.

'I put on more weight. Obese, they call it nowadays. I think I was looking for comfort . . . .'

'That's enough of that,' Justin decided, pressing stop. And I agreed. I sensed he'd rather regretted showing it to me. Seeing it perhaps through my eyes. Yes, technically it was a good video, but it was like reality TV. It was cringe-making. After watching it, I felt like the person I'd been accused of being. Snooping. Digging up the family dirt. I actually felt dirty, as if I needed to wash my hands, brush my teeth.

'She's quite formidable,' I said. 'I'm not sure I'd want her to be my therapist.'

'God forbid.'

I couldn't resist probing a tiny bit. 'So you do still talk to your mother? I mean, on the phone.'

We'd moved up close together in order to watch the video. Thigh inadvertently touching thigh. He must have suddenly become aware of this, and slid away.

'Sure. She likes me to phone her. She's a bit of a control freak. She likes to think she's watching over me from afar. Suits me, that it's afar. That it doesn't get too close.'

'And you felt comfortable with Lizzie?'

'Lizzie was always like a second mother to me. It was Lizzie who used to walk me to school and back, and look after me in the holidays. I had to explain to the other kids that she wasn't my mother, she was my Aunty Lizzie. One of them actually asked me if I was an orphan. But it was Philippa who used to do what she thought were the important things, like turning up at open evenings, at the school. She wouldn't trust Lizzie for that. She'd go there all dressed up and puffed out, and then she'd come home and give me a dressing down for under-achieving.' He gave a rueful chuckle. It didn't quite mask how much he must have dreaded those open evenings. 'In all fairness, she didn't have it easy. She had this job in a fashion shop in Norwich, and she didn't drive in those days, so she was catching trains every day, then having to come back and sort things out at home. Brian was one of the old-fashioned type, he didn't think cooking and cleaning were men's work. And then when I was about thirteen she decided I needed sprucing up, a bit of discipline, so she started working nearer home, in one of those residential care places. She hated it. She used to say she how much it sickened her, the smell of piss, being around people who didn't know their own names any more. She said she wanted to work with people who had a life. That's when she started training to be a counsellor. Those were the worst years. Philippa practising on me, trying to be my therapist as well as my mother. Trying to make me something I wasn't. Trying to undo the damage she thought that Lizzie had done. She failed abysmally of course.'

That was quite a monologue. He put his hands to his face and ran his fingers down his cheeks. I didn't know what to say. I looked away from him.

'Sorry if I'm getting a bit emotional. I didn't mean to unload all of that onto you.'

'I did sort of ask, didn't I?' I couldn't help thinking it was Philippa, not Lizzie, who'd done the damage. I had this sudden feeling that I wanted to make things better for him. I was conscious of a pain, deep down in my gut, that was almost sexual. More than anything, I wanted to put my arms around him, hold him close, but instead I inched further to my half of the sofa, scared of being intrusive. After hesitation, I leaned towards him again, and put my hand briefly on his knee.

'Thanks for telling me all that. I'm feeling a bit choked. A bit inadequate.'

'Sorry,' he said again.

'No need to apologise.'

'Let's change the subject,' he said. 'What's on TV?' He picked up the remote, and started flicking through the channels, in an attempt to neutralise that unexpected interplay of emotion between us.

We'd only shared a living space for such a short time, and already I knew more about Justin and his family than I normally got to know about a man in months or even years. I wasn't sure I was ready for this. I wasn't sure such a deluge of knowing things about someone so soon was actually healthy.

***

I think Justin must have felt this too. The next few days, I didn't see very much of him, and he seemed to be keeping his distance again, or maybe avoiding me. I too was conscious of setting boundaries. It was as though we both decided we'd moved too close too soon. He'd opened a door and given me a glimpse inside, and then he'd closed it again. Not locked, just closed it. That was the way it felt. I believed he'd open it again when we were both ready. For now, it was a strange sort of in-between time, when we both seemed to sense that maybe some sort of a relationship between us was imminent, but we weren't quite ready to acknowledge or surrender to it.

Or maybe I was being too self-absorbed, too introspective, referencing his behaviour to myself. Maybe it was simply that he had other things on his mind.

Such as the inquest into Lizzie's death.

I'd forgotten about this. Although my mother had said something about the death certificate being an interim one, I'd lazily assumed the funeral had been the end of it all, as far as formalities went. Like any other death.

A couple of weeks after he'd shown me the video, I was sitting at the table eating an oven-ready pizza, and he was ironing a white shirt and a well-worn suit. He seemed subdued. 'The inquest's tomorrow,' he volunteered. 'I thought I'd better get kitted out for it.'

'Good luck,' I said to him, realising immediately that this would have been more appropriate for a job interview than an inquest.

He frowned. I could sense the tension around him, an invisible armour.

'It's just a formality, though, isn't it? I mean, everyone knows how she died.'

He shrugged his left shoulder. He was ironing with his right hand. 'There's not much doubt about that, yes. I gather there was a bit of a puzzle at first about how she got hold of the tablets, bearing in mind she wasn't on any medication. The police kept asking me about this, about whether I knew if she was taking anything. I told them Lizzie didn't even like taking aspirin if she could help it. Philippa's theory is that she nicked the tablets from their bathroom cabinet, one of the times she'd been over there for a meal. Brian gets morphine on prescription, for his back troubles, and he'd got into the habit of stockpiling it. He's that sort of person, careful, saves stuff for a rainy day. Lizzie could easily have found it, when she'd been to use the bathroom.'

'So she must definitely have planned it, what she was going to do.'

'Seems that way.'

I pushed the remains of my pizza away from me. 'How are you getting to the inquest? Do you need a lift? I could take time off from work, I could say I'm going to the dentist.' I wanted to do something helpful. To be involved in some small way.

'Thanks, but it's all sorted. Philippa and Brian are coming to pick me up.'

So Philippa would be knocking on the door. *My* door, I couldn't help thinking. It occurred to me, perhaps for the first time, that if Justin and I were to have a relationship, I'd have to take Philippa on board as well. The real Philippa, not just someone in a video. I found the notion decidedly scary.

'So you and Philippa and Brian. Who else is going to be there?'

'One of the police, I've already met him. He was one of the guys who came to the house. He'll be the one presenting the report. He seems quite decent. And the coroner, of course. I don't know who else. But yes, it'll be straightforward, I think. No surprises. It's not like a trial. That's what I've been told. It's just to establish who it was that died, and when and where and how. It's not about accusing anyone of anything.'

'I don't suppose you have any photos of Lizzie?' I asked him. I had my own mental picture of how Lizzie would have looked, some sort of ageing hippie, but I wanted to have it verified.

He shook his head. Then he remembered, 'There's the funeral programme, there was a photo on that.'

He took his freshly ironed clothes upstairs, then came back down and handed me a crumpled funeral programme – an A4 sheet folded into three – before he disappeared upstairs again. My mother must have had one too, I was surprised she hadn't shown it to me. But then, after the funeral, we'd been so busy salvaging stuff from the house, we hadn't really talked.

On the front of the programme was a black and white snapshot of Lizzie Brown as a child. Her hair was in two plaits, and she was wearing shorts and holding a kitten that looked desperate to be anywhere else. On the back was a head-and-shoulders colour photo of a much older Lizzie Brown. She had long auburn hair, rather unkempt, with just a trace of grey. Her head was tilted to one side, and there was a hint of laughter in her eyes that reminded me of Justin's, although, of course, she was the *step* grandmother, not related.

I glanced through the programme. It began with music: Bach, Partita No.2 for Solo Violin in D Minor, Sarabande. A welcome speech was followed by tributes from Philippa and Kate. Then a poem by Rabindranath Tagore, Bengali poet and philosopher, which was printed in the centre of the programme. My mother had mentioned something about a lovely poem. The Reflection and Committal had been sandwiched between Bob Dylan singing 'Forever Young' and Nina Simone singing 'Angel of the Morning'. And then there were some closing words from the speaker, and finally an excerpt from Autumn, The Four Seasons, by Vivaldi.

It did seem like a good funeral, if there is such a thing. I almost wished I'd been there, though at that time of course I had no connection with the family, nor even much of an interest. There's something about funerals – at least the ones I've been to – that makes you wish you'd taken more time to get to know the person who's died. That summary or distillation of a life. So it had been with my father's, even though I thought I knew him as well as anybody. My grandparents'. My aunt's. All prefixed with 'my', their existence had been rooted in my own perceptions. It took death to open my mind to other facets of them.

I was still sitting there with the programme in my hands when Justin walked past me to go to the bathroom. He touched me lightly on the shoulder as he walked past. 'You're looking reflective.'

I didn't tell him that at that moment, for some reason, I'd been thinking of Sarah. Of how I'd missed going to her funeral. Oliver would have been there, and all the other staff who were close to her. It occurred to me that her mother probably hadn't been there either, if she was so ill. Her father of course had died long ago. I was thinking again of that dark, musty house, and how it had made me feel.

I turned my thoughts back to Lizzie. I asked him, 'Who arranged all this? The funeral service. It seems like a lot of thought went into it.'

'I think it was a joint effort between Philippa and Kate. I guess more Kate than Philippa. If it had been left to Philippa, there'd have been less music, more psycho-babble.'

'She looks a nice person. Lizzie. I can see why you got along with her.' And then I added, 'I'll be thinking of you, tomorrow.'

***

As Justin had foreseen, there were no surprises at the inquest. No evidence of any third party involvement in Lizzie's death. They seemed to have bought Philippa's theory, about the morphine tablets being taken from the bathroom cabinet. It would have been so easy, unfortunately. 'It rather amazed me,' Justin said, 'impressed me, anyhow, that the coroner must be dealing with this sort of thing all the time, day in, day out, and yet he didn't sound jaded or mechanical. He sounded human, that guy, as if he really cared about Lizzie. You know, respected her. And about the way it was for all of *us*. As if we all mattered.'

It struck me then that one of the things I liked about Justin was his ability to see the bigger picture, how it was for others, not simply be bogged down in his own little corner of the world. Maybe this was something I could start to learn from him.

Thirteen

It was almost two weeks later that our relationship took a leap forward. When we actually started to *have* a relationship, rather than being two separate people living together.

When I returned from work that Friday, I was surprised to see Justin at home. Normally, on a Friday evening, he'd be propping up the bar at The Kings Arms, before sweating beer on a friend's sofa. Well, that's how I imagined it. It was years since I'd spent a Friday evening in North Walsham.

My bowels had been a bit erratic all day – one of the symptoms of PMT – so I muttered a quick 'hi' and rushed past him to go to the bathroom. When I emerged, I could see that he had something to tell me, the way he was darting around, like a dog ready for walkies. 'I've just heard I've got a job.'

'That's good news.' I was still feeling the after-waves of my stomach cramps. 'What sort of job?'

He shrugged, disappointed, no doubt, in my lack of excitement. 'Assistant caretaker at a primary school.' He spoke flatly.

'When do you start?'

'After half-term, soon as possible. Once they've had me checked out by the police. It's just routine, has to be done.'

'Of course. Justin, that really *is* good news. I didn't even know you'd been for an interview.'

'Oh, I've been to a few more than one. I haven't even bothered telling you because it's usually negative. For once I must have managed to seem enthusiastic.'

I laughed. 'Well done.' So, a caretaker in a primary school. In Oliver's world, the world of artists and academics, or in fact in the world of my brothers, with all their financial aspirations, this would seem such a small success. For Justin though, and for so many other people, drifting between low-paid jobs and unemployment, it was the difference between marginalisation and acceptance. Even I, with my cosy, unchallenged life, was aware of that. I felt genuinely pleased for Justin. Touched that he'd wanted to share his news with me. More so now that my stomach was settling, and I could start to focus on him.

'I was going to cook some pasta. Do you want some?' He was suddenly twitchy, ill at ease, obviously embarrassed to have been so excited about a job.

'You're not going to see your friends this weekend?'

'I can't really be arsed.'

'Why not save the pasta and I'll treat you to a meal somewhere?'

'OK. Sounds good, why not? And when I've got some money coming in I'll be able to start treating *you*, once in a while.'

'I'll look forward to that. Just give me time to have a shower and change, and then I'll ring for a cab. We might have to do some serious drinking tonight.'

***

We went to one of the Indian restaurants in Magdalen Street. Justin's choice.

He was wearing his usual jeans and a battered leather jacket. I too was in jeans: tight ones, with a T-shirt that showed my cleavage, under a fitted blazer. I'd washed my hair in the shower, and put fresh make-up on, more than I'd use in the daytime. Bright red lipstick, which I knew wouldn't survive the first glass of wine.

Justin chose a chicken madras and I opted for a chicken passanda. I ordered pilau rice and brinjal bhaji

90

for us to share, and a bottle of Rioja. And some poppadums for while we were waiting. The waiter sloshed wine in both our glasses.

Indian restaurants weren't part of my trail with Oliver. I'd been missing them. I'm always seduced by the theatrics, how the waiters burst from the kitchen like a team of magicians, speed over with the trolley, and then, with a flourish, download those various shiny dishes on to the starched tablecloth. As soon as the hot spices waft upwards, to my nostrils, whether hungry or not, I'm hooked.

I made up my mind to steer the talk away from all the bad stuff. Tonight was a celebration. 'I've been meaning to say to you, I've heard you playing your guitar in your room and it sounds good. I mean, *really* good. It's great that you've got a job, but you can still play music as well, can't you, in your own time?'

'I know. I mean, I know I can carry on with the music. Not that I'm good. I try though. I think maybe it's in the genes. Peter, my grandfather, used to play guitar in a folk group. His day job was teaching.'

'Your grandfather? Lizzie's husband?' I couldn't keep her name out of the conversation any longer. I was still trying to fit the family jigsaw together.

'That's right. I spent quite a lot of time around him when I was young. I haven't seen much of him since he split up from Lizzie. I don't think he plays music anymore.'

'Do you write your own songs?'

'Mostly. Have you ever listened to a guy who calls himself Bonnie 'Prince' Billy? His real name's Will Oldham?'

'I think I picked up a CD of his, when I was in Lizzie's kitchen. I mentioned to you I took a few. I haven't played it yet though. Is it one of yours?'

He shook his head. 'My stuff's mostly downloads. I bought that one for Lizzie, for a present. I've tried to model myself on his style, not exactly copied it, but my own version of it. I like the way his songs sound like he's having an intimate conversation with someone. Sort of relaxed. Idiosyncratic.'

'I'll listen to it. Will you sing some of your own stuff to me sometime?'

'OK. Sure. What do you normally listen to?'

'Mostly quite mainstream I suppose. Adele. That sort of thing. And I like Laura Marling. Well, you saw what I had in the car.' Music's a bit like art is for me. Other people have tastes, preferences, seem to know what they're talking about. I don't. 'We didn't have much music on at home,' I explained. 'We weren't that sort of family, we were always too busy talking. Or watching TV. When I was young, my mother used to listen to Joni Mitchell, and once I sang Both Sides Now in a school concert. You know, the one about how clouds get in the way. I was only about seven, and I couldn't sing for toffee, but I must have looked cute on the stage. My mother made me a special dress for it. I still have the photo somewhere.' I didn't mention I liked Billie Holliday. I didn't want to think about Oliver.

'Joni Mitchell's classic.'

We had a bit of a comfortable silence while we tucked into our meals. And then we started talking again, but I can't remember what about. Once we were into our second bottle of wine, things started to blur. I should have a tolerance by now, but alcohol tends to make me forget a lot of the detail. I vaguely remember reaching out to Justin across the table, clasping his hand. Letting my thumb trace circles around his palm, rather like the way Oliver used to do with me. There's nothing new in the way relationships unfold, it's the way the clichés evolve and mesh together, the process of it all, that makes each time it happens something special. At one point, I asked him whether anyone had ever told him what beautiful eyes he had, and he told me I was an amazing woman. Hardly the stuff to win an originality contest. At another, slightly later point, my ankle was rubbing against his, and he had his hand under the table, on my knee, then on my thigh.

I paid the bill with my credit card, and then I phoned for a cab to pick us up. I was a bit wobbly walking out of the restaurant, so it was good to feel Justin's hand around my elbow, steering me. We sat together in the back of the taxi. I nodded off to sleep, and woke up outside my house with my head on Justin's shoulder. He settled the fare before I had time to fumble around in my handbag.

***

There was a bottle of brandy in the kitchen cupboard that I kept for special occasions, and I poured us each a glass. But we'd only had time for a couple of sips before Justin had his hands on my shoulders and was kissing me, his hot spicy breath blended with mine. I had my hands under his T-shirt and I could feel the hairs on his back and chest. His fingers wriggled under my bra, and I undid the fastening at the back and slipped off my T-shirt, letting it drop to the kitchen floor. I unbuttoned the flies of his jeans, felt his hard-on, and then I took his hand and led him upstairs to my bedroom. I was conscious of subverting a pattern. With Oliver, things had always happened the other way round. I'd always let Oliver decide on the bedroom moment, then I'd follow meekly, like an obedient child.

The rest of our clothes fell in a heap on my bedroom carpet, and as it was cold we started to make love under the quilt, side by side, facing one another, exploring each other's bodies, and before long I was astride him and we kicked the quilt out of the way. I enjoyed the boniness of him, his smell, his differences from Oliver. I tried to put Oliver firmly out of my mind. We were both out of practice, and it wasn't the most accomplished sex I'd ever had, but it felt real. When Justin came, with a little suppressed cry and a shudder, I lay beside him, encircling his body with my arms. We stayed like that for a while, and he seemed to be asleep. My arms were starting to feel stiff, but I didn't want to wake him, I didn't want the separation. And then he roused himself, and rolled over. Suddenly cold again, I retrieved the quilt. I curved my stomach and thighs around his bottom, resting my left arm across his waist. Before I too went to sleep, I told myself that I'd finally found the person I needed.

Fourteen

Not long after Justin started his job at the school, I went down with a cold. On the Monday afternoon, I was aware of a persistent click in the throat, and when I woke up on Tuesday my voice was an unpredictable croak or squeak. There was no way I could go into the office sounding like that.

By now, Justin and I were sharing my bed on a regular basis. It felt right and comfortable and, although we still enjoyed a bottle of wine, we no longer needed alcohol to fuel our relationship. I told him to keep his distance if he didn't want my germs, he couldn't be taking time off from work when he'd only just started, but he laughed and hugged me and said the damage was already done if it was going to be.

I wasn't exactly bursting with energy, but I didn't feel ill enough to stay in bed. Wearing a sweater over my pyjamas, old fluffy slippers on my feet, I curled up on the sofa with my laptop and, after checking what my friends were up to on Facebook, for something to do I searched for Philippa's video. I was still curious to hear the rest of her story. I thought it better to watch it on my own, without embarrassing Justin. I googled 'Philippa Morgan Therapist' without success, and then I remembered that Justin's surname, Morgan, was the name of her first husband, Ricky. Philippa's name was in Lizzie's funeral programme, but I'd given it back to Justin, and I didn't want to start raking through his stuff. I rang my mother and asked her if she knew Philippa's surname. 'It's Johnson,' she told me. 'Why?'

'Just something I'm checking out. I didn't want to ring Justin at work.'

'By the way, she did call round and apologise, for what she'd said about you. I do respect that, at least, when people have the courage to come and apologise. She said she was pleased that Justin had got a job, and maybe you'd been a good influence.' I couldn't help puffing myself up a bit when she said that, although I didn't really think Justin's progress was down to me. 'I asked her in for coffee and we had a chat about this and that, and I told her what you'd said about Lizzie's paintings, that we might be able to sell them. She seemed quite keen on the idea. She told me she's going to investigate the village hall, where she lives, she says we wouldn't have to pay for it. Apparently she's on the committee.'

'It's about time something was done with those paintings. You can't keep them in your garage forever.' Personally, I'd lost interest in them.

'Your throat sounds dreadful. Are you taking something for it?'

'Yes,' I lied.

So I scrolled down the Philippa Johnsons, and it wasn't long before I found the link I was looking for.

***

THE VIDEO

' ... *I put on more weight. Obese, they call it nowadays. I think I was looking for comfort. Of course, this had the opposite effect. Even Ricky was starting to go off me. I seem to remember him using the word 'grotesque'. A big word for Ricky, who couldn't normally manage more than one syllable at a time.*

'I didn't do too well with my GCEs. Not surprising, what with all the issues I was having. Even so, and even though my physical appearance had a lot to be desired, I managed to get a job, working in a women's fashion shop in Norwich. It was a bit depressing

standing there every day amongst all those clothes I couldn't fit into, but I was a good salesperson. I'd tell people that something looked fabulous on them, and they'd believe me. I made twice as many sales as the other girls.

'And then I became pregnant. I was only seventeen when my son was born. I had to give up my job when I had the baby, but luckily I was able to find another one quite soon afterwards, because my stepmother, Lizzie, was able to take over the childminding. A year later, Ricky and I got married. We rented our own little flat. And at first everything seemed fine. I had Ricky. I had my baby boy. We had our own place. I had my job. But it wasn't long till Ricky's personality started to change. He started knocking me about. And I could tell people were looking at my black eyes and thinking 'I told you so', even if they weren't saying it. Nobody in my family had ever taken to Ricky, and maybe they were right after all. So I didn't have much choice but to go back and live with my father and Lizzie, tail between my legs.'

Philippa looks downwards at that point. The camera zooms in on her hands, the clasping and unclasping of her fingers.

'It wasn't ideal, of course, but I was out in the daytime, working, so Lizzie and I weren't under each other's feet all the time. I registered on the list for council housing, and a year later they found a flat for us, me and little Justin. It was a bit run-down on the outside, and the stairs smelt of cats and God knows what else, but inside I kept it immaculate. A place of my own. Somewhere I could feel proud of.

'It was probably a result of all the stress I'd had over the past few years, but I'd lost a bit of weight. And I started thinking positively about my life. I stopped feeling like a victim. And when you open your

97

heart and mind, you start to make space for the good things to happen.

'So I met my husband, Brian. He was a breath of fresh air. He didn't see me as a fat person. He was able to see beyond that, through all those layers of fat, and all that awkwardness and insecurity, to the inner me.

'When we first met, he was just doing odd jobs, then he started working for a company, fitting kitchens. But he had ambition and started his own business, employed a couple of people. He was a hard worker. And of course, I was still working too. We saved up some money and managed to get a mortgage on a two-bedroomed house. I lost more weight, and I started to find my own dress style. People told me I dressed with panache. I love that word, panache. We had our circle of friends, we socialised, had barbecues, invited people round for dinner parties. I started to feel like a real human being instead of a social outcast. And things just got better and better.

'And so, let's cut a long story short. Fast forward to the present, and you can see me now. OK, I'll never be a catwalk model, but I'm at home in my own skin, and when you're comfortable in your own skin you're at home in the world. I've learned to feel good about myself. There's no trace now of that miserable fat teenager I used to be.

'And over the years, I've come to realise that we all have our problems. We all have obstacles preventing us from being the people we were meant to be.

'Think about yourself. Like I used to do, you might imagine that there's something wrong with the way you look. Or you're not clever enough. Or you're too shy, or you have a stammer, or there's something you're afraid of. Crowded places, open spaces, heights, flying. Or you have habits you want to lose. Smoking,

or drinking too much. Or bad habits in relationships. Repetitive patterns. Feeling like a victim. Not being in control of your own life.

'So listen to me. I trained to be a therapist so that I could help others, people like you. I can help you to overcome whatever your problems might be. Just as I overcame mine. If I could do it, and I seemed to have all the odds stacked against me, then you can do it too. It's all about believing in yourself, in your own specialness. Nobody needs to be a victim. Discover who you really are, believe in that person, and once you really believe in yourself, then you'll start to shine. You're beautiful. You're unique. Believe that, and anything's possible. Whatever you dream of. You can do it. Trust me.'

Philippa looks out from the screen, eyes shining with tears. There's no doubting her sincerity. Nor the message of her life story. No one can deny that the plain fat teenager, with all her problems and awkwardness, has become a strikingly attractive and confident woman.

The video ends.

On the screen are details of how to contact Philippa Johnson. And underneath, in large capitals, two words.

TRUST ME

Fifteen

As I first watched, it struck me what an unhappy person she'd been. I felt rather sorry for her. Angry, too, because she didn't seem to have a lot of love for her baby, Justin. He just seemed something that had happened to her, incidental. But then, at the end, when she started talking about that beautiful uniqueness we all have, I watched how she started to glow with some sort of inner light. It wasn't just the clothes and the make-up, it was something within her. The transformation seemed both credible and incredible.

I deleted my search history.

I made myself a coffee and wondered what to do next. It wasn't often that I had a free day, and I was feeling too ropey for housework.

I'd been meaning to do something with the dresses I'd rescued from Lizzie's house. I thought I could perhaps take photos of them and show them to Simone, who owned a vintage clothes shop, called Lacy Daze, in Norwich Lanes. She'd be able to put dates to them, tell me how much they were worth, and then maybe I'd talk to Justin, decide what to do with them.

I opened my wardrobe. One of my obsessive compulsions is having my coat hangers all face the same way, with the hooks pointed outwards. But two of the dresses were hung with the hooks facing inwards. I was rather drunk, of course, when I hung them. But I was surprised I hadn't noticed this before.

I took my dressing gown from its peg on the bedroom door and threw it on the still unmade bed. I replaced it, one by one, with the four dresses, carefully smoothing the collars and arranging the pleats in the skirts. They looked like ghosts, disembodied. I'm no photographer, and there wasn't a lot of room to manoeuvre between the door and the bed, so it took me a while to work out how to get everything in the frame, but eventually I had the photos more or less right. They'd serve the purpose if we decided to sell the dresses on eBay. I returned them to my wardrobe, this time making sure the hooks on the coat hangers were all pointing the same way.

I downloaded the photos to my laptop, then sent them to a USB flash drive so Simone could look at them on her computer screen. I'm not sure why I didn't want to take the actual dresses; perhaps I was afraid she'd offer to buy them from me. They weren't mine to sell. And for some reason I wasn't ready to part with them.

***

I went to Lacy Daze the following Saturday afternoon.

My cold had cleared up quickly, and it felt good to be going out into the city centre, even though the day was murky and there was a damp November chill in the air, making the festive Christmas windows look rather desperate. I hadn't started thinking about Christmas, not really, though I'd vaguely wondered whether I'd be spending any of it with Justin. I'd never shared Christmas with a man. Sharing Christmas, I thought, must make a relationship feel real.

When I walked into her shop, Simone came towards me with arms outstretched and gave me a kiss on both cheeks, as if we were close friends. I'd once helped one of the tutors organise a student event there, which had given Simone some publicity in the press, as well as the students. Since then, I'd been in there a couple of times on my own, just browsing. Simone's one of the most attractive women I've known. People talk of someone having a smile that lights up a room, and she has a smile like that. And her shop sets your senses reeling from the moment you step through the door. It's more of an installation or a happening than a shop: as you move around, your reflection follows in strategically placed antique mirrors, and the sense of times past is conveyed in ornately framed sepia photographs dotted around the walls. There's an old hinged trunk with garments spilling out, and peacock feathers bunched in a ceramic vase. And there's always some sort of retro music playing in the background.

'How *are* you?' she asked me, looking as though she really cared about the answer.

'I'm good thanks.' And I was. Feeling good. There was hardly a trace left of my cold. Those few days off work had been a welcome break. And Justin had more than filled the gap in my life left by Oliver. Goodbye heartache.

I'd already phoned Simone and told her about the dresses, making sure she wasn't taking a day off, leaving an assistant in charge. She had a computer on her counter, and I gave her my flash drive. I stood beside her and watched as the images of the dresses appeared on screen. I watched her slim, beautifully manicured hands as she pointed out the various details.

'This blue one, with the white print, it looks as if it's probably silk, it's hard to tell though from the photo. I'd say it's 1960s. It's something you'd wear for going out at a weekend, not something you'd wear every day. This next one's *lovely*. Again it's hard to pick up the detail from the photo – is that a net petticoat?'

She turned to me, and I nodded, breathing in her perfume. Something French and expensive.

'I'd say it was a dance dress from the 1950s. And – oh *look* at this one, it's exquisite – that lovely little lacy bodice. I'd say early 1960s. These would probably sell for about seventy or eighty pounds, if the condition's as good as it looks on screen. And this navy blue one, I *love* it, you could go out in this one today and you wouldn't be out of place. It's very demure, very classy. I had one almost identical to this in the shop a while ago, in fact . . .'

She hesitated, frowning slightly, then nodded, frowned, nodded again, as if in debate with herself. 'Do you know, I think it's the same dress. See that little stain, it looks like it could be a splash of bleach, just there on the right hand side, near the hem. Even in the photo, it shows. I had to reduce it because of that. It sold for forty-five pounds, I think that was what I asked for it. I remember this very pleasant elderly lady coming in to buy it, she said it was for her daughter, but she sort of blushed, and I had a feeling she was buying it for herself. I told her if it didn't fit her daughter she could bring it back . . .'

'How long ago was that, you sold it?'

'A couple of months, something like that, it may have been a bit longer. It's definitely 1950s. Interesting details, the grey buttons down the bodice, those two little pockets on the chest. Lovely print, little red flowers. Why is it, you have these dresses? What do you want to do with them?'

'Nothing at the moment. I've just borrowed them from someone. I think she inherited them. I told her I'd do some research on them.'

'That's interesting.' She raised her eyebrows. 'But surely she hasn't died, that lovely lady who bought the dress from me?'

'Unfortunately, yes. If it's the same person.'

'Oh how *sad*. She seemed so . . . *hopeful*, somehow. I'm remembering her quite clearly now. She had . . . I don't know . . . a look in her eyes, almost as though she were in love.'

103

So Lizzie had bought this dress not long before she died. And she'd been looking hopeful. Almost as though she were in love, to quote Simone. Not the sort of expression you'd expect from someone who was planning to kill herself.

***

Back home, I went to my bedroom for another look at the dresses. I could still hear inside my head the lilt of Simone's voice as she'd talked about them. I imagined her long fingers, fondling the dresses, appreciating them. I looked at the blue silk one first, stroking it with my forefinger, careful not to snag it with my fingernail. Then the grey one with the white netting underskirt. And the pink chiffon one, with the lacy bodice. And finally the navy dress with the little red flowers. The one with the stain of bleach that Simone had pointed out to me. The one that an elderly lady – presumably Lizzie – had bought from Lacy Daze. I looked at the details on the bodice that Simone had drawn my attention to. The grey buttons. The two little pockets.

I'd been in such a hurry to look at the dresses again, in the light of Simone's comments, it took me a while to notice that one of the dresses – those dresses that I remembered carefully hanging just those few days ago, with the coat hanger hooks pointed outward – was now once again facing the wrong way round. Everything else in the wardrobe was hung correctly. Perhaps I hadn't been as careful as I'd thought. Maybe my cold had left me confused.

***

I turned the coat hanger round, in line with the others, and then, without really thinking what I was doing, or why, I wandered into the little bedroom behind mine, at the back of the house, the room that nobody used. When Ellie lived in the house she used to call it my shoe room, because it was always piled high with shoes I'd grown tired of or that didn't fit me. My relationship with shoes was like my relationship with men, I used to joke. I never seemed to get it quite right.

In addition to shoes, the room was cluttered with a long-neglected exercise bike, some cardboard boxes, and a few stray handbags. More recently, I'd found space there for Lizzie's paintings, her sketchbook, and the two portfolios.

These were what I was looking for.

I knew a lot about Philippa. Rather too much. Now I wanted to know more about Lizzie.

I'd flicked through the sketchbook before, but today I had time on my hands, and so I looked a bit more closely. There were lots of detailed sketches of flowers. Lizzie enjoyed flowers. I remembered my mother saying that she'd seen her at the market, buying flowers, the day before she died. Other pages seemed more like a notebook, with various scribbles and doodles, and what appeared to be shopping lists for art materials. There was the torn-off corner, where I'd written my contact number for Justin. Then there were some slightly worrying sketches of what might have been Lizzie's own body parts. A sagging breast. Curvy lines, that could have been labia, surrounded by pubic hair. Sketches of what looked like a woman's reproductive organs, with tree-like structures growing out of them. Scribbled underneath were some strange titles: 'Love at First Sight', 'Heaven and Earth', 'Fruit of my Womb'. Ironic, perhaps? Whatever the intention, they made me feel rather uncomfortable. It was like watching Philippa's video, as if I'd intruded into someone's private spaces. Worse because, unlike the video, Lizzie's sketch book wasn't meant to be shared.

I hadn't yet opened the portfolios, not even a peek. I'd been far too busy, what with work, and Justin moving in, and the weekly visits to my mother. And, to be honest, I hadn't been all that interested. I'd seen enough of Lizzie's paintings, and I thought the contents of the portfolios would be more of the same. Earlier versions, perhaps. Less finished.

I unzipped the larger of the two. It obviously hadn't been open for quite a while. It was slightly sticky to the touch, the stickiness coated with a permanent layer of dust. Some of the sleeves were stuck together with the remains of spilled paint. The pencil drawings were mainly landscapes, nothing out of the ordinary. There were one or two scribbled drawings of a young girl, presumably Kate, and then there were others that interested me more, of a very young child, a boy, most likely the young Justin. I zipped it up again, propped it back against the wall, and opened the smaller, A3 portfolio.

This one was much newer, the pockets undamaged. It still smelt of plastic. The drawings were all black charcoal, with the occasional touch of blue, and they appeared to be a series. A live model, with the face missing, in different poses, and wearing . . .

Yes, there was no doubt – the model was wearing the dresses that hung in my wardrobe. And although the poses were feminine, the arms and legs were muscled and masculine. In some, the model sat on a chair, with crossed legs, or with legs provocatively apart. In others, the model stood, weight on one leg, with maybe a pointed toe, a bent knee, the suggestion of a wiggle.

I looked at all the sketches, and then I looked at them again, and my stomach rose and dipped as I tried to make sense of them.

Because I knew those legs, those arms.   The model was Justin.

Sixteen

LIZZIE'S STORY

I've never been a writer. If I see a flower, or a landscape, or a face, I don't want to write about it, I want to draw it or paint it. But now I need to write. I need to write all this down. I'm growing older, and somebody has to know the truth. I need to explain how things happened. Because that's how it was. Things happened. Philippa says we have choices, but we don't, not really. I don't believe so. Not about the big things. The little things, yes. Whether we go shopping today, or leave it till tomorrow. Whether we put butter or margarine on our bread. Whether we get up now, or stay in bed another hour. All those little everyday choices. I can spend fifteen minutes at the supermarket, deciding what sort of cheese to buy. But with the big things, it's as if it's all decided somewhere else. We might seem to make decisions, but it's other people's voices in our head, telling us what to do.

Take school for instance. All through primary school I was told that if I worked hard I'd pass my 11-plus, and I'd go to the grammar school. I didn't know why it mattered so much, but it seemed important to everybody else, my parents, my teachers, and so I did work hard. In any case, I enjoyed my schoolwork at that time. I liked learning about English proverbs, and doing mental arithmetic that seemed like puzzles. I liked history because it was all about stories, and I liked the New Testament, and the Old. I was always reading, and of course I was always drawing and painting. And I did pass my 11-plus, but I didn't go to grammar school, because they built this brand new comprehensive school just down the road, and everybody had to go to that, whether they'd worked hard or not. My mother felt cheated, she'd always longed to have a daughter at the grammar school. As it happened, I was quite excited to be going to a brand new school, instead of that decrepit old grammar school, but I pretended not to be. I felt as if it was my fault, going to the wrong school. And after that, I stopped working so hard. Why bother, if at the end of the day you just had to go where they sent you.

I didn't have any academic role models. We lived on a council estate, near Wolverhampton. My father worked in the office of a tool manufacturing company. My mother was a housewife. My aunt cleaned rich people's houses. That was the way things were.

I had a friend called Beth and we did everything together. We sat together in all the classes. We walked to school and home together. We did our homework together. And then we left school together and went to work. We were sixteen at the time. It was easy to get jobs in those days, if you weren't too fussy about what you wanted. Beth worked in an office for British Rail. I worked for an insurance company. We were still best friends. We used to go dancing at the Queens, or to the cinema, and we'd listen to records for free in a little shop in the Arcade. We'd drink coffee in the Milano, and put coins in the juke box. We started to go to jazz club and folk club. Anywhere we could listen to music, meet people, have a drink or two. After we'd given some of our wages to our mothers for keep, we'd spend the rest on clothes and having a good time.

We were always going out with different boys. Just a bit of kissing and snogging. I was still a virgin. And then Beth settled down with a regular boyfriend, and it wasn't long before they were engaged, then married. Some years later, they went to live in Australia.

I started going around with girls I'd met at the folk club. They went to art college, and they wore strange clothes, different from other people, though I suppose it was their own sort of uniform. A tribal thing. They mostly wore black. Black stockings, and long black jumpers. I started to copy them. Instead of dressing up when I went out in the evening, I'd dress down. I'd wear jeans, and a duffle coat I'd bought from one of those army and navy shops. Lots of eye make-up but no lipstick. Up till then I'd always had long hair, but I suddenly had it cut short. Really, really short. About half an inch all over. And I lost weight. With hindsight, I think I may have been a bit anorexic. I stopped eating bread and potatoes and cakes. I didn't tell myself I was going to lose weight, I just did. And my periods stopped for a while.

I left my job at the insurance office. I don't remember it being a decision. I just left. I don't think I even bothered handing in my notice. I went to live with Jen, one of my new friends. She was the middle one of three sisters, and her mother was an artist, and it didn't matter what time we came in at night, or whether we came in at all. I worked in one of the coffee bars, part time, and I did some life-modelling at the art college, and that was how I met Leo, one of the final year students. I fell in love with him straight away. I lost that virginity I'd been hanging on to so desperately, as if it was something precious. He persuaded me it didn't matter. I'd never been in love before. Before that, I would go out with someone a few times, then become bored, and make some excuse not to meet. But when it came to Leo, I couldn't let go. I followed him when he went to live in London. And we stayed friends for years and years. Just friends, that's all. We were never a couple, the way most of my old school friends had become couples with people. He believed in free love, and I did too, or so I thought. Some of the time, we lived in the same squat. And then there were times he moved out and went to live with someone else, and it was OK, because we didn't own each other, people weren't other people's property.

Maybe it was because of the anorexia and the missed periods, and maybe it was because I once caught a dose of gonorrhoea from someone, but, although I never went on the pill, I never seemed to get pregnant, and I thought I was probably infertile. But then, when I was twenty-nine, coming up to thirty, I suddenly fell pregnant. I hadn't been having sex with anybody for a while, probably not for about six months, because I heard women saying that it was really just a man's world, that all this so-called free love was fine for men, but not so great for women. And I realised I wasn't really enjoying sex all that much after all, I was really just going through the motions, pretending. And then Leo suddenly came back into my life, after he'd spent almost a year travelling around Europe with another woman, and we slept together this one night, and the next thing I knew I was feeling sick in the mornings, and hating the smell of instant coffee. I sort of guessed what was going on, and I went to see a doctor and he confirmed that I was pregnant. And I was jumping around with excitement. I didn't even consider an abortion. It felt like a miracle. Not only was I fertile after all, but the baby was Leo's. I was to have the child of the person I'd loved for all those years.

At that time, I was living on my own, in a little bedsit in Notting Hill. I was working in an office again. But when my landlord's agent came to collect my rent, and saw that I was pregnant, he gave me two weeks' notice to leave.

I told Leo I was going to be homeless – I think even then I was half-hoping we might live together – and he put me in touch with a friend of the girlfriend he'd been travelling with. Her name was Meg, and she was a folk singer who lived in Norwich with her boyfriend Dave and their two young children, and she didn't have a problem about sharing their house with a single mother and her baby. So that was how and why I moved to Norfolk. I never saw Leo after that.

But I had my baby. I had my beautiful Kate.

Meg used to sing in a folk group with Dave and another guitarist, Peter. And that was the man I eventually married. After his wife left him to go and live with another woman, he used to be always turning up at Meg and Dave's house, and he was lovely with Kate, like a father to her. He was a teacher, so he knew all about children, what their needs were. There was this one really bad time for him, when his son was killed in an accident, and we all supported him through that. He had a daughter, Philippa, and he was worried about her. He said she'd been moody ever since her mother left. He asked me to move in with them. I knew I couldn't spend the rest of my life living with Meg and her family, so I did. I didn't love Pete, but I thought I might grow to love him, a bit like an arranged marriage, except that we were doing the arranging ourselves. I was in my thirties by then, and I'd had enough of being single.

Seventeen

When Justin returned that evening, he seemed in a happy mood. He came in whistling. 'Do you fancy a Chinese take-away? Or shall we go out somewhere?'

I was sitting at the table, drinking coffee. I'd brought the portfolio downstairs, and I had it on the table in front of me. He looked at me when I didn't answer, and then he seemed to register the portfolio. I opened it up. 'These are you, Justin, aren't they?'

I was waiting for him to say that yes, he'd done some modelling for Lizzie, she'd wanted someone to model the dresses and she didn't have a woman to do it for her. And then I would put the portfolio back upstairs, and we'd have a meal, and I'd forget about it.

He didn't. He looked down at his feet, and then he looked me straight in the face and said, 'Yes, they're me. Lizzie bought the dresses for me. I'm a transvestite.'

'You're what?'

'Don't make me repeat it. Telling people isn't easy.'

'I feel sick.'

'I'm sorry.' Sorry for what, I wondered. Sorry I felt sick? Sorry he was a transvestite?

'I suppose . . . I suppose you can't help it.' That sounded banal. Worse, condescending. I was desperately trying to process this new information. It didn't fit the Justin I knew. Despite his weird background, he'd seemed so normal, so regular. I felt deceived. Suddenly I felt angry. 'Why didn't you tell me?'

He sat down opposite me at the table. I could see a nerve twitching in his right cheek. He put his elbows on the table, his head in his hands. He raised his head, and looked at me briefly, and then he looked down at the table, where the portfolio lay open between us.

'The problem is, when could I have told you? When's the right moment to tell someone? That first time I met you, when we were driving along in the car? I don't think so. The day I moved into your home? Over the dinner table? Before the first time we had sex? See what I mean? Every time's an impossible time.'

'Before I fell in love with you would have been good.'

'So how was I to know? It wasn't something I was expecting.'

'I know. It's just . . . it's just that what I loved about you was you always seemed so real. You always seemed like one of those what-you-see's-what-you-get sort of guys.'

'I'm sorry,' he said again.

I closed the portfolio, as though, by shutting away the images, I could pretend this conversation wasn't happening. As though we could go back to being ordinary everyday people, at the start of a normal relationship.

'I'm still the same person,' he said. 'It's just now you know that once in a while I put on a dress. You don't have to see me in a dress, if you don't want to.'

This wasn't a time for eating out. I said, 'Let's have a Chinese take-away.'

While he went to collect it, my mind tumbled over itself, considering alternatives. I could be the sort of narrow-minded person I hated, and ask him to find somewhere else to live. That wasn't an option. We could carry on living in the same house but resume separate lives. That would be almost as impossible. Or we could continue having a relationship. We could work through this. I could try to come to terms with this aspect of Justin. I'd only known him a short time, but already I couldn't imagine life without him. This seemed the only way forward.

But we had to have a dialogue.

Over our meal, I continued to ask questions, to try to understand. 'So Lizzie knew all about this side of you? She didn't have a problem with it?'

'She may have found it difficult at first. I don't remember. Lizzie always tried to be cool about everything. As I said, she bought the dresses for me. I think they appealed to some romantic side of her. She enjoyed buying them. She seemed to enjoy seeing me in them. She liked to do those sketches of me. I might have been biased, but I thought they were rather good. She thought so too. She bought that portfolio especially for them.'

I tried to visualise Lizzie adjusting the dresses on Justin, deciding what pose he would take up next. It seemed strange behaviour for a grandmother and grandson. Even for a *step* grandmother and grandson. But, as he'd said, Lizzie had tried to be cool.

I couldn't imagine telling my own mother about this side of Justin. Already I'd sensed she didn't entirely approve of our relationship. She'd always expected me to end up with someone academic, or financially successful. Someone rather like my brothers, I suppose.

And as for mothers, I was curious how Philippa – that full-on, rather overwhelming person I'd watched in the video – had taken to the idea of a transvestite son. I asked him, 'What about Philippa?'

'As far as I know, she doesn't know. Not about *now*. When I was young, like eight or nine, I used to sometimes dress up in Kate's stuff, quite openly. It was all a bit of a joke in those days, nobody seemed to mind, apart from Kate, she was a bit miffed, she didn't really like the idea of someone else wearing her clothes. I suppose she was about fourteen at the time. And then when I was a bit older, and Lizzie was looking after me, and Kate wasn't around, I used to sneak into her room and do it then. I used to try things on. Shoes, tights, dresses, whatever. There was this one time, Philippa was there and she came up and found me. Slapped me across the face, told me I was disgusting.' He winced at the memory.

'How awful.'

'I was pretty screwed up at the time, because the thing was, I had to keep on doing it. I couldn't just stop, it wasn't an option. And it was around that time that Philippa started to keep me away from Lizzie. That was when she decided to work nearer home, that she was going to be a full-time mother with a part-time job, instead of the other way around. She seemed to be watching me all the time.'

'How awful,' I said again. And then a thought occurred to me. 'Talking of jobs, what would happen to yours? If they found out?'

'Transvestism isn't contagious. Or illegal. I'm not a paedophile or something.'

I took a deep breath. I didn't want to say this, but I had to. 'Justin, I know you've been into my wardrobe. Well, they're your dresses, not mine. But I just wanted you to know that I know about it.'

'I shouldn't have done that.'

'It doesn't matter. But I'll give you back the dresses and you can hang them in your own room. It's better that way.'

I wasn't sure whether I wanted to sleep with Justin that night. He followed me into bed, and I wasn't going to push him out, but I kept my distance. He wasn't the Justin I'd been attracted to. It wasn't just the transvestism. He hadn't showered, and he smelt of beer and Chinese food and sweat.

Neither of us could relax. I was aware of him stiff and awkward beside me. I could tell he was turning things over in his mind. 'If it hadn't been for those dresses,' he said finally, 'we wouldn't have met.'

'What do you mean?'

'Remember when I met you that first time, in Willowherb Close? When you came running over and told me you'd been going through stuff in the house.'

'Of course I remember.'

'And I mumbled something about CDs, but what I'd really gone back for were the dresses.'

'If I hadn't taken them first, they'd have been all scrunched up in your rucksack?'

'I was only going to take one of them. I figured out I'd have to find a way to hide it. Living in other people's houses, it wasn't going to be easy. None of my mates know I'm a transvestite, and I wanted to keep it that way.'

'Which one would you have taken?' It seemed an odd question to ask, but for some reason I needed to know.

'Probably the pink one.'

I almost laughed. 'So, Justin, I take it you've never actually gone out in any of these dresses?'

'Just a couple of times, I've been to a tranny club in London. The first time I went was last February. And then the next time was that weekend, when Lizzie died.'

'That's awful.' I seemed to be saying the words 'that's awful' an awful lot that evening.

'Mm. I know. I mean, none of that had anything to do with her dying. Apart from the fact that I wasn't there to stop her.'

'You can't blame yourself for that.'

117

'I don't. I'd have been out of the house, anyhow, for most of the Friday. I always was. It was always my day for going to the pub, and I'd often end up in one of my mate's houses. Sitting up all night with a few cans of beer, talking shite. I suppose what upsets me the most is I was in London, having a good time, wearing a dress that Lizzie had just bought for me. She was the only person who'd seen me in it till then. And there she was, like that . . .'

He was lying on his back, and I turned towards him, laid my arm across his stomach. At that moment, all my shock, disgust even, seemed to melt away, and I felt such an ache within my body that it seemed it would burst, like when you bite into an over-ripe tomato. I leaned over and kissed him, and I wasn't sure whether the wetness on his face was sweat or tears. I put my lips to his, and tasted the beer on his breath. I didn't mind, any more, that he'd brought those smells to bed with him. I stroked his stomach, his groin, and then I cradled his penis, felt it grow hard in my hand, and we made love gently, as if aware of each other's fragility.

He might have this strange, mysterious side to him, but he was still the man I was in love with. That hadn't changed.

***

And I don't know why, but as I lay there asleep, beside Justin, I had a dream about Oliver and Sarah. We were in Lacy Daze, all three of us, and Sarah was wearing a pink dress. Oliver was frowning. That way he did when he didn't quite approve of something. 'It's not your colour,' he said. She looked like the awkward schoolgirl Sarah, not the attractive adult, and I watched her as she stumbled out of the shop, in that pink dress, looking miserable and ashamed. I was trying to find

118

the words, to say to Oliver, let's go after her, tell her it's all OK. But he just stood there, staring straight ahead, ignoring me as though I wasn't there. And I wanted to go running after her myself, to say something important, something she needed to hear, but I had that jelly sensation in my legs that's such a feature of dreams, and all I could do was stand there feeling helpless. Letting her go.

Eighteen

LIZZIE'S STORY

It felt strange at first, living and sleeping with a man. After Kate was born, in fact from the time I became pregnant, I was almost celibate. There'd been a couple of one-night stands, both meaningless. When I moved in with Peter, I wasn't madly in love with him, and I don't think he was with me. I think we were both people who'd lost the ones we'd really loved, and we hadn't fully recovered. But now the love of my life was my daughter, Kate. I loved her passionately, the way a mother loves her first and only child.

Peter was fond of her too. I mentioned he'd been like a father to her. He didn't love her with the passion that I did, of course. He'd already had two children with Sandra. One of them, sadly, had died, and the other was Philippa. He cared a lot about Philippa. He was worried about her.

I did try to become fond of Philippa, but it was difficult, impossible really. She was already a teenager, awkward and stroppy, and she'd had a mother of her own. I did attempt to have some sort of relationship with her, truly I did, but she didn't make it easy for me. She was strangely unlovable.

It was the way she sat sprawled in that armchair – the one she always sat in – and seemed to be watching me all the time. Looking at me in a way that seemed to say, 'What's the silly cow doing now!' I talked to Peter, and he said I was being over-sensitive, that she was just a teenager, going through a difficult phase. But the fact was, she *stared*. It was unnerving. It was as if she could see things about me I didn't know myself.

She still does that. She still looks at me in that way. Even though we're both so much older, and supposed to be friends. I'm not sure she even realises she's doing it.

Back then, I tried hard to be friendly with her. Her hair was brown in those days, long before she had it dyed blonde. It was naturally curly, and I thought it could have been her best feature. But she had it cut short, and it didn't suit her. God knows, I didn't know much about teenage fashions, but I thought maybe we could start to bond if I talked to her about clothes and make-up and hair-dos. So I said to her, 'You've got lovely hair. Have you ever thought of letting it grow a bit longer?' And she looked at me, in that way of hers, and said, 'What's it to you?' It was always like that. If I spoke to her, she just stared at me, and either ignored what I'd said, or came back with something dismissive.

When I first moved in with Peter I was a vegetarian. I'd been one for a long time. But that didn't go down too well with my new family. Whenever I cooked anything, Philippa used to look at it as if it was poison. She'd pick something up with her fork, stare at it, put it back on her plate. And then she'd leave the table. Peter said it was OK, she was used to cooking for herself. So she'd stomp off to the kitchen and fry chips and beefburgers. The kitchen reeked of cooking oil that had been used over and over, and it made me want to gag but I didn't say anything. Gradually, though, I stopped trying to be a vegetarian, and started cooking chicken and fish, and after a while I was cooking and eating anything and everything. It made life easier that way.

And I had my own daughter, Kate, who was delightful. It wouldn't have been natural if I hadn't taken pleasure in her, spending lots of time with her, reading books and planting acorns and lemon pips and making models and collages out of all sorts of odds and ends I could find around the house or garden. And all the time, Philippa would be watching us. Even when her boyfriend Ricky was there, and she was sitting on his lap and smooching with him, she would still be staring at me out of the corner of her eye. Yes, I know, I'm sure it was hard for her, when her mother left. And I'm sure she felt jealous of the closeness I had with Kate. But, as I said, it wasn't as if I didn't try to be friendly with her.

Well, as I wrote earlier, the relationship I had with Peter was what you might call expedient. We liked and respected each other. He was a father to Kate, and although he could have been a bit more supportive of me where Philippa was concerned, he was mostly kind and attentive. He had a good job at the school, he'd been promoted to head of department, and he didn't expect me to go out to work. And he didn't make demands as far as housework was concerned. I was a mother to Kate, and I cooked, and I bought vegetables from the market, where they were cheapest, I even grew some in the back garden, and I bought clothes from charity shops. Financially, I was low maintenance. And I think that having me there made him feel better about himself. It must have given his self-esteem a knock when Sandra left him for a woman. I had long hair – it's always been long, except for that one time when I had it cut really short – and I wore long skirts in those days. I always looked feminine, whereas Peter told me Sandra had been going around in baggy jeans and no make-up. We had friends round to the house, or we went out to visit people, usually his colleagues from school. I think everyone saw us as a good couple. But there was one thing missing. Although we went through the motions in the early stages, we never really had a sexual relationship.

I was happy that way, and I thought Peter was too. But then, when he told me he was going to live with Serena – a young maths teacher who worked at the same school – I started to wonder if this had been an issue for him all along.

I was fifty-six at the time, and he was fifty-nine. There were just the two of us by then. Philippa was long gone, living with Brian and Justin in their little village, and Kate was in Brighton with James. I think Peter must have been going through that crisis that men seem to have, when they find themselves attracted to someone much younger. And, it's true, I *had* been letting myself go a bit. I only put make-up on when we were going somewhere special, and I wore old clothes around the house because of my painting. I had much more time for painting by now, with just Peter and me in the house, no children to look after. I'd met Serena, and I could see how she was attractive to him. I was a bit upset at first, because it wasn't something I'd expected – as I said, I thought that Peter was happy with the way things were. But, if truth be told, we'd spent most of our marriage living separate lives under the same roof. So Peter left, and I carried on living in the house, and nothing much had changed. The mortgage was paid off, and he sent me money till I started getting my state pension. I still had my art. I still spoke to Kate on the phone. By now we had very different lifestyles, but we were still mother and daughter, there was always something to talk about. I still saw Justin, usually when he'd been out drinking with his friends and he needed somewhere to sleep for the night, what with Philippa and Brian living out in the sticks. I never minded him turning up, whatever the time of day or night, I was always pleased to see him.

And then, for some reason, Philippa started wanting to be my friend. She said she was angry with Peter, for leaving me. She seemed to feel sorry for me. She seemed to think I was lonely. I didn't need any of that, I didn't need her anger, or her sympathy. She'd turn up uninvited and have coffee with me, and it was usually on a Friday morning, and gradually that started to become a routine, so I had to make sure I was always at home on Friday mornings, waiting for Philippa. She'd say, 'See you next week,' and I really didn't have a choice. And once in a while, she'd invite me over for a meal, and Brian would come and pick me up, while she was busy in her kitchen cooking something elaborate. She always has to make a song and dance about her cooking, wanting everyone to praise it.

She kept telling me that it wasn't too late, I wasn't too old, that I could still meet someone new. Someone who loved me. Well, I had no wish to start a new relationship. I couldn't see anything wrong with the life I was living. By now, she'd trained to be a therapist, and I couldn't help feeling as though she was practising on me, sort of experimenting. If I'd met someone new, she'd have notched it up as one of her successes. But anyhow, I listened politely when she told me I was still an attractive woman, and I suppose in a way I was enjoying the attention.

And then she had this idea for Justin to come and live with me. She said he was taking up space and that she needed a room where she could meet her clients, and that I'd be doing her a really big favour. But mainly, she said, it would be better for me to have someone else around. It wasn't healthy, being there on my own.

Well, I didn't argue with her. I'd spent a lot of time looking after Justin when he was young. More time, in fact, than Philippa ever had. So it wasn't as though we were strangers to each other. And Justin said it would suit him better living in the town. It seemed to be a good arrangement for all three of us. So he moved in, with his few bits of clothes and his guitar. And, although I'd been fine on my own, I found it was even better having Justin there.

So thank you for reading this so far, and for being patient. But there's an important part of the story I've missed out. I'll come to that soon. It's the hardest part to tell. But if I don't tell it, somebody else might tell it first. And they might tell it differently. So I want my version to be told. I want to tell the truth. I want it to be written down.

Nineteen

Once I knew about Justin, about his transvestism, I realised I needed to learn everything there was to know about it. I needed to make sense of it all. Sense of what it meant for Justin. And how it would be for me, living with him and loving him.

So I did the obvious thing you do when you want to know about something. I turned to the web.

Most of the information I found was supportive and sympathetic. For instance, one website said that men who dressed as women were often attracted by qualities that were supposedly typical of women. Non-violence, gentleness. They wanted to escape from the pressures of being stereotypically male. They wanted to enter a world that was non-macho, non-aggressive. All that seemed fine to me. Because what had drawn me to Justin was how easy he was to be with, almost like a good woman friend, with the sexual attraction a bonus. There were none of those gender power games between us. He was genuinely affectionate and caring. Not only that, but he seemed to have a sort of intuition about how I was feeling, what I needed.

The sexual, kinky side of it – all that stuff about being turned-on by women's tights and underwear – I found harder to take on board. Sexually, I've always been rather straight and unimaginative. I've had my own comfort zone, never felt the need to stretch the limits. And so I didn't delve too deeply into any of this. I realised I wasn't ready, and that, quite frankly, I probably never would be. I asked myself did this really matter, as far as our relationship was concerned, and told myself it probably didn't. After all, if I was going out with a guy who liked football, it didn't mean I had to go to all the matches with him, or even pretend a superficial interest. So I reasoned.

However, I was curious how other women had coped, so I searched for the personal experiences of women in relationships with transvestite men. I found there were women who'd only learned of their husband's transvestism after many years of marriage. There were others who'd had to confront the truth in the early stages of a relationship, and who wondered how it would be to settle down and have a family. Having children had never been high on my agenda, and yet I felt strangely reassured by the prospect that it was possible, in fact not at all uncommon, to have children with a transvestite partner.

I devoured all this information obsessively at first, and then, once I'd found out most of what I needed to know, I let it rest. I didn't go into denial, exactly, although I have to admit I wasn't in any hurry to see Justin in a dress. He told me that he spent time on his computer chatting to other transvestites, and I knew I had to accept there was a side to his life I'd never be part of. But, for the rest of it, I just wanted to return to us being *us*. Without that 'transvestite' label hanging between us like some sort of hurdle I had to be continually jumping over.

***

Meanwhile, Christmas was drawing closer, and I wanted to know how I'd be spending it. Over the years, my family Christmases had shrunk. In the early days of my brothers' marriages, they'd both turned up in cars loaded with wives, babies, presents, contributions of food and drink, but as time went on, and with at least two of their children having a tendency to car sickness, they'd decided they didn't want the hassle of driving all the way to Norfolk and back. So in recent years there'd been just me and my parents and then sadly, last Christmas, just me and my mother, trying to be cheerful.

I was relieved when my mother told me that Joshua, the elder of my brothers, had invited her to spend Christmas with him and his wife Patsy and their two daughters. They lived near Oxford. She'd be going by train and staying there for almost a week.

I was welcome to join them too, of course, but I said I'd like a quiet day at home. I mentioned to Justin I'd be free on Christmas Day. And, just as I'd hoped, he shrugged and said why not spend it together.

There were still Justin's parents, Philippa and Brian, to consider, and we said we'd visit them on Boxing Day. It was, after all, supposed to be a family time. I found the idea of this unnerving, but at the same time I was curious to see Philippa, actually in the flesh, in real-time.

I told Justin that, as he nearly always did the cooking, I'd sort out food on Christmas Day. 'Only don't expect me to do the whole Nigella Lawson thing,' I warned him.

I went to the supermarket and bought some ready-mades. A pre-stuffed turkey breast. A reduced-price Christmas pudding. Different sorts of cheese. Crackers and mince pies and mixed nuts and chocolate biscuits. Wine and beer. A bottle of brandy. I almost bought a small tree, but then I thought better of it and didn't. This was all about now, not about trying to recreate Christmases past. Carry on like this and I'd be making chains out of gummed paper, hanging a stocking at the end of the bed.

***

I'd been unbelievably nervous about the day – a sort of rite of passage, my first Christmas with a partner – and

I wanted it to be perfect. We ate croissants with honey for breakfast, and exchanged presents. Nothing expensive, because Justin hadn't been working long, and I didn't want to embarrass him by going overboard. We had a mid-morning drink of special offer champagne, and switched on the CD player. We listened to Justin's hero, Bonnie 'Prince' Billy, and to another singer he introduced me to, called Bon Iver. Justin told me that his real name was Justin Vernon – another Justin – and that Bon Iver was adapted from the French words 'bon hiver', meaning good winter. Apparently he'd recorded most of the CD while holed up in a hunting cabin in Northwestern Wisconsin. It might have been down to the mood I was in at the time, and being snuggled up with Justin, but I thought it one of the most haunting and beautiful recordings I'd ever heard.

We kissed and hugged rather a lot. After a late Christmas lunch, Justin took out his guitar and played a song he'd written, and the words went something like: *There has to be a way / To share our differences / I'm not looking for paradise / Just a place to feel free / You and me.* The weird thing with songs is that you don't have to be too deep. You can get away with unexceptional, almost banal lyrics and, with the addition of a few chords, a bit of falsetto, make them sound meaningful.

We drank wine, and ate mince pies, and the day outside became dark without ever really becoming light, and it was evening, and we drank and ate some more. I'd never actually had a weight problem, but I told myself I'd better start watching out for the slippery slope.

Finally came the moment I'd been dreading. He asked me, 'Would you mind very much if I put on a dress?'

Well, it was Christmas. I felt apprehensive, in fact more than apprehensive, terrified. But I nodded. 'Go ahead.'

He disappeared upstairs, and eventually reappeared after what seemed an awful long time to be changing a few clothes. He was wearing the grey dress with tiny cream flowers and a black waistband. I suppressed an urge to laugh. He sat beside me, right leg crossed over the left, showing the white net petticoat. I had to say something, so I said 'Do I call you Justine?'

'Actually it's Jane. That's what I call myself, when I'm in a dress. She's sexy, but naïve at the same time. A bit prim and proper, but she can be quite frivolous sometimes, when she wants to be.' A bit like me, I couldn't help thinking. It hadn't occurred to me that this female side of Justin would have a personality of her own. He shrugged, self-conscious. He'd shaved that morning, and I noticed how finely chiselled his face was, with its slightly prominent cheek bones. He looked surprisingly androgynous. Tentatively, I put my arm around his shoulders, and then, later, I laid my hand on his bony knee, and he humoured me by watching *Strictly Come Dancing*. We drank brandy and picked at the nuts and the cheese and crackers, playing at being normal, it seemed, when in fact we were anything but.

As bedtime approached, I asked him if he could put his usual clothes back on.

He laughed. 'You want to see me looking like a man again, before you let me into your bed.'

'Something like that.' It was true. I wanted to make love to Justin the man, not Justin the transvestite. I'd had a glimpse of that other side of him. And for now a glimpse was all I wanted. All I could deal with.

Twenty

If Christmas Day had been as near to perfect as I could have hoped for, give or take a bit of cross-dressing, Boxing Day was rather different. The complete opposite.

Just the simple act of leaving the little oasis of our home – and it was really starting to feel like *ours* by now, not *mine* – seemed to break the spell that had held us so close the day before.

It was typically unChristmassy weather, damp and drizzly, and, as we drove to Philippa and Brian's home, the Norwich suburbs blended greyly into the North Norfolk countryside, sharing the same nondescript bleakness.

We didn't take presents – I thought we should, but Justin said they'd all decided about ten years ago to drop the tradition of exchanging presents nobody really wanted. But we took a bottle of wine and a box of chocolates, and I bought flowers at the petrol filling station.

I realised how little I knew about Justin's parents, apart from what I'd learned from the video. 'What's Brian doing nowadays, workwise?' I asked, as I drove.

'He had to give up working full-time, he has these back problems. I mentioned to you before about the medication. The morphine. He keeps himself busy doing a bit of freelance stuff with computers, sorting people's issues out. He's good at that. He's a technically minded sort of guy.'

'So neither of them has a full-time job.'

'I don't think they're short of a bob or two. They had an inheritance from Brian's parents, and Brian's quite shrewd when it comes to money. He's quite a clued-up guy.'

We'd never actually spoken much before about Brian. It was apparent that Justin respected his stepfather. He sounded rather ordinary and down-to-earth, which was probably all to the best, living with Philippa.

The house was one of those modern brick-and-flint semi-detached places that had been built to look like a traditional Norfolk cottage. Lots of terracotta pots with brown and withered plants, that must have looked pretty in the summer. Philippa opened the door with a flourish and welcomed us. Or, rather, she welcomed *me*, if you could call it that. Justin, clutching the supermarket carrier bag with the wine and chocolates, slid silently past her into the house, like a cat. She stood there, taking up space with her large frame, and her eyes – as heavily made up as they'd been on the screen – seemed to bore into me, noting every flaw in my skin, every smear of toothpaste I might have missed, every flake of botched mascara. Finally she said, 'You must be Melanie. I'm Philippa. I've heard *so* much about you.' I couldn't imagine how. Or when. She held out her hand for me to shake, and I quickly transferred the flowers to my left hand. She pressed her thumb hard into my palm, so I could feel the imprint of her finger nail. I couldn't help wondering if there was some sort of weird symbolism going on, a bit like those freemason rituals I've read about.

'Let me take your jacket,' she said, as soon as I had both feet in the hallway.

I gave her the flowers, and she muttered an absent-minded 'thanks', taking them from me as if they were a bit of a nuisance she'd have to deal with. I followed her into the living-room, where Brian was already pouring a beer for Justin. 'What would you like to drink?' she asked me, without telling me what the choice was. Perhaps they had a fully stocked drinks cabinet, like people often do who only drink on special occasions, because nothing ever gets emptied.

'I'm OK, thanks. I'm driving. I'll wait and have a glass of wine when we're eating.'

'What about fruit juice? Or elderflower cordial?'

'Elderflower would be great. Thanks.' Though I could have done with something seriously alcoholic at that moment, to take the edge off the awkwardness. Justin wasn't helping. He just stood there, with his back to me, talking to Brian, who'd apparently bought some new hi-fi equipment. They were discussing technical matters that I knew would be way over my head. Philippa handed me my elderflower cordial, then retreated to the kitchen. I sat myself down on one end of a cream coloured leather corner sofa. It smelt new. I sipped the cordial, feeling out of place and ill at ease. For something to do, I cast my eyes around at the décor.

There were scatter cushions with geometric designs, which seemed little used. An imitation sheepskin rug lay on the laminated floor. There was a black ash bookcase with glass doors, and geometric prints on the walls that looked mass-produced, and appeared co-ordinated with the cushions. A fireplace flickered with simulated flames. Two large scented candles were burning on the glass coffee table. Everything seemed artificial and somehow unpeopled, like one of those show houses on new-build estates. It was the total opposite of Lizzie's house, with its many layers of clutter, and it lacked the ageing homeliness of the stuff my mother surrounded herself with, carefully transferred from one house to the other.

Philippa reappeared and sat next to me, and I wished I'd made more of an effort to talk technology with the men. As in the video, she was dressed in a loose smock over black leggings. Smocks and leggings seemed to be her thing, only on this occasion the smock was turquoise and gold, and she was wearing a string of black beads. Avoiding her eyes, I looked down at her shoes, a flat ballerina style, also coloured gold, and I noticed she had a rather strange tattoo on her left ankle. Despite her size, her calves and ankles were slim and shapely.

I'd made a bit of an effort, too. I was wearing a little red dress, and matching red shoes with small heels, which she suddenly noticed. 'I hope those heels of yours don't scratch the floorboards.'

'Sorry.' Already she had me apologising. 'It's probably best if I take them off.' I eased my feet out of my shoes.

'I'll put them by the front door. Would you like to borrow a pair of slippers?'

'I'll be fine like this, thanks.' Without my shoes I felt two inches shorter, diminished, even though I was sitting so it shouldn't have made any difference.

She rejoined me on the sofa. She seemed to have moved up unnecessarily close beside me, in a way that made me feel uncomfortable. 'I've heard a lot about you,' she said again.

'So what's Justin been saying about me?' I asked her, trying to keep it light.

'Oh, Justin hasn't had a lot to say. Does he ever? But Joyce and I have had a few little chats.' My mother's name, Joyce, sounded strange coming from Philippa's lips. I felt a bit uncomfortable, at the implication there was some sort of cosiness, camaraderie, developing between them. It ought to be good, I supposed, if our mothers became friends. Even so, I'm afraid I found the idea rather unnerving.

'So you're going to organise a show of Lizzie's paintings?' I wanted to deflect her. I didn't want to be the subject of this conversation. I didn't like the way she kept looking at me.

'We're thinking about it. I hear you work at the art college?'

'That's right.' I was suddenly finding it hard to focus. It occurred to me that the shakiness I was feeling was because I was hungry, not just nerves. We hadn't had breakfast. I'd been wanting to save my appetite for the lunch, after all that gorging we'd done Christmas Day. I suppose it's what they say: appetite grows with eating.

She seemed to read my mind. 'The meal's almost ready. You must be hungry. I'll just go and finish things off.' She stood and turned to Justin. 'You haven't even taken your jacket off. Go and hang it in the cupboard, for God's sake darling, make yourself at home.'

I didn't like the way she called him 'darling'. It sounded false and inappropriate. But at least she'd moved away from me, and I could start to breathe more easily again.

***

We ate in the dining-room, which was almost completely filled by the table and chairs. Lunch was salmon, with butternut squash mash and side salad, followed by trifle made with black cherries, yoghourt, and sponge dipped in madeira wine. At any other time and place I would have enjoyed it. A love of cooking seemed to be in the family genes. Philippa made rather a big deal of listing all the ingredients. I was conscious of Brian, sitting opposite me, often wriggling and shifting his position. It must have been the problem with his back. He was short and skinny – the opposite of Philippa. Philippa would easily dominate

135

any household set-up, and I couldn't see Brian being much of a contestant. Philippa was sitting to my left, and Justin to my right. He refilled my wine glass more times than I should have let him, bearing in mind I was driving. We touched legs, conspiratorially, under the table, and he smiled at me. I began to feel a bit more relaxed. Brian told a couple of unfunny jokes, and Philippa was starting to look flushed.

Afterwards, both Justin and I helped Philippa carry the dishes into the kitchen, and I offered to help her load the dishwasher, but she insisted we left everything for her to sort out in the evening.

She then produced a game called Linkee, which she told us she'd ordered from Amazon especially. She said it was as new to her as it was to the rest of us, so an equal playing field.

It turned out to be a sort of trivia quiz. Somebody was appointed Questions Master, and we all had to write down the answers to the questions, keeping them secret. The aim was not simply to answer the questions but to solve the link. For instance, if the answers to the questions were 'Yesterday', 'Hello', 'Madonna' and 'Jude Law', and the clue was 'Fab Insects', the link was that all the answers related to songs by the Beatles. Once somebody identified the link, they had to shout out 'Linkee'. If correct, they'd be awarded a letter, and the person who won enough letters to spell LINKEE was the winner.

I've always been a dunce when it comes to any sort of quiz. Other people's minds seem to go into overdrive, while mine gets stuck between gears and wobbles around going nowhere. Philippa, Brian, even Justin, were all shouting, entering into the spirit. Philippa won the first game, Justin the second. I had the feeling Brian could have won if he'd wanted, but that he was holding back, giving the others a chance.

I'd barely come up with a single answer, let alone a link. As the third game started, I said 'Count me out this time', and asked if I could use the bathroom. As soon as I stood, I realised I was on the point of wetting myself, I'd been hanging on so long. Philippa mumbled 'up the stairs, first door on the left', or was it 'first door on the right.' I was in too much of a hurry to pay attention.

***

I opened the wrong door first, then found the right one, and made it to the loo with not much margin for error. It took me a while to empty my bladder. I could hear the three of them shouting and whooping downstairs. Philippa was shouting the loudest. As I returned to the landing, I went to close the door I'd mistakenly opened, and then I couldn't resist having a peep inside.

It was obviously the therapy room. The room that had once been Justin's bedroom. It must have been furnished and decorated for the purpose. The walls were a pale blue. There were two chrome and leather armchairs, facing each other, and between them a glass coffee table, similar or maybe identical to the one in the lounge. On the coffee table, there was a flask of water, a candle, a box of tissues, and what looked like a diary. There were abstract prints on two of the walls. Not the geometric patterns that she had downstairs, but more curvy and swirly. There was also a framed calligraphic text, with the words 'Feel the fear and do it anyway.' I remembered Ellie reading a book of that title, telling me it had changed her life. I could never quite see how a book could change anyone's life.

After the warmth downstairs, it felt unheated in this little room, and I started to shiver in my short sleeves. Gooseflesh prickled my arms. But I wasn't ready to go back down and rejoin the party. Losing every game was not much fun.

Besides, I was idly curious about Philippa's therapy. The room seemed set up ready to go, with its flask of water, but reminded me of an amateur dramatic society stage set. Justin had said she only had one or two clients on a good week. I had a feeling she wouldn't care to admit this, that she liked to pretend that she had a full diary. I could imagine her being one of those people who, if somebody's watching, search their diary laboriously, as if struggling to find a slot, even though there are a lot more spaces than there are appointments.

I picked up the diary from the coffee table, and had a quick glance through. I didn't want to pry into details, just get a general picture of how busy she was.

The pages looked very empty for the whole of December. There were a couple of isolated appointments in November, and September looked equally barren. I flicked through to the back of the diary, where she had a list of what were presumably her clients' names, email addresses and telephone numbers.

There were only about seven in total, and most of these had been crossed out.

It was one of the crossed out names that sprang out at me, and I started to shiver with shock and nausea, not just cold.

The name, written in upper case, was SARAH BANNISTER. The name of my dead friend.

There were two phone numbers next to her name: a Norwich landline number, and a mobile number underneath it. Hands shaking, I leafed back to the earlier pages of the diary. There was a Sarah entered on the 4th January. Then the 11th, 18th, 25th. Another on the 1st February, then the 8th. I carried on turning the pages. Every week. Every Wednesday. Until 25th April. All these entries had a little tick beside them, presumably indicating that Sarah had turned up for her appointments. She appeared to have been Philippa's most faithful client. There was one more, on 2nd May, which was crossed out. Then the entries stopped.

Sarah had killed herself on 1st May. The date stuck in my mind. May Day. Just over three weeks before my birthday. It had been a strange birthday. I remember I went out in the evening for a few drinks with Rachel, and I tried to have a laugh with her, the way we always did, but all I could think about – apart from feeling gutted that I hadn't heard from Oliver – was Sarah. Her birthday would have been two weeks after mine. When we were teenagers, my mother had once organised a joint party for us, between our two birthdays. But there'd be no more birthdays for Sarah.

Could this really be what it seemed? Had Sarah – if it were indeed the same person – have been coming to Philippa for therapy all those weeks? Had she in fact been to see her just a few days before she died?

***

For a moment, I'd lost track of time, almost forgotten where I was, what day, whose house. I hadn't shut the door to the room, because all I'd intended was to have a quick glance around. I hadn't noticed the sudden quietness downstairs. I still had the diary in my hand when I became conscious of Philippa standing there in the doorway, glaring at me. Her eyes flickered from my face to the diary and back to my face. They settled on my face.

'I see you've been doing a bit of snooping.'

I shut the diary and put it back on the coffee table. There was nothing I could say. I couldn't even bring myself to say 'sorry'.

And then she flipped. She still looked flushed from the wine. Her eyes sparked with venom. Her lips, under the red lipstick, snarled. Her blonde hair flared out, an angry mane.

'Get out of my house,' she said, quietly and menacingly at first. Then, louder, 'Get *out*.' And finally, raising her voice to a nasal screech, 'Get out of my fucking *house*.'

I didn't wait to be told a fourth time. Although her body was filling most of the doorway, I pushed past her, and ran downstairs.

Justin must have realised what was happening, or at least caught the gist of it, and he'd beaten me to the front door. He grabbed his jacket and mine from the cupboard where they'd been hung, and put my shoes in front of me so I could step straight into them. He'd even thought to pick up the handbag I'd left on the sofa.

I could hear Philippa coughing, and I thought, childishly, I hope she chokes herself to death.

I fumbled in my bag for the car key, and once the doors were unlocked remotely, Justin opened mine before whizzing round and letting himself into the passenger seat. I turned on the windscreen wiper. All the other windows were steamed up, but in any case all definition had gone, everything was blurred. I was a bad naughty child, who'd been told off, and only had myself to blame.

I'd drunk much more than I should have done, and I wished I didn't have to drive, but I had no choice. Hand trembling, I switched on the ignition. I half-expected Philippa to come running behind us, shaking her fists, like some crazy caricature in a cartoon.

'Sorry.' My voice came out in a whisper.

Justin put his hand lightly on my knee, as I drove.

'Sorry,' I said again. 'I fucked things up for us, didn't I?'

He shrugged, sighed. 'She didn't have to over-react like that.'

'I *was* in the wrong though.'

'We all do wrong things sometimes.'

It was Justin being so nice that finished me. I pulled up in the first available lay-by and I just sat there, chin cupped in my palms, forehead pressed against the steering-wheel, eyes stinging with tears, my whole body shaking. I could feel Justin's hand between my shoulder blades. I sat there for as long as it took me to stop shaking, to feel strangely sober, depleted, and rather sick.

And then I drove us the rest of the way home, and we didn't talk.

Twenty One

SARAH'S DIARY

4th January 2012

I knew I had to do something, about the fear and anxiety that continued to plague me.

I wondered whether therapy would be the answer. I thought it unlikely. I'd tried it once before and it hadn't done anything for me. Years ago, when I was feeling a bit desperate, I went to a rather dowdy, self-effacing woman who wore a skirt and cardigan, the sort of clothes my mother used to wear. She worked at home, and obviously didn't bother dressing for the job. She even wore bedroom slippers. How could this woman possibly help *me*, when all the time I was sitting there I felt like telling her to smarten up, get a handle on her own life, stop poking around in other people's. My mother always said that counsellors were nosey parkers, that was why they got into the business. If this person was typical, then I couldn't help agreeing with her.

Even so, I thought that maybe it was worth giving it another go. Things are different today. Now we have the internet, we don't just walk into a situation blindfolded. We do our research, we find out what's on offer before we part with our money. Just like when we're buying a computer or a washing-machine or something.

I know the diagnosis. All I need is the cure.

I searched on the web for therapists in Norfolk. I decided it would be better to find someone out in the sticks. I don't want to be bumping into this person when I'm out and about in the city in the evening, or at lunchtime, with people from work. I'm not one of those people who'll be banging on about what 'my therapist said'. It's going to be a totally private affair.

I found the website of someone called Philippa Johnson. She has a video on her website, talks about her own life and how she's overcome her problems. This must have taken quite a bit of courage, putting herself in the picture like that. And I liked the way she presented herself, visually. Presentation's important. I knew she wouldn't come to the door in bedroom slippers. She was a professional.

But what really hooked me was how she said, at the end of her video, 'Trust me.' Easy words to say, but the way she looked at me, out of the screen, she seemed to mean it. And trust has never been a big part of my life.

So I emailed and made an appointment, and I drove to her house. It's a modern house, pretending to be much older; brick-and-flint, semi-detached, in a village called Dartingham. Not somewhere I would choose to live, but it's off the beaten track, just as I wanted. Away from the rest of my life. No prying eyes.

It was grey and cold, and I was wearing a fitted jacket over my long velvet skirt. I had a scarf wound several times around my neck. She opened the door. I would have recognised her anywhere. She was dressed in a loose black smock, appliquéd with palm trees and parrots, over mid-calf black leggings. Her hair, instead of being loose like it was in the video, was pinned back with an assortment of clips. Apart from that, she looked pretty much the same.

I wasn't sure of the etiquette but I held out my hand for her to shake. She gave a little nod, looking straight into my eyes, and took my hand, holding it tightly and firmly. I fought an impulse to turn away. I could feel her fingernail digging into my palm.

A dog was barking, and I couldn't stop myself giving a little shudder. I have a dislike of dogs that verges on terror. She noticed, of course, and said, 'The dog's not mine, it's next door's. Always yapping. Dreadful creature.' I felt that we were allies when she said that. United against dogs. Then she said, 'My therapy room's upstairs,' and she led the way.

The room is painted blue, with minimal furniture. Two leather armchairs face each other diagonally, and between them there's a glass coffee table, with a flask of water, two glasses, an unlit candle, and a box of tissues. On two of the walls there are these dreadful abstract prints that masquerade as art, the sort you might buy in Homebase. On another wall, pride of place, ornately framed, are the words: 'Feel the fear and do it anyway.' I once read a book with that title. At first it seemed to help a bit, but then I just went back to being the same old me, always anxious and fearful.

She told me to sit down. I did as instructed, and crossed my legs in front of me. She sat in the opposite chair, and crossed hers. She was wearing black ballerina pumps, and her ankles seemed very slim for the rest of her body. I saw the tattoo on her left ankle. It looked like a scarab, one of those Egyptian beetles that have some sort of supernatural meaning.

She just sat there and waited for what seemed like an awfully long time, though it was probably only a few seconds. I tried not to fidget, not to give away any body language. I felt scrutinised, as though she was already garnering insights into what I was about and how I ticked. She had her arms folded, and I realised that mine were too. I'd folded them tight against my chest, as if protecting myself. Finally, she broke the silence. 'So tell me, what's on your mind?' She was looking not just *into* my eyes, but more *beyond* them.

'May I?' I leaned forward and poured myself some water. It gave me something to do while I decided how to begin. I fiddled with the glass, changed my mind about it, straightened up and looked directly into her face, and the words came out, as though rehearsed. 'I think I have impostor syndrome.'

She blinked, looked slightly disapproving. Perhaps it was a strange way to begin. Perhaps I should have waited for her to make a diagnosis, not pre-empt it. That was supposed to be *her* job, not mine. Then she looked at me again, with those piercing eyes. 'Impostor syndrome,' she repeated. And, after a pause, 'So what exactly does that mean for you?'

'If it means what I think it means . . . well, what I feel like is that I'm play-acting all the time. I'm pretending to be someone I'm not. And I'm constantly nervous. Anxious. Always afraid of being found out. Like the emperor's new clothes. Suddenly everybody's going to realise what I really am, and they'll all be muttering about me and laughing behind their hands.'

She didn't say anything at first. I started to wonder if she was a bit out of her depth. Or maybe she thought I was trying to be too clever. I know I sometimes give that impression. It's a defence mechanism. Always trying to be one step ahead. She scratched her right wrist with her left hand fingernails. Finally, she asked me, 'What's she like? This person you say you're pretending to be. The person wearing the emperor's new clothes. Can you describe her for me?'

I thought for a moment. 'She's good at what she does. She's talented. She works hard. People find her interesting.'

'OK. Now how about substituting the first person pronoun? Try saying: *I'm good at my job. I'm talented. I work hard. I'm interesting.*' I gave a little smile, almost a snigger. I couldn't help it. It felt like

145

being in a self-esteem class for adolescents. They probably have such things nowadays, there's a lot more support, more pampering, than there was when I was young. 'Go on,' she said. So I repeated everything, feeling more than a little ridiculous.

'OK. That's on hold. It's not going to go away. It's *you.*' She folded her arms. 'So let's start looking at why you have trouble believing it.'

I took a sip of water. It was warm, and tasted rather stale, as if it had been there on the table too long.

'I watched your video,' I told her. 'I listened to what you said, about how you had all those problems when you were a teenager, and how you managed to transform yourself. I thought it was very brave of you, to share all that. I have a similar story. When I was young, I was very plain, very shy, very awkward. I had trouble relating to other people. My mother didn't like anyone coming round to the house, and I felt I was never going to be normal, like everyone else. I did have one friend, who I went around with, and she was the opposite of me, always outgoing, always chatting to everyone, never seemed to worry about anything, and I was just this timid shadow. And then, when I left school, and I went to sixth form college, I started to be a bit more confident. I attached myself to a little circle of friends who had a sort of alternative lifestyle. The way they dressed, what they talked about, the music they listened to. I started to dress the way they did. I felt as if I belonged with them. And I made up my mind I wanted to go to university and study art. It felt like the right thing for me to do.'

'And you did that?'

'I went to Newcastle. I enjoyed the course, it was brilliant, everything seemed to go well, the tutors liked me, I got my degree. I had a boyfriend, he was on the same course, and afterwards we rented a flat together.

146

Our relationship didn't last, but we split up amicably. We're still in touch. He moved to Birmingham and I came back to Norfolk. And workwise I've been lucky. I have a really good agent, and she's got me lots of commissions. I illustrate children's books. That's what I do, the main thing. But the money I earn from this isn't consistent, and a friend suggested I did a bit teaching on the side. So a couple of years ago I started working as a part-time tutor. That was a mistake. A big mistake.'

'And why was that?'

'I'd actually been looking forward to starting the job, it felt like a new challenge, and I guess I felt like I'd be putting something back in the pot, you know, sharing my skills. But then, on my very first day, I had to see the course administrator about something, and it turned out she was this person who used to be my friend at school. The one who always made me feel like I was just her shadow. It was as if my past had come back to haunt me, or maybe more like I'd walked straight back into my own past. And I shook hands with her and pretended everything was fine, but of course it wasn't. It wasn't fine at all. I could see her looking at me, as if I was Cinderella and she was one of the Ugly Sisters and she'd caught me out at the ball. Not that she's ugly, of course. And she's been perfectly polite and professional with me. We haven't said anything to each other, only about work, we've never actually mentioned the past. But whenever I see her, I have the feeling she's seeing the person I *was*, all those years ago. And, of course, that's the person I really *am*. Underneath all the success, all the veneer, that's what I am.'

'So that's when it started? This impostor syndrome? When you saw your old friend.'

'To be honest, it must have been there all along. But I used to have it under control. I thought if I worked hard, if I just kept on working, it would go away. Or maybe, if I worked hard enough, I'd become the person I'd been pretending to be.'

'I see.'   She clasped and unclasped her hands. Clasped them again. I looked down at my lap, and realised I'd been doing the same.   Clasping, unclasping, clasping.

'And there's something else.'

'What's that?'

'The old school friend I was telling you about. We're in love with the same man.'

It was the first time I'd actually acknowledged this, even to myself. Suspected it, maybe. Acknowledged it, no. But it was true, of course it was.

'I just *know* we are. I can tell. It's so obvious.' I was conscious of a tremor in my voice, as if I was on the verge of crying. I swallowed, contained it, before I continued. 'I've watched, in a meeting – we have these course meetings every couple of weeks – the way they look at each other, my old friend, and the man I've been in love with for years. He's a part-time tutor like me, he teaches photography. He was the friend who suggested I applied for the job, we both started working at the university at the same time. Anyhow, whenever we're in a meeting, they exchange glances across the table, this man I'm in love with and my old school friend. A little smile, maybe, or a raised eyebrow. As if they have a secret. And then she looks at *me*. As if she's warning me. As if she's saying, *Of course he loves me more than he loves you.* And I just sit there, and everything starts swimming, and anything I was going to say to the meeting goes completely out of my head, and everybody seems to know what's going on, and they're all trying to look somewhere else, it's all so

148

embarrassing, and I want to run away and hide. It's so *demeaning.*'

I hadn't actually put words to any of this before, it had just been a creeping suspicion, like a mole, burrowing underground, in the dark. Now that I'd brought it to the surface it was threatening to overwhelm me. I'd been so sure I wouldn't need that box of tissues. Nobody'd seen me cry. Not since I was fifteen. Almost sixteen.

And, of course, I can't stand the idea of sharing Oliver with *anyone*. But with *her*, it's unbearable. I didn't say that, but I thought it. The thought of them having sex together. The thought of Oliver touching her, the way he touches me.

'Mm. That's a tricky one.' She looked at her watch. 'Our time's nearly up.'

Surely she must have noticed that my eyes were brimming with tears.

Stopped midstream, I started to jump out of my chair, afraid of overstaying my welcome. 'Don't be a nuisance to people,' my parents always used to say to me.

'Whooa, hold on a moment, we're not quite there yet. And we don't want you to leave here feeling negative. Remember those affirmations you said at the beginning. What were they? I'm good at my job, I'm talented . . . Say them to me once more before you go.'

This wasn't what I wanted to do at all. I wanted to go on talking, now that I'd started. To verbalise all those thoughts and feelings I'd been keeping under wraps. To have someone listen to me. To understand.

To give me a hug, even. I wanted to be held by her, the way no woman had ever held me.

Only men had held me and hugged me.

149

But I repeated, mechanically, like one of the times tables: *I'm good at my job. I'm talented. I work hard. I'm interesting.* I almost spat the words out. Did she really think that, by saying them, I could actually believe them? Like there really is a Father Christmas. I might be fake, but I'm not an idiot.

'Well done. I take it you'll be coming back to continue our work?'

Our work. An odd way of putting it. It sounded like a business transaction.

I hesitated. I wasn't sure. I hate to feel pressurised by anybody. Particularly when I'm feeling emotional and insecure.

She waited, looking into my eyes, behind my eyes. Behind the tears. Stripping me down to all my vulnerability and helplessness and hopelessness. I nodded.

'Same time next week?'

'Please.' The pathetic whisper of a small, frightened child.

'Some people find it helpful to keep a diary. You might want to note down your exchanges with this person, this old friend. Write down any feelings that surface, what triggers them, how you deal with them. Just a suggestion. It's up to you. I'm going to write up my notes now. Do you mind letting yourself out?'

I didn't. I needed some air. I still felt like crying. I *was* crying, to my surprise and shame. I couldn't stop myself.

And now that I'm thinking about it, writing about it, the reason I was so upset, it wasn't just the thoughts that had surfaced. About Oliver. About Melanie. That was part of it, but only part. It was also the way the session had ended so abruptly. As if, after I'd started to open up to her with all my hurt and my hang-ups and my needs, she didn't really care. 'Do you mind letting

150

yourself out?' she'd said, dismissively. Time and attention given, then taken away. Isn't that how it's always been? People seem to want to be nice to me, care about me, like me even, but then I'm thrown out on my own feeble resources again. Cast aside, avoided, an embarrassment, forgotten.

And as for those pointless affirmations, it was like giving a couple of fruit gums to a child. Suck these, for goodness sake, you'll soon feel better. Only you don't.

I cried all the way home, disregarding speed limits, the scenery a blur of skeletal trees and hedges. I was still crying as I drove into Norwich, just about remembering to stop at traffic lights, green and red almost indistinguishable, splayed and watery at the edges. I parked my car, fumbled for my keys, ran up the stairs to my apartment, collapsed on the sofa and cried some more. All those tears I'd kept inside me for so long had suddenly found a way out, and couldn't be contained. The phone rang, and I ignored it, even though it might have been Oliver. Or my mother. And when I'd finally finished crying, I filled a large glass with water from the fridge, and drank it in thirsty gulps. I felt sick, and I had no desire to eat.

It was much too early for bed. And I didn't feel like watching TV. But I had to do something.

I found a notebook I'd bought for work.

So I'm beginning my diary with this account of how I started therapy, and why. I'm writing it down while the meeting's still clear in my head. There must have been more than that, we said, over the hour, but those are the parts I remember, the parts that stand out. And I'm not sure how I feel or what I think about it now, it's all mixed up. I'm not sure whether I actually *like* her or not, my new therapist. But at least she's different from that one I went to before, in her old skirt and bedroom slippers. At least she has presence, she seems confident. As if she knows what she's doing. And that's what I so much need to believe.

I need to believe I'm in safe hands.

.

Twenty Two

4ᵗʰ January 2012

I'd been looking forward to a new client.

They don't know how thin on the ground they are these days. Sometimes I almost forget I *am* a therapist. A qualified therapist, no less, though only just. That's something else they don't know: that I didn't exactly pass the course with flying colours.

The course leader wasn't helpful. She seemed to think that I lacked authenticity. She said she wasn't entirely sure about my commitment to helping people. What was it she said? That I knew the tune but not the words? Or was it the other way around?

She also said I didn't seem to have resolved my own issues. That if I wanted to be a working therapist, I'd need a lot more therapy myself. I would also need a good supervisor, someone to help me understand my reactions to my clients. Someone I trusted, she said.

Frankly, I've never trusted anyone. Except Brian, maybe. Even Brian, I'm not always sure about. Life has taught me there are no certainties when it comes to other people.

I didn't want more therapy. I'd had enough. I didn't want a supervisor either. So when I finished the course, I made a decision. I wasn't going to join a professional organisation like the BACP. I was going to set myself up independently.

Let's face it – most people, when they decide they need a therapist, don't even know or give two hoots about the British Association for Counselling and Psychotherapy. They just want someone to listen while they spout off about themselves and their problems. Someone who says what they want to hear. Someone who makes them feel better about themselves. And I reckoned I knew enough about therapy to give them what they wanted.

So I put a few adverts about in the local papers. Brian fixed me up a website. I told my tale of woe to Justin's video camera. Up close and personal, the way they like it. Sincere. A little bit tearful. Fuck my course leader for saying I was inauthentic. How dare she!

Almost every client who's come to me – and there've been quite a few over the years, though most of them have only come for the first session, which I offer free – have said how *brave* I was to talk on that video the way I did. Yes, I was brave. It wasn't easy. But if I'm honest, it was also therapeutic. I named names. Sandra, Lizzie, Ricky. In a way, I was punishing them for what they'd done to me. I had a lot of anger. I wanted people to see my point of view. To be on my side.

But this is just preamble. I was going to make some notes about my new client, who I shall call by her initials, SB. And I can't say I really took to her.

As a matter of fact, I found her rather annoying. It was the way she sat there, legs crossed, arms folded. Rather prissy. The way she looked around the room, and then at me. As if she was judging everything. The way she helped herself to water, kind of slow motion. The way she came out with that baloney about impostor syndrome.

Isn't that what life's all about – pretending?

Only a newborn baby hasn't learned to pretend. We have to pretend, for our own survival.

And she seemed so smug. 'I'm good at my job. I'm talented. I'm interesting.' Blah blahdy blah. Oh, and the way she said, in that prim little manner she has, 'I illustrate children's books. That's what I do.' Sounds like a cushy little number to me. Not like standing in a shop all day, flattering people who already think they're the bee's knees. Pretending to actually give a shit. Or looking at old women's shrivelled-up bottoms. Shovelling food in their toothless mouths. Pretending to *care*.

She seemed as if she wanted to impress me, but I wasn't buying it.

She's another of these arty-farty people. Banging on about her 'alternative' friends. As if ordinary people aren't good enough for her.

Rather like Lizzie.

But those issues she has about her old school friend – that might be worth looking into.

She started to get emotional at the end, and that was to be avoided. That's why I cut the session short. My sort of therapy's about positive thinking. About conquering fear and negativity. The last thing I want is people sitting there sobbing and snivelling. Whenever I've had a sniveller, I've told them to look for another therapist. Mostly it's just a performance, anyhow, all that weeping and wailing. I can do it myself. I can turn it on. A tear here, a sniff there. The whole theatrics if necessary, to get results, or to make people feel guilty. But it has to be calculated. Controlled.

She has potential, this client. I just need to get her onto my wavelength. It might even start to be interesting.

Twenty Three

The problem with starting a relationship is that there are no instruction manuals. Not for the particular combination. Like how to have a relationship with your new lodger who happens to be a transvestite and who also happens to have a mad scary mother.

If I had the right number for the model, I could download the manual. As it was, I was troubleshooting randomly. I couldn't figure out whether we needed more space away from each other, or less. More talking things over, or just going with the flow. Whether we had a future together or we didn't.

Whenever he was out, I soaked up his favourite music. Over and over again, I played Bonny 'Prince' Billy. There was a song of his called Love Comes to Me, and I didn't really understand the lyrics, but I learned them by heart, sang along with them, cried along with them.

I thought it might help if we socialised more, started to share each other's circles. Well, maybe not the tranny ones, not yet. So we asked a few people round for New Year's Eve. Rachel, Ellie and Paul, Karen and Dave. I even invited Kathleen from work, knowing she lived on her own and didn't have much of a social life. Justin's friend Mick came down from North Walsham, we said he could sleep over. And Glenn and Rita, who Justin had been staying with before he moved in with me. They looked nothing like I'd imagined them. I'd heard Justin's words 'baby crying' and 'post natal depression', and I'd stereotyped them as some downtrodden couple, struggling to meet the bills, like on reality TV. Instead they looked like models. They brought champagne – the real stuff, not just fizzy wine – and Rita kissed both of us on both cheeks, even though she didn't know me. I said I was so glad they'd been able to get a babysitter, and she told me her mother was there with Clary, so sweet of her to give up the evening, and they'd promised to be back in time to have a midnight drink with her.

It was good to have some noise in the house, and fortunately we didn't have to worry about this. The house next door was full of young students, who were having their own, much noisier party. The house on our other side had been empty since the old man George had died.

Justin and I started dancing first, to give things a kick-start. Besides, we'd been drinking steadily while waiting for everyone to arrive, and we needed to sweat some of it off. It was the first time I'd danced with Justin, and I thought how well our bodies moved together. I think we were both showing off a bit. Seeing Justin like that, as if through other people's eyes, I was hyper-aware of his delicate bone structure, his laughing eyes, his tall slender body. It was hard to recall how I'd once thought him unexceptional and unnoticeable. I was wearing skinny black jeans with a tight-fitting glittery T-shirt, and I'd long since thrown off my shoes, and I guessed that I was looking pretty good as well.

Then everyone was dancing, and nobody was with anybody in particular.

I went to the kitchen for a refill, and Rita followed me. 'Thanks for rescuing Justin,' she said. 'He's a sweetie, but I wasn't in the best frame of mind for having someone else living with us.'

'He told me there were a few problems. It must have been really hard with a new baby.'

'That's right. She's much better now, thank god. Hardly cries at all, except when she's hungry.'

I filled my glass up to the brim, and took a gulp. I wiped the wine from my lips with the back of my hand. 'Have you got a glass?'

'I'll get myself some tap water in a minute. I don't drink all that much. Anyhow, I'm on medication.'

'OK.' I had a sense she wanted to tell me something.

'I suppose he's told you that I went a bit crazy when I found he'd been poking around in my wardrobe.'

'No, he hasn't told me that.' I clearly remembered him saying that none of his friends knew about his transvestism. That he wanted to keep it that way.

'I mean, I know it's just what he does, he can't help himself.'

'So you know about . . . ?'

'The cross-dressing. Course I do. Everybody knows. Well, maybe not quite everybody. But it's what he does, isn't it, it's no big deal.'

I nodded. I took another gulp of wine, and went back to join the others. I left Rita in the kitchen. I managed to stop myself from saying, 'The tap's there. Help yourself.' Bloody tap water people, they always have a way of sounding superior.

***

Midnight came and went, and with it all the kissing and the New Year wishes. Kathleen had left soon after Rita and Glenn, she didn't make it to midnight, but nobody else was in a hurry to go anywhere. I needed the bathroom, but Rachel was in there, throwing up, and didn't seem as if she'd finish any time soon. I walked out into my tiny overgrown garden, disregarding the freezing sogginess under my bare feet, and crouched down amongst the weeds and the brambles and discarded junk. I was drunk enough not to care if anyone saw me. The brambles pricked my ankles. When I pulled my jeans back up, I realised they were spattered with pee.

I pushed past our friends, still dancing and partying, and went upstairs to change into my joggers. 'I felt like changing into something more comfortable,' I'd say, if anybody noticed.

I'd overdone the wine, and everything was spinning. I lay down on top of the bedclothes, and I must have dozed off because the next thing I was aware of was Ellie leaning over me, saying, 'We're about to go. Are you alright?'

'I just needed to lie down,' I mumbled, and followed her downstairs. Everywhere smelt of wine and weed and sweat. Karen and Dave were asleep, entwined on the sofa. Justin and Mick were sitting at the table, talking incessantly, their voices overlapping across the wreck of empty wine bottles and glasses. I kissed Ellie and Paul, wished them yet another happy new year before they left in a taxi, and then I wandered into the kitchen and made myself an instant coffee.

My mobile was flashing on the surface where I'd dumped it, and I checked for missed calls and texts. Surprisingly there was a text from Oliver: a simple 'Happy New Year'. No kisses of course. Even more surprising, as I didn't know she had my number, there was one from Philippa. She'd typed, 'Let's draw a line under what happened boxing day. All the best for 2013.'

I went back upstairs, and changed my glittery T-shirt for an old, baggy one. I left my joggers on in case I needed to go back down. I pulled the duvet up to my chin. This time, I couldn't sleep. I was aware of the voices downstairs: Justin's and Mick's. Rachel's too. She was laughing. That high-pitched ultra-female laugh she has. She'd obviously recovered from her bout of vomiting. I thought about the two texts. I supposed I ought to send one back to Oliver, but I couldn't be bothered. I'd washed that man right out of my hair, as Mitzi Gaynor sang in South Pacific. We used to have the video at home, it was one of my mother's old favourites, and I sang along with it when I was a child. It used to drive Joshua and Jake mad with me, so I'd sing that song over and over, around the house, just to wind them up. As for Philippa, my mother had said she was good at apologising. And so she should be. But I've often thought the best apologisers are the people who are always acting badly in the first place. OK, I was out of order looking at her diary, but the way she'd screamed at me was enough to give me the horrors for a lifetime. Perhaps she was one of those split personality people. Perhaps she couldn't help it. The way she'd flipped reminded me of Kathy Bates in the film Misery. One of my favourite films of all times, it was so creepy.

There'd been no text from my mother, she wasn't a texting person. She'd probably ring me in a few hours, her idea of time to get up in the morning, regardless of whether it was New Year's Day. She was still in Oxford with Joshua and Patsy and the girls, and no doubt they were all tucked up in their beds.

I suppressed an urge to ring or text her. Wake her up, like I was a child again, waking from a nightmare. I missed her suddenly. I missed them all.

Joshua was five years older than me, and he'd always seemed a bit remote. I'd been closer to Jake, who was only two years older. I wished we still talked to each other, really talked, the way we used to when we were young. I could have told him about everything that was playing on my mind – Sarah, Philippa, Justin – and whatever worries I'd had he would have listened and then told me not to be so daft. He'd have blown it all away.

Yes, I suddenly realised, I missed my family. Not the way it was now, with me always feeling like the one who hadn't grown up, when everybody else was settled and sorted. My family as it had been, in the old house, noisy around the meal table, everybody being who we were, no inhibitions or criticism.

And then, once again, I started thinking of Sarah. How nervous and awkward she'd been at first, but then how she used to come round to our house more and more, gradually starting to relax amongst us, almost one of the family. How I'd suddenly decided I didn't want her to be my friend any longer. So cruel and unfeeling. Nobody likes to be discarded like that. It must have been particularly hard for Sarah, not having any other friends or brothers or sisters. Living in that dark house with those weird parents.

I thought of that time in the office, not long before she died, when I'd bragged about my trip to Paris with Oliver. There are times when I'm not a nice person.

And I thought of her name in Philippa's diary. Nobody would ever know what they'd talked about in that blue room with the jug of water and the box of tissues, they'd be sworn to confidentiality. From what I knew of Philippa, and what little I knew of Sarah in the months before her death, it seemed like a strange mix. I couldn't imagine the private and rather uptight Sarah confiding in someone like Philippa. Had anybody else ever known that she'd been going for therapy? Had she given any clues, that she was thinking of suicide? Or was it unexpected, a mystery, like it was with Lizzie?

I needed to find out what really happened, and why. Somehow I owed this to Sarah.

***

I fell asleep with those thoughts, and when I woke – it must have been nearly morning – Justin was there beside me. I rolled over and put my arm around his body, and then I took it away, remembering. He half opened his eyes. 'Justin, there's something I need to talk to you about.'

He sighed. 'Can't it wait?' But he knew me. He knew when I wanted to talk I had to talk.

'You know when you told me you were a transvestite. You said none of your friends knew about it. That's not true, is it?'

He sighed again. 'Not exactly, no.'

'What do you mean, not exactly? Rita and Glenn know. Presumably they're not the only ones.'

'A few people know. They might have told other people. I don't know. It started when I was still at school. I used to talk to people. One or two. Hardly anybody.'

'So why did you tell me nobody knew?'

'I don't know. It wasn't something I really thought through before I said it. I guess I just didn't want you thinking you were the last person to know something about me.'

'Why?'

'I'm not sure. I think maybe I wanted you thinking it was our secret. That you'd be more protective about it. And about me.'

I just lay there, waiting for him to continue.

'Anyhow, all sorts of people know about it now. I mean, in connection with Lizzie. I had to tell people where I was that weekend.'

'I suppose.'

'You know that first time we met. I've already told you it was the dresses I'd gone back to the house for, not the CDs. Well, when you offered me that lift, I felt torn. I thought the dresses would still be in there, I

162

didn't think you'd have found them. I badly wanted those dresses. But then you were standing there, looking frazzled and stroppy and gorgeous, all at the same time, and I wanted *you*. So I chose the lift.'

I had nothing to say to that. I put my hand on his stomach.

'And then, when you dropped me off at the station, and you said there was a room in your house, I had to bite my tongue, or I'd have jumped at the offer straight away, like a salivating dog. So I waited a couple of days, before I phoned you. It was true, things were a bit fraught at the time, with Glenn and Rita and the baby, but I exaggerated a bit. When I rang that evening, and you said I could move in the next day, my heart did a few somersaults. I'd only met you that one time and I was crazy about you. Still am.'

'Me too. About you.' I didn't bother telling him how that night, when he'd phoned, I'd been eating my heart out for Oliver.

'I don't think you were at first. I think you were curious about me. But I knew we had time on our side. And if we were living in the same house we had to keep on seeing each other.'

'Justin.' I spoke into his chest, tasting the sweat that beaded his body hair. 'Can you promise me one thing? That you won't lie to me again. Ever.'

'That I can't promise. People lie all the time, or at least tell untruths. That doesn't sound as harsh as lying. For example, we're always telling people we're fine, when we're not.'

'We're all going to end up in hell,' I murmured. 'That's what a friend told me once. That we'd end up in hell if we lied. Only Jake told me there's no such place as hell. That hell itself is just one big lie.'

'It's just a state of mind, isn't it? Hell. Heaven. What's that quote, about nothing's either good or bad but thinking makes it so. Wasn't that Shakespeare?'

'Was it?' I said, not caring. Suddenly all the lies, and the half-lies, what was true and what wasn't, seemed unimportant. The only truth at that moment was I wanted Justin. My body was crying out for him. So we started the New Year with our lovemaking. I'd always had a secret superstition that, if I woke up to New Year's Day with someone, we'd still be together at the end of the year. I'd been proved wrong before. This time, maybe it would really happen.

I gave Justin a long, hard kiss. Just for luck.

Twenty Four

LIZZIE'S STORY

Just for the record, I'd better make it clear that there's never been anything going on between Brian and me, although I know Philippa's had her suspicions. Because of that other time. But I'm not the sort of person to misbehave with a married man. If you read this when I'm dead, I want you to believe me, because Philippa may have given you a different version.

As it happened, I was the one who introduced Brian to Philippa, all those years ago. At that time, Philippa was living in her little council flat with Justin. Peter and I decided we needed someone to make us some bookshelves, and one of the neighbours I used to chat to, someone who's long since left the area, recommended Brian. He was a freelance carpenter. That was before he started working for a kitchen company.

So he was in and out of our house for a week. Peter was at work and Kate was at school, but I had Justin there with me, he was just a toddler then, so that Philippa could be in Norwich, working in the shop. I wasn't painting so much in those days, there was enough to do with looking after Kate, when she was home, and Justin during the daytime. It was summer, and I had a tan from spending so much time in the garden. I remember one day offering Brian a glass of cider, and we sat outside while Justin messed around in the little sandpit Peter had made for him. Peter loved being a grandfather to Justin. I was wearing shorts, and I was conscious of my tanned legs. I could see Brian looking at me, and although he was younger than me I could tell he found me attractive. As I wrote earlier, Peter and I never had much of a sexual relationship, and maybe I had my needs. Maybe I was flirting a bit. But nothing happened, of course, because Justin was there, and Brian had to get on with the job.

A few weeks later, we met again. North Walsham is that sort of place, it's not that small, but the odds are wherever you go you'll meet at least one person you know. It was still hot and summery, it must have been a good year for sun. We were at some music-in-the-park fundraising event. Peter was playing in the group, with Meg and Dave. They moved to Somerset not long afterwards, and that was that as far as the group was concerned. A shame, as Peter was a good guitarist, and he pretty much stopped playing after that. I was sitting on the grass with Philippa and Kate and little Justin. Brian came walking past, and then he spotted me and came over. He appeared to be on his own. I could see him looking at Philippa. She was wearing some sort of sundress, and she'd lost quite a bit of weight around then. She looked better than I'd ever known her. I took Kate and Justin to buy ice-creams, and by the time I came back it was obvious that Brian and Philippa were onto something. When Peter finished playing his gig, we went home with the children, and left Philippa to work her magic with Brian.

So you see, that was the second big favour I did her. The first, I'll come to later. Anyhow, I introduced Philippa to Brian, though I've never bothered to remind her of it. Even though, whenever I'm at their house, I can see her eyes on me whenever I'm talking to Brian. As if she doesn't trust us together. We talk about things that Philippa's not interested in, like music and politics, and I think he enjoys the conversation, but I suppose she feels a bit left out. And then she stomps off to the kitchen, and I can hear her clattering around, and when she comes back she's watching me again, in that way she has. Well, one of the ways. Sometimes she looks at me, her eyes all aglow, as if she's about to pounce, as if she's on the point of finding something she's been looking for. At other times, she looks at me as though I'm cat shit.

There was one time, a few months ago, she really flipped. I hadn't seen her do that before. When she was a teenager, she didn't have tantrums. If ever she was angry or upset about something, she just looked daggers at people, and sort of folded in on herself. I'd been having problems with my computer and Brian offered to come and look at it. He fixed it for me, but it took longer than we expected. Justin was out, at the time, I remember. I made coffee, and we sat there drinking it on the sofa, it's the only place to sit because I use my living-room as a studio, and I need every surface I can lay my hands on. I just keep the sofa free so that Justin and I can watch television in the evenings. And suddenly in burst Philippa. She couldn't just phone, of course, she had to drive over, as if she wanted to catch us in the act. She has her own key to the house, she always has done. Fair enough, it used to be her home for long enough. She said to Brian, 'You're looking very cosy. I came to see if you'd got lost.' He squirmed. I wanted to smooth things over, so I said, 'He's been working hard for the last couple of hours, I thought it was time for a coffee.' She turned to me then, and that was when she flipped. 'Time for a coffee!' she said. 'Is that what you call it? Time for a fucking coffee!' She was almost screeching. I felt embarrassed, more than upset. Embarrassed for Philippa. Embarrassed for Brian. I couldn't see what all the fuss was about. All we were doing was sitting on the sofa together, chatting. I stood up. I said, 'Do you want a coffee, Philippa?' She said, 'No I don't want a fucking coffee.' Then she said, 'I know the sort of person you are. Brian's a bit old for

167

you, though, isn't he? He's not all that much younger than you. Only ten years younger. That's not enough for you, is it? You like them young. Much younger. Don't think I've ever forgotten. And don't think I don't know what goes on between you and Justin. You're just a dirty old woman. Ugly and desperate and old.'

She obviously has problems. She calls herself a therapist, but I reckon she needs some therapy herself.

Brian just glanced at me, threw me a little apologetic grimace, and followed her out like a lamb. I felt sorry for him. It probably wasn't the first time she'd flipped like that. He didn't seem so shocked.

And the next Friday, she came round to see me as if nothing out of the ordinary had happened. As if she'd forgotten that she'd said those awful things. The only difference from usual was that she didn't give me an overdose of positive thinking, like she normally does. She just kept looking at me, fixing her eyes on me, as if she knew something I didn't. And she said something rather strange. She said, 'Whatever we do or we don't do in life, we all have to die. Sometimes it's a blessing, that we know that.'

Twenty Five

SARAH'S DIARY

25th January 2012

Is it possible to be in love with two people at the same time?

Because I still love Oliver, of course, but now I find I'm in love with my therapist. With Philippa. I believe this is normal. To fall in love with one's therapist. See, I'm a walking, talking, real live cliché.

The fact that she's a woman, well that's a first. I've never felt attracted to women. Unless, of course, you count the French teacher I had a crush on, but that was just an adolescent thing. I look at women, admire them sometimes, aesthetically as well as intellectually or artistically, but there's never been a sexual element. Then, last week, I actually dreamed we were making love. We were caressing each other's bodies. I could almost smell her. A sort of milkiness. I woke up with an orgasm. I put my hand between my legs and I was hot and wet.

Even more bizarre is that, aesthetically, she's not the sort of woman I'm attracted to. She has style, but no subtlety. No class. She's much too in-your-face. All that make-up. That dreadful tattoo. And those awful abstract prints in her room, they actually hurt my eyes. I want to say to her, take them down, I'll give you something better.

Maybe I'll offer her something of mine. Although I'm an illustrator, mainly of children's books, I'm also a printmaker. Most of my stuff is monochrome. It invites you to bring to it your own imagination, your own interpretation. It would be ideal for a therapy room.

But I won't, of course, because I couldn't bear it if she looks at it in that put-down way she sometimes has. When people reject my art, they reject me. I'm terrified of rejection. Especially by someone I love.

Today we had our fourth session together. And I suppose it's ironic, because I started therapy with the intention of getting in touch with my real self, but I'm now finding I have less and less of an idea where that self begins and ends.

I've spent a lifetime trying to be the person other people want me to be. My parents. They wanted me to be not much seen and certainly not heard, so I became a mouse. Melanie, when she was my friend, she just wanted a puppy dog, someone to follow her around, do whatever she wanted me to do. The friends I had afterwards, I copied them, I became a member of the pack. Chris, who I met at university and used to live with, he seemed to value me for what I was, but then he met somebody else he valued more, so I guess that didn't really count. And as for Oliver, I've worked hard for Oliver, at being the sort of person he likes to hang out with. Interesting, a bit mysterious, with hidden layers of sexuality. He actually said those words about me once. I really believed he loved me, until I saw that he was attracted to Melanie, who's about as mysterious as an empty wheelie bin.

And now I find myself turning up for therapy with one main thought in mind, which is to give Philippa what *she* wants from me.

The problem is, I'm not sure exactly what she wants.

When I went for my second session, I was feeling even more apprehensive than I had been on that first occasion. I never thought anyone would have such power over me, to make me feel like that. Cry like that. I'm normally so in control of my emotions. The last

170

time I let my emotions get the better of me was twenty years ago. That awful birthday party at Melanie's house. And I don't even want to think about that.

I almost rang and cancelled the session. I still felt cynical. Those ridiculous affirmations. *I'm good at my job. I'm talented. I work hard. I'm interesting.* I felt like throwing up. If she asked me to say all that over again, I would have to say no. I would have to be honest. I'm not there to play silly games with her.

But she didn't. She must have realised that it was too simplistic for me.

I'd done what she'd suggested: written about an exchange I'd had with Melanie, in the office, and how it had made me feel. I didn't write about it in this diary. I wanted to present it to Philippa, like homework. I suppose I wanted her to grade me. A, B or C. Or so many marks out of ten.

***

This is what I wrote:

I go into the office because I need to find out about a student who's transferring from another course. I need to make an appointment to meet her, and see some of her work. Find out her motivation. It's a busy day, a group tutorial in the morning, and then individual tutorials in the afternoon. I don't have much time. But Melanie's talking to Graham, one of the Graphic Design tutors. He's quite old, he's reached that point where he really doesn't give much of a shit about anything, he's just waiting to retire, and everyone else can't wait for him to go. It seems like they're just chatting. Nothing urgent or important. He's moaning or complaining about something, that's mostly what he does. But she carries on talking to him, ignoring the fact that I'm standing there waiting. I feel myself getting angry. I fidget. I walk over to the window, look outside. I'm going to have to interrupt. But I don't, I decide it can wait. I start to walk out of the office. But then she calls out, 'Sarah, did you want something?' I feel like being sarcastic. Saying something like: 'No, I don't want anything, nothing at all, I just came here to pass the time of day.' But Graham's looking at me, and I don't think he likes me much. I think he finds me too serious. Too intense. If he hadn't been there I would have said it. So I tell her what I need to say, about the student, and Graham shuffles out, and Melanie becomes all polite and efficient. And I just say, 'Thanks Melanie.' And I carry on with my day. But I feel put-down, put in my place, as if I've been a nuisance. I take that feeling away with me.

***

So when I went to see Philippa, that second time, I started to hand her the piece of paper, written in my handwriting. I don't like my handwriting, but I've never been able to change it. It reminds me of the schoolgirl that I was. It's timid and back-sloping.

'You read it out aloud to me,' she said.

So I did as instructed, feeling rather stupid and awkward. My voice sounded squeaky, like a child's. Maybe that had been her intention. She wanted me to realise how trivial it all was. To put things in perspective.

'As if I've been a nuisance,' she repeated. We didn't discuss anything else I'd written. She just pounced on that one sentence. 'Is that something you feel quite a lot?'

That was perceptive of her. I nodded.

'I think it's time for some more affirmations. How about: *I am not a nuisance. I have a right to be in the world. I have a right to ask for what I need.*'

I looked at her, said nothing.

'Go on.'

I repeated the words. Those other affirmations hadn't worked, they'd just sounded nonsensical. This time there seemed to be some sort of sense in it.

'Well done. And now I want you to do something for yourself. Whenever you start to feel as if you're being a nuisance to people, I want you to think those words in your head. Imagine yourself saying them out loud. Will you do that?'

I nodded again.

She had her palms together, in front of her chest, as if she was praying. I realised I was doing the same.

And I noticed that her eyes had misted with tears. She really felt for me. She really cared.

And then I realised that my own eyes had misted too. And I think that was the moment when I started to fall in love with her.

At the end of our session, she left me to find my own way out, as before. But she stood up, and held my hand, and dug her nail into my palm, like she did when we first met. 'Feel that,' she said. 'Remember what it feels like. And when you start doubting yourself, let your hand do the feeling, as you remember it, and let it convey that feeling to your mind. And tell yourself: *I am not a nuisance. I have a right to be in the world. I have a right to ask for what I need.*'

And now I do this all the time. When I'm at work, in a meeting, I say, *This is important. I need you to listen to me.* When I'm with Oliver, I say to him, *I need more of your time.* Or I say, *I need you to make love to me.* And he does. And I think of Philippa's nail digging into my palm.

173

And even while we're making love, Oliver and I, or I'm in a meeting, or whatever, I'm notching up these little successes, and in my mind I'm reporting them to Philippa. I'm doing it all for her, as much as for me. Because I want her to be pleased with me.

Twenty Six

'What's this all about?'

I'd picked up a paperback book that was lying on my mother's coffee table. It was entitled *How To Do Less & Live More*. The blurb on the back said something about how we clutter our lives with more and more things to do when by doing less we could discover a deeper meaning in life, and live it more fully. Which was pretty much what had been said in the title. The two hundred and something pages in the middle probably found different ways of saying the same thing. That's how it had been with a couple of the books that Ellie had lent me, when she was trying to sort my life out for me. It didn't look like the sort of book my mother would normally read. She'd never been one of those self-help junkies. Besides, she'd always looked for more to do, rather than less, even though she liked to moan about never having enough time for herself.

'Philippa gave it to me, she thought it might be helpful. I don't think it's really my cup of tea, only she keeps saying I need to slow down a bit. She says I'm in denial about my own needs. She says I should put myself first for a change.'

'Oh yes. I was forgetting she's your new best friend.' I wasn't forgetting at all, and I couldn't help the sarcasm. I was remembering how Philippa had said, rather smugly, 'Joyce and I have had a few little chats.'

'Oh I'm not sure about that. I think she means well though.'

'Does she?' Philippa's so-called friendship with Lizzie hadn't ended very well. And ever since I'd discovered that Sarah had been going to her for counselling, I couldn't help wondering whether her brand of therapy hadn't been quite as effective as it should have been.

I put the book back on the coffee table. 'I suppose she's told you what happened on Boxing Day?'

'She mentioned you had a bit of an altercation. It was just one of those things that happen, she said. She told me she wanted to draw a line under it. As a matter of fact she rang me when I was in Oxford. I gave her your mobile number so she could text you.'

'I thought so.'

***

Things had been a bit strained between me and my mother over the past few weeks. I think she still hadn't forgiven me for not consulting her before Justin moved in with me. The fact that we were now in a relationship hadn't pleased her too much either. It seemed rather irrational, that she could sit and chat cosily with Philippa over cups of coffee, and yet disapprove of me having anything to do with her son. But I stuck to the routine of our Sunday lunches, even though I'd far rather have been chilling out with Justin. Traditions, once established, are hard to break. Besides, although she might have become a bit sniffy with me lately, she still needed me. She wasn't the sort of person to enjoy spending Sundays on her own. Nor, for that matter, any other time on her own.

The book was wrong, at least in the case of my mother, and so was Philippa. It was being busy that kept her going, kept her alive. It wasn't in her nature to sit around brooding, being introspective.

Too much thinking and worrying about stuff wasn't a habit of mine, either, not normally. But these weren't normal times. The two suicides, Sarah's and Lizzie's, had twisted together, like intertwining shadows,

176

sometimes behind, sometimes ahead of me, but never entirely out of my consciousness.

And I wasn't comfortable about Philippa planting books in my mother's territory, as if she was trying to change her. She'd always seemed pretty much unchangeable, secure in her own skin, but now, having witnessed Philippa at her most extreme, I wasn't so sure. Philippa wasn't your average friend. The word *evil* came to my mind. There was something evil about her.

***

Later that week, Ellie and Paul came round to share a stir fry with us. As usual, Justin did the cooking. It seemed we were now a member of the couples club. It felt strangely reassuring, as if I'd finally made it as a grown-up, but I reminded myself that I must phone Rachel to arrange some time out, just the two of us. We'd been buddies in singledom for a long time, and it wasn't in my nature to neglect somebody. Well, not since that time as a teenager, when I'd abandoned Sarah, and look how that had come back to haunt me.

'I was thinking the other day,' I said to Ellie across the table, 'how you were always reading those self-help books. Do you still? Or do you find now you've got to where you wanted to be, you don't need them anymore?'

'There's always room for change.' She and Paul exchanged a conspiratorial smile, in that irritating way that couples sometimes do. As if they *know* something. I made a mental note never to find myself doing that with Justin.

'I suppose. Though don't you sometimes think too much poking around in the psyche isn't a good idea? I mean, couldn't it actually tip you over the edge?'

177

'I don't think the books do that. They're sort of universal, aren't they? They're written in a way that anyone can apply them to their own life, so it's up to people what they take from them. I suppose, if people start looking too deeply into themselves, they might stir things up that were best forgotten. I've done some of that myself, I daresay. But I think if you're a certain sort of person you'll do it anyhow. I mean, it's you who buys the books, they don't come looking for you.'

'I guess. I suppose it's the same with therapy? Like it's a certain sort of person who goes to a therapist? Because you have to go out there and look for one, don't you? Browse the web or whatever. They don't come knocking at your door, like Jehovah's Witnesses, do they? And might it be dangerous sometimes? Giving another person all that power, to go poking around inside your head. What do *you* think, Justin?' I turned to face him, and he visibly squirmed. I could tell he thought I was being confrontational. Fracturing the lazy bonhomie of the dinner party. 'Justin's mother's a therapist,' I explained to Ellie and Paul.

Justin shrugged, refusing to be drawn. Trying to hide his irritation. Then Paul said something inconsequential, probably to stop things getting too deep and personal – Ellie had certainly had more than her share of therapy over the years – and the conversation drifted.

***

It was not long after they'd left, and I was wondering if there was anything worth watching on TV before we collapsed into bed, when Justin said, 'I'm thinking of going to a tranny club next weekend. Would you mind very much?' For a moment he looked like the insecure adolescent that I'd first met, rather than the grown-up man I was starting to depend on.

'I guess not,' I said. I didn't want him to go of course. And I didn't want to be reminded that we weren't such a straightforward couple after all. That, like a cat at night, he had this mysterious other side to him.

Even though I knew now that some of Justin's friends knew about his transvestism, I had no intention of telling any of mine. Not yet. My inhibitions were more about me than about him. He was the first man I'd ever shared some sort of a normal life with. I didn't want my friends to think he was a weirdo. I thought it might reflect on my own credentials.

'I wasn't sure whether I wanted to go or not,' he went on. 'Not after what happened to Lizzie the last time I went. I mean, I know what I was up to that weekend had nothing to do with Lizzie, with what happened, but it felt almost like I was being punished. But it's actually quite important for me to do this. It took me years to pluck up courage to take the plunge and go to one of those things.'

'Of course you have to go. It's a big part of your life. I understand that.' I felt my dishonesty stick, like a herring bone, in my throat. 'Well, actually I don't understand, but I'm trying to.'

'I know you are.' He kissed me on the forehead. 'You could come with me if you wanted. Get to talk to a few people. Find out a bit more about it.'

'Thanks, but I don't think so. Not just now. Maybe some other time. It's not just about me not being ready, although I'm probably not. But I think it's something you need to do on your own. I mean, it's good if we do things on our own sometimes, I think that's healthy, it's how it *should* be. We don't have to be joined at the hip.'

179

I really meant this. I've a tendency to be a clinger, and it's not something I'm proud of. It's probably a mark of my own insecurity with people, though I've no idea where that comes from. But I've often thought that my parents' marriage lasted so well, with so little conflict, because they trusted each other, respected each other's differences. He had his wildlife photography and his golf. She had whatever she was involved with at the time: Women's Institute, quilting bees, parent-teachers associations, and so on.

'Anyhow,' I added, 'I've been meaning to catch up with Rachel. It's time we had an evening out together.'

What I didn't tell Justin was that there was someone else I planned to see at the weekend. Someone I'd tried, with surprising success, to banish from my mind.

Twenty Seven

I said, earlier, that I'd been wondering about the quality of Philippa's therapy. Surely, if it had worked, then Sarah wouldn't be dead. Or, if Sarah had seemed suicidal, Philippa should have picked up the signs. If she'd been concerned for Sarah's safety, she could have told someone. But the more I thought about this, the more I started wondering whether the therapy had been not just remiss but positively harmful. Philippa couldn't be trusted. There was something unbalanced about her.

I still had that cartoon image of her in my mind, the mad crazy woman chasing me out of her house. By making a cartoon out of her, I could keep a safe distance. Otherwise, I'd find myself inflating her into some sort of monster, lurking in the shadows, ready to pounce. She'd found her way to my text messages. Now I dreaded her turning up at my mother's front door when I was there on a Sunday, or worse, at my own front door. She was Justin's mother, and I couldn't avoid seeing her again forever. But my fear and dread of her was growing out of all proportion. Just as, before, I'd been haunted by images of Sarah, now I found myself plagued by visions of Philippa. And this was something I couldn't talk about to Justin. I couldn't give voice to my suspicions. I didn't want him to know that she was crawling and wriggling through my head, like worms.

I'd even started dreaming about her. Mini-nightmares. Ridiculous ones. Like the one where we were in a field, and she was running around with a golf club, smashing the heads off the daisies. She spotted me, and came charging towards me, wielding her golf club, until a super-sized blue butterfly flew into her face, distracting her. And then the butterfly morphed into a dress, a blue one with a billowing skirt, and it was Sarah who was wearing it. Sarah and Philippa were flailing around, dancing wildly, or fighting, I wasn't sure which, and I could only watch and tremble. 'Just a dream,' I said to Justin, when I woke us both up, and he opened his eyes, kissed me, rolled over, and went back to sleep.

I needed to see Oliver. Not to talk about my fears, or my nightmares, he'd just think I was the crazy one. But to find out what he knew about Sarah during those last weeks before she died. To find out whether she'd mentioned seeing Philippa, whether she'd talked to him about her therapy.

***

I knew he often worked in his studio on a Saturday.

I parked my car in Rouen Road and walked the short distance to Oliver's studio, in a converted industrial building, just off King Street. I had no idea whether he'd be there, but I wasn't going to wait to be invited.

And as it happened, he *was* there. Busy, of course. The outer door to the building was unlocked, and opened to a tiny square-shaped area with two doors leading off it. One was inscribed with the name of a graphic design company, the other with Oliver Foster, Photographic Studio. I pressed the bell, and Oliver came to the door. He looked surprised. He seemed not actually displeased to see me, but it was obviously not the best moment to turn up unannounced.

'Oliver, I know this is a bit impromptu, but there's something I really need to talk to you about.'

I watched him take a step back, not so much physically as mentally, needing to maintain his distance.

'It's not about us. You and me, anything like that. It's something else. I think it's quite important.'

I saw the flicker of irritation across his face, before he contained it. 'I'm just finishing a shoot, how about coffee afterwards?' I didn't think coffee afterwards was such a good idea. Here, in the studio, it felt more like business. Besides, I didn't want anyone I knew to see me out with Oliver. Not now I was in a relationship with Justin.

He must have seen me hesitate. 'Or, OK, you're welcome to hang around, if that's what you'd rather.' In the spacious white-walled studio behind him, I could see an attractive young black woman in a tightly-fitting dress posing against a white backdrop.

So I loitered in that draughty little no man's area that smelt of new paint, while he finished his shoot. It must have been at least half an hour. It was bitterly cold. I was wearing a padded bomber jacket over my jumper and jeans. I kept my hands in my pockets. I was starting to wish I'd agreed to meet afterwards for coffee.

At last Oliver came to the door again, held it open as the model came out, wearing a long, expensive-looking coat over her dress. She acknowledged me with a brief smile as she passed me by and went on her way. I gave a little meaningless nod in her direction. I surprised myself with my total lack of jealousy. Oliver was still holding the door open, and I walked past him, into the studio. He grabbed a couple of chairs, unfolded them. 'Can I make you a coffee?'

I thought it might warm me. My fingers were numb with the cold. 'Please.'

With all the waiting, I'd had too much time to think about what I was going to say. I'm not very good at planning and forethought, I'm much better at being impulsive. If I plan too much, I start to doubt myself.

He passed me a mug, and I pressed my hands around it. He didn't have one himself. He sat beside me. 'So what's all the urgency?'

'Something I've been wondering. Did Sarah ever say anything to you, about going to someone for therapy?'

That wasn't what he was expecting. I watched the little wrinkles chase themselves across his face, the way they did when he was considering how to deal with something a bit out of the ordinary. It was one of the things I used to love about him, those glimpses of uncertainty behind his usual veneer.

'Why do you ask?'

'I'll tell you why in a minute. Can you answer my question first. Please,' I added. I didn't mean to sound so abrupt.

'OK. The short answer's no. She didn't actually say anything to me about it. I think I might have suspected something though.'

'What do you mean?'

'I don't know. Just little things. Some of the things she said. Her vocabulary seemed to change. She started coming out with what I thought was pseudo-psychological jargon. I thought either she was seeing somebody, like a therapist, or she was reading the wrong books.'

'Mm. So did her actual behaviour change at all? Did *she* change?'

'I'm not a psychologist, Melanie. This is all a bit too subtle.'

'Can you try and think about it? Please. It's quite important. I don't think I ever mentioned this to you, but Sarah and I were friends, a long time ago. We were at school together.'

'She told me that once.' He sighed. 'I'm assuming, though God knows why you're bringing all this up now, that you're trying to find out what led up to the suicide. Nobody knew, not exactly. There was a lot of stuff going on for Sarah last spring. There was a lot of stress around the job, there was for all of us. Nobody knew quite what would be happening this year, all the changes. It was all getting a bit dog-eat-dog. You must have known something about what was going on. And then on top of all that her mother was seriously ill with cancer. She wasn't particularly close to her mother, but she was the only daughter and I think she felt the call of duty. She'd always been a bit, I don't know, fragile. It was probably all too much for her. That's what everyone seemed to think.'

'But you say you suspected she was going for therapy?' I persisted.

'Like I say, her vocabulary changed. Also, this would have been quite early last year, she became a bit, I'm not sure how to explain. Not distant, exactly, but it was almost as though she'd be with me and she'd be talking to someone else at the same time. I've known people before, my wife was one of them, she was always in and out of therapy, and it's as if they're constantly processing everything that's happening to them so they can take it to the therapy room.'

He stared down at the floorboards between his legs, as though he was reading something that was written there. 'The way it was with Vivienne, she had to stop going for therapy in the end, even though it was really hard for her to break it off. She told me it felt as though this other person had penetrated her mind, that she couldn't think for herself any more. It was like she had to ask permission for every little thought that she had. That was what she said to me, afterwards. I found it all a bit incomprehensible.'

It was the first time Oliver had spoken to me about his former wife. The first time he'd even mentioned her name. I found myself wishing we could continue along that track. I'd always wanted to know more about his past life, so I could understand him better. But I had to return to the subject of Sarah and Philippa.

'So, OK, you're saying Sarah's vocabulary changed. That she seemed to be talking to someone else. All of that. But was *she* any different? Say from the beginning of last year.' I was thinking of the dates in Philippa's diary. 'Was she more confident, or less? Happier or less happy? I mean, apart from her concerns about her mother, stress at work, all the rest of it.'

'To begin with, I'd say she possibly started to be a bit more assertive. She'd never been a very confident person, but she started to have more of, what you might call, a sense of entitlement. The last time I saw her, she seemed a bit agitated. And maybe I wasn't quite as supportive as I should have been.' He sighed. 'You know my limitations. So why have you suddenly got this bee in your bonnet?'

'I can't tell you the whole story, but I happen to know someone who's a therapist, and I'm pretty sure Sarah was seeing her. From the beginning of last year up until the time she died. I can't say any more at the moment, but this woman, this therapist, there's something really scary about her.'

'You think this therapy she was having might have had a bearing on the suicide?' He frowned with the effort of unpicking.

I nodded. 'I think it's possible.'

'If what you're saying is true – and I have no idea about that – then this has serious implications. She could be doing all sorts of damage to people.'

'I know. Although I don't think she has many clients. Not at the moment, anyhow. She might have done once.' I wasn't going to say to Oliver that Sarah

186

was possibly her last, or at least her last regular one. Going by all the empty pages in the diary. They say there's safety in numbers, and it struck me at that moment just how risky it had been for Sarah. Alone in the lion's den.

'If you really want to know about Sarah, what was playing on her mind in those last weeks, it might be worth having a word with Carol. Carol Willoughby, d'you know her? One of the Fine Art tutors.'

'Yes, I know Carol. Well, I don't really know her, but I'll try and speak to her. I'll give it a go.'

'They were good friends, they used to go out together sometimes. If Sarah had confided in anyone about this, it would probably have been Carol.'

'Thanks Oliver. You've been helpful. Thanks. To be honest, I didn't expect you to take me seriously.'

He gave me a smile then. One of those smiles that used to melt me. 'Are you coming to my private view? Here in the studio, in a couple of weeks?'

'I didn't know about it.'

'Well now you do.' He smiled again. Then he looked at his watch. 'I have to go.'

'Me too.'

We both stood, and he kissed me on the lips. His lips had always been slightly moist. I could taste the familiarity of him. There was still an emotional connection for me, how could there not be, but the feeling passed almost as suddenly as it came.

Twenty Eight

SARAH'S DIARY

15th February 2012

I wrote that I'm in love with Philippa.

I ache inside every time I think of her. She's become the centre of my life, even more so than Oliver. Last weekend, I was in bed with Oliver, and I dreamed I was with Philippa. I felt so guilty. I know he has sex with other women, that Melanie's probably only one of them, but I've always been monogamous. When I love somebody, I'm with them totally. Not just in practice, but also in my mind. I've never understood people who aren't. Until now.

As I wrote before, the ridiculous thing is she's not the sort of woman I even like. I know I shouldn't say this, but normally I'd rather look at skinny women than fat ones. And once I even caught a whiff of sweat, as if her personal hygiene isn't what it ought to be. But there's something seductive about her. Those eyes, the way they seem to look right into my soul. And sometimes, when she's sitting there opposite me, listening to what I have to say, I want to just curl up in her lap and have her stroke my hair. More, I want to sink my head into her cleavage. Even more, I want to kiss her lips – those wide, sensuous lips. And then I want to put my hand inside her smock, stroke her breasts. I want to put my fingers in her vagina, feel the wetness of it. I want to caress her clitoris with my tongue. I want to taste everything about her. The salt of her tears, the scent of shampoo in her hair, the sweat under her arms. I even want to taste her menstrual blood.

There – I've written it. I can't believe I just wrote that. And I had to stop writing and masturbate.

She's married of course. That in itself is enough to put a safety rail between us. Between fantasy and reality.

And no one but me is going to read this. Ever. I shall make sure of that.

Don't we all have stuff we can't share with anyone else? This goes for memories too. The bad ones.

Philippa doesn't encourage me to talk about memories. She says you can't change the past, only your perception of it. You have to learn to live with whatever's happened to you.

She says that too much dwelling on the past is counter-productive. You end up blaming people – usually your mother – for what you are, instead of taking responsibility for yourself. And of course, I do blame other people. I do blame my mother.

When I was a child, she never listened to me. She talked *at* me. She told me how to behave, what I should say to people. I never felt as if she cared about me. I remember once, I was running around the back garden, on my own, chasing some imaginary friend, and I slipped over and cut my knee on a stone. I went into the house, I wasn't really crying, maybe sniffing a bit, because it hurt. My mother was just sitting in an armchair, I think she had a book on her lap, but she wasn't reading it. I just stood there, waiting for her to notice me. And all she said was, 'It's just a little graze, go to the bathroom and wash it. You know where the plasters are, on the window ledge.'

She couldn't help being the way she was. I realise that now. She didn't mean to be cruel. She was depressed. Clinically depressed. She had what they used to call endogenous depression. It was something inside her that would never go away. 'We all have our cross to bear,' she used to say to me, 'and this is mine.'

But unfortunately, we all had to bear it with her.

189

When she was having one of her bad days, we just crept around her. The slightest noise used to set her off, so if I made a noise she'd start screaming at me. And my father never stuck up for me, never took my side, he felt beholden to her. He said that once, when I actually plucked up the courage to say it wasn't fair. He said he felt beholden. An old-fashioned word. But that was how it was for us. Everything about my family was old-fashioned. Everybody I knew at school watched television, and talked about what they'd seen. We didn't even have a television, we just sat and read books, or sometimes played cards. And the other girls all had a computer, and games they played on it. They all went on holidays abroad. The only holiday I remember having with my parents was once when we went to Scotland. We should have been there for a week, but it rained all the time, so we came back early. My father used to say we were lucky living so near the sea, we didn't need to go on holiday. But I don't recall us spending a lot of time by the sea. In the summer there were too many tourists. In the winter it was too cold. That was what they said.

My mother never worked because of her illness, as she used to call it, so we didn't have as much money as other families. We didn't even have a car. My father worked as an accountant for a small firm. He never said how much he earned, but I'm sure it wasn't much. My mother was almost always at home. Apart from housework and making scones – we were always eating scones, they were dry, they used to stick in my throat, but I had to eat them or she'd be upset – she filled her time doing jigsaws and tapestry. She used to buy those kits from the hobby shop. Sewing by numbers. Nothing that stretched her imagination. I sound disparaging, I don't mean to be. Or perhaps I do. If she was up to it, she used to go into town on market day. She'd dress up for it, in a skirt and her best shoes. That was the highlight of her week. Some days, she didn't even get out of bed.

My father died not long after I'd gone to university. He was knocked down by a taxi, and died in hospital. I don't think he had a very strong survival instinct. He can't have had much of a life. Strangely, my mother seemed less depressed after he died. I suppose she had to be, with no one there to look after her. She moved back to Yorkshire, where she was born, to be near her older sister and her family. Her sister died a few years ago. Her niece, her sister's daughter, calls in almost every day to see her. I'm grateful to Anna for that. She has cancer now, and Anna tells me that she's very frail. I must make the effort to go and see her sometime soon. Before she dies.

She couldn't help it that she didn't love me.

I was crying a bit when I told Philippa about my childhood. I watched her, to see whether her eyes would water in empathy, the way they did that time before. But all she did was push the box of tissues towards me. I longed for her to come over and give me a hug.

I put my face in my hands, and then, when I looked at her again, she said, quietly, 'What would you like to say to your mother before she dies?'

I was going to say, 'Why didn't you love me?' But then I said, 'I forgive you.'

Philippa nodded. And then she said, 'What would you like to say to yourself? To that little girl you used to be.'

I thought for a moment. 'You'll be all right.'

And I am. That's what I've tried to be all these years. I've tried to be all right.

'That's good. That's what you need to say to yourself. I'm all right. Nobody else is going to say it

191

for you. Your mother isn't going to say it. It's down to you.'

That's true, of course. And of course she's right not to hug me. It wouldn't be professional. And she *is* professional. I have to remember that, and keep my emotional needs to myself. Besides, I'd rather die than let her know the way I feel about her.

Twenty Nine

I asked Justin to go with me to Oliver's private view. I didn't feel like going on my own, and besides I wanted Oliver to see me there with Justin. To know that I had a new life.

Justin was a bit reluctant at first, he said it wasn't his scene, and then he joked about me wanting to parade my 'bit of rough'. But in the end he came with me, and it was fine. People who turn up at private views are usually too busy networking to take any notice of someone who's not part of the scene.

I hadn't told Justin that I'd recently visited Oliver in his studio. Now, transformed from that cold, empty room to an exhibition space, it was almost unrecognisable, with people milling around, chatting in their various little groups, and, of course, Oliver's photos on the normally bare walls. They were all portraits, all black and white, with lots of shadows and subtle lighting effects, like in a film noir. Young people, old people, black people, white people.

I couldn't help but be impressed. And I couldn't help being more than a little bit thrilled to see a photo that Oliver had once taken of me.

I clearly remembered that day. He'd had me posed outside a derelict building not far from his studio. He took ages, trying to get the result he was aiming for. There was a cold wind, and he'd made me take my jacket off, so I was only wearing a strappy little top with my jeans. It was a wonder the goose pimples weren't visible in the photo. My hair was longer then, and a windswept mess, but that was the way he wanted it.

When I saw the photo hanging there, I grabbed Justin's arm and said, 'That's me,' like a child, and he grinned, in a sort of proud-fatherly way. And, well, there haven't been very many moments of fame in my life.

***

I knew there'd be a portrait of Sarah too, and of course there was.

It was blown-up to almost life-size. She was standing in a doorway, looking out. Behind her, a darkness that led to nowhere. Her feet were bare, slim and white, and she was wearing a mid-length dress that emphasised the boniness of her ankles. The dress was fastened up to her neck, and her hair was loosely tied up, with wisps escaping around her face. Her expression was hard to define, but there was an unexpected confidence and assurance in the way she seemed to be staring straight at the camera, eyes wide open. Her neck looked very long and very white, with a dark shadow in the little hollow at its base. An image flashed through my mind of Oliver kissing it. She looked – and I'm afraid it hurt me to think this – *loved*.

There was something familiar about that dress. It didn't strike me immediately, because of the absence of colour. But then I looked harder at it. Wasn't it one of the dresses I'd rescued from Lizzie's house? The ones now hanging in Justin's wardrobe, where they belonged. Could it be the navy blue one, with the tiny buttons and the little square pockets? The one that Simone said she'd sold to an elderly lady. The one which, now that I thought of it, had been lying on top of the heap on my bed when Oliver came round to look at Lizzie's paintings. Could he have recognised it, and was that what prompted his strange behaviour when he came into my room?

***

Now, though, he was darting around from one group of people to another, in his element, star of the show. When he first saw me there, he'd said, 'Melanie, lovely to see you, glad you could come,' and I'd said, 'This is Justin,' and they'd briefly shaken hands. And then he'd moved on.

I was suddenly aware of somebody beside me. 'It's a lovely portrait. He really got the essence of Sarah.'

It was Carol, the Fine Art tutor, who Oliver said had been a close friend of Sarah. 'It's lovely, yes. I was just wondering about the dress. You were friends, weren't you? Do you remember ever seeing her in it?'

I hardly knew Carol, but from what I'd seen of her I knew she liked to talk, she wasn't one of those people who keep too much of a distance. She answered me, in her rather husky voice. 'I do as it happens. It was a navy blue one, with little red flowers all over it. I remember it well, because after she died I sorted all her clothes out, there was no one else to do it. I took that one and a couple of others to that lovely vintage clothes shop, Lacy Daze, do you know it?'

I nodded.

'Well, obviously I couldn't pocket the money I was given for the dresses, they weren't mine were they, and I wasn't sure what to do with it. So I sent a cheque to cancer research. It seemed to be the best option.'

'Carol, I know this isn't a good moment to talk, but everyone's always so busy at work, there's never any time. Did Sarah say much to you about her state of mind before . . . you know? And I know you must have been asked this already.'

'I have. A number of times. And the answer's no. I was as shocked as everyone else. I knew she was stressed, like all of us, and I knew she was worried about her mother, but I didn't know she was suicidal.'

'She didn't mention she was having therapy?'

'No. Never. She was a private person, even with me, and I was supposed to be her friend. Why are you asking? Is there something you know that I don't?'

'Maybe. It's just a thought. Something I found out by accident. I know, or sort of know, a woman who's a therapist. I think Sarah might have been seeing her.'

'If she was, I'm pretty sure nobody knew about it. Otherwise she'd probably have had to be at the inquest, wouldn't she? She, if anyone, would have known something about Sarah's state of mind, what you were asking me just now.' She gave a little gasp, put her hand to her mouth, like children do when they've suddenly remembered something they should have done, something they'd forgotten about. 'There was just one strange thing. I didn't even think about it at the time when everybody was talking about Sarah. It was afterwards, I suddenly had this memory of her feeding stuff into a shredder, it must have been just before she died. She was in the library, and I remember wondering why she was there, why she wasn't using the one in her own department. When I came up behind her, she looked kind of, I don't know, almost guilty. Secretive. She was holding these sheets of handwritten paper, I assumed it was something to do with the students, but on reflection I suppose it could have been something of her own, a diary or something. Don't people sometimes keep a diary when they have therapy? Whatever it was, there was something a bit frantic about her, the way she seemed to be desperate to get it all shredded. Anyhow, just a thought. I must go, there are people here I need to speak to.'

I turned round to look for Justin. We'd become separated around the time I'd spotted Sarah's portrait. He was chatting to a former photography student, who was now one of the technicians on the course, and who at this moment had his arm around a very pregnant girlfriend. 'Do you know Martin?' Justin asked me, as if he was the person who belonged here, not me.

I nodded, and smiled at Martin.

'He's from North Walsham,' Justin told me. 'One of my mates from the pub.'

'That's a coincidence,' I said, rather inanely. I was still thinking about my conversation with Carol.

'That's a good portrait of you.' Martin flicked his head in the direction of the wall where it was hanging.

'I remember how bloody freezing I was at the time.'

'Oliver's good at getting what he wants from people.'

I wasn't sure whether Martin was referring to Oliver's photography, or to his attitude to people generally. It was true on both counts. I said to Justin, 'When you're ready, there's a photo I'd like you to see.'

'We're off now, anyhow. Too many people.' Martin gave his girlfriend a little squeeze, and she nodded. She looked tired, as if she was more than ready to escape.

I led Justin over to the photo of Sarah. 'That's my old school friend. The one I told you about, who committed suicide last year.'

'She's beautiful.' He used the present tense.

'She was wasn't she.' I was waiting for him to identify the dress, but I had to prompt him. 'That dress she's wearing, do you recognise it?'

He frowned. 'I suppose it looks a bit like . . . like that one of mine. It's hard to tell though, with it being black and white.'

'I know. I think it *is* that one of yours. Somebody took it to the shop, Lacy Daze, after Sarah died. That's where Lizzie bought it from.'

'That's bizarre. So when have you been doing all this detective work?'

'I'll tell you about it sometime. Not now. When we're back home.'

Only I didn't. We went for a pizza, and we shared a bottle of wine to top up the free glasses we'd been drinking at the private view, and by the time we were home we were ready to tumble into bed.

I knew that sometime I had to talk to Justin about the connection between Philippa and Sarah, my concerns. I didn't want to leave him in the dark. Not that I wasn't in the dark myself, it was all so nebulous, a flicker of a question here, a shadow of an answer there. The problem was – as Justin had once said to me in another context – there's never a right time for certain things to be told. And, whatever Justin thought of Philippa, she was still his mother, and blood, so it's said, is thicker than water.

Thirty

PHILIPPA'S NOTEBOOK

9th May 2012

I have a very clear and strong sense of right and wrong. That's why I've befriended Lizzie ever since my dad, Peter, left her for that young Pakistani woman. He should have known better. He should have remembered what it felt like to be left. The way it was for him and me and George, when Sandra went off and left us. And, what I mean by right and wrong, I'm talking about leaving for the wrong reasons, the wrong people. Sandra left us for that woman, Marianne. Women aren't meant to be with other women. We're not designed for it. Bluntly, a vagina is meant for a penis, a penis for a vagina. And as for mixed-race marriages, that's wrong too, in my opinion. I'm not racist, I just believe different coloured skins belong in different countries. Lizzie doesn't agree of course. Anything goes as far as Lizzie's concerned. I've had lots of arguments with her about this.

I didn't want to see Sandra after she left us, but Dad made me. He said she was still my mother. He used to take me there, to see her and Marianne in their little love nest. And I suffered for that, because of what happened when I was away from home. But that's another story.

Likewise, I didn't want to visit my dad, after he set up home with Serena. I took Lizzie's side. More to spite my dad than because I gave a shit about Lizzie. I was much angrier about it than she was. It annoyed me, the way she seemed to accept what had happened, just shrugged and carried on with her life. I kept telling her she wasn't too old to meet somebody else, but she told me she didn't want anybody else, she was happy living alone. I didn't believe her. I still don't. I believe that all that art stuff she's always working on is just a substitution. Besides, when I sent Justin to live with her, that proved it. Because she formed an unhealthy relationship with him. I've actually seen evidence of that.

She doesn't know I know. I went to the house once, when she was out. She always waits in for me on Friday mornings, but this wasn't a Friday. I just happened to be in the town, and thought I'd pop in and see her. But she wasn't there, so I let myself in. I thought maybe I'd fix myself a coffee, make myself at home, surprise her when she came back.

We always have our coffee at the kitchen table, so I never go further into the house, not normally. But to pass the time I decided to take a peep in the living room. I've never seen such a mess. I don't think it's ever seen a duster since dad left. I don't know how people can live like that. It made me feel quite ill, just looking at it, but I had a quick look round, trying not to breathe in too much of the dust. It used to be my home, after all. She always said she used the room as her studio, but I hadn't imagined anything quite that bad.

She had a drawing on an easel, something she'd been working on, and I wasn't paying much attention to begin with. But then I took a closer look – just idle curiosity – and, well, to say I was shocked was an understatement. I've had a few shocks in my life, but this one took the biscuit.

It was a drawing of a figure in a dress. No face. It should have been a woman, but instead it was a man dressed up in women's clothes, and I knew straight away it was Justin. I just knew. He'd always had a peculiar side to him, been a bit too partial to girly clothes. I'd caught him in the act when he was young,

200

but I thought he'd have grown out of it by now. And as for Lizzie to be colluding with him, encouraging him, well that – that was disgusting.

My first thought was to tear up that obnoxious drawing. Only I didn't. Because then my rational mind took over, and I thought it might come in useful as proof of inappropriate behaviour. I wanted Brian to see it, because he's always thought that Lizzie's the bee's knees. He's told me he thinks she's intelligent. To be honest, I think he fancies her, though I can't imagine why. She's much too old for him. And those tatty old clothes she wears, they're a disgrace.

In fact, a couple of weeks ago I almost caught them in the act, Brian and Lizzie. Brian had gone to sort out a problem with her computer, that's what he said. I didn't believe him. He gave me a kiss as he was leaving. Well, anyhow, a peck. He hardly ever kisses me these days, so I knew he had a guilty conscience. He was gone a long while. I went round there, and sure enough, there they were, snuggled together on the settee, in the middle of all that clutter. I forgot to take a look to see whether the easel was still there, with that disgusting drawing. I was livid. They must have already had their fun and games. They had that moony, self-satisfied look on their faces.

I said I have a clear sense of right and wrong, and that's another thing that's wrong, in my book. Older women with younger men. It's going against nature. Like men in women's clothes. Like mixed race marriages and homosexuality.

***

So, I was going to make some notes about my client, SB.

All that, that I just wrote, was going off at a tangent. But it shows my state of mind, what I'm having to deal with. So I think it excuses my inattentiveness, you might say, to my client. Just this one time. Every other time I gave her my full attention. But on this one occasion I lapsed.

She came on 25th April for her weekly session, and I really didn't feel like seeing her. I had problems of my own. All I could think about was Brian and Lizzie together, and Lizzie and Justin and whatever they got up to in that disgusting house.

Of course, if I'd known I wouldn't be seeing SB again, I would have made more of an effort.

She was the first client I ever had who wanted to keep on coming back to me, week after week. I suppose I should have been touched by that, but I wasn't. I'm not the sort of therapist to try and hang on to my clients. Some therapists, I know, nurture a dependency in their clients that lasts for years and years. But if they're so dependent, they're not cured, are they? Me, I prefer to go for the quick fix. Usually my clients have their first session with me, their freebie, and then they make another appointment, and I give them a few affirmations to take away with them, and off they go, cheerio. But this one was different. The first time she came, she wasn't very cooperative. I thought I probably wouldn't see her again. But she surprised me. Every week she kept on coming back for more. And every week, she started snivelling. That was all she did. Snivelling and talking about her unhappy childhood. Feeling sorry for herself. Wanting me to feel sorry for her.

At first I thought she was starting to improve. She was starting to say her affirmations as if she meant them. *I am not a nuisance. I have a right to be in the world. I have a right to ask for what I need.*

But then it seemed that all she wanted to do was dwell on the past. She kept on telling me her mother never hugged her. So what did she want from me? Hugs and kisses? Well, that's not my job. My job was to help her to give herself a hug, if that's what she needed, or to find someone else to do it for her. What about that man she told me she was in love with? Where was he when she needed a cuddle? I thought we might have explored that rivalry she had with her old school friend, but she clammed up about that, she didn't mention it again after that second week.

Besides, I don't believe in hugs. My mum used to hug me all the time, after she'd made up her mind she was leaving us. It was her way of over-compensating. She was just being sentimental. If she'd really loved me she wouldn't have left me.

Back to my client, SB. She told me her mother was dying of cancer. She seemed upset about it, though I can't think why, not if her childhood was as miserable as she said it was. She said she'd forgiven her, but she was obviously lying. She needed to let go of the past. She needed to let her mother die in peace. That's what I tried to make her understand.

So, that day, I wasn't really in the mood for her. She came in with that intense look on her face, and said she had something she wanted to tell me. Something that happened to her when she was a teenager. Really, how fascinating, I was thinking. She said it was really hard for her to talk about it, she'd never told anybody before, but she wanted to share it with me. As if she thought she was offering me a special gift. Well, frankly, I didn't want to know. I didn't want to hear about some trauma from her fucking past. Every week, I'd been telling her to move on. But she was sitting there, dithering, twiddling her hair. Fiddling with her bottle of Evian. Yes, after the first week, she always brought her own bottle of water with her, and put it on the coffee table. As if my tap water wasn't good enough for her. So she sat there, hesitating and faffing, working herself up to start on this big revelation about her dreary life. And I just yawned, I couldn't help it.

She said, 'Are you bored with me?' She sounded surprised, anxious, as if she couldn't really believe I found her boring. So much for that impostor syndrome she was supposed to have. I think she really did find herself fascinating, and imagined everyone else did.

I said, 'Sorry, I'm not feeling too good today, I've got a splitting headache.' And I rubbed my forehead convincingly.

And then of course she went all apologetic. She said, 'It's me that should be sorry. I'm being insensitive. I should be aware you have your issues too.' And then she said, 'Would you like me to go?'

I said, 'No, no, let's finish the job now you're here.' I'm not normally as abrupt as that with my clients. It's not the way I usually speak to them. I'm a professional. But, like I said, she'd been winding me up with all her snivelling. We weren't making progress. I was getting impatient. Frankly, I'd had enough.

She said, 'Is that all this is for you? Just a job?'

I didn't answer. I thought it might be healthy for her to show some anger. She'd been playing the victim for long enough. But then her face puckered up, and I said, 'You're not going to start crying again are you?'

She said, 'Don't be so beastly.' Beastly. Whoever uses words like 'beastly'?

She stood up, her eyes filling with tears. She stood there, looking at me, shocked and accusing, as if I'd physically punched her in the face. And then she said, 'I am not a nuisance. I have a right to ask for what I need.' Just like I'd taught her to. Loud and clear, if a bit shaky. I was smiling to myself. The therapy hadn't been a total failure after all. And then she said, more quietly, 'I need us to give each other a hug.'

Well, frankly, that was the last thing I needed or wanted. So I just sat there. It's not like me to be indecisive, but I didn't know quite how to deal with this. I said, 'I think you'd better leave.'

And she looked at me, like a wounded cat.

I couldn't stand the way she was guilt-tripping me. I said, under my breath, so that she wouldn't hear me, 'If things are really that bad, there's always suicide.'

And then she let herself out. I could hear her running down the stairs, opening and slamming the front door.

That was April 25th. I had her pencilled in for the following Wednesday, May 2nd. I wasn't sure whether she'd turn up, but I half expected she would, what with her masochistic tendencies. But she didn't, and she hadn't let me know. I knew then that I wouldn't see her again.

And strangely, although she'd been winding me up, I was in fact slightly disappointed that losing her had been so easy. Perhaps she hadn't needed me as much as I'd believed. So I googled her name, just out of curiosity, to see if anything came up, what with her being a professional illustrator and so on, and I was shocked to find out that she'd committed suicide, on May 1st. Just a few days after I'd last seen her. Apparently all the staff and students where she worked were shocked and upset. The head of department said that she had been a well-loved and enthusiastic tutor, as well as a successful illustrator. A colleague said she'd had a fine mind and was an inspiration to them all, and would be greatly missed. Somebody else said that she was a perfectionist, who found it hard to live up to her own high standards, and that she was also carrying the burden of her mother's terminal cancer.

Well, she'd talked of being an impostor, but she apparently succeeded in fooling most of the people most of the time. As far as I was concerned, she was just a cry-baby. I hadn't wanted her to die, though. I'd wanted her to move on and start taking responsibility for herself. But it was her choice. We all make our own choices.

And, if I'm absolutely honest, I think the therapy did have an impact. Maybe she'd been wanting to die all along, and the therapy gave her permission to make that choice.

In any case, when I learned of SB's death, I did have a sense of my own power. Lots of things happened to me when I was younger. My mother leaving. George killed in that accident soon after. Lizzie moving in and taking over the house. Ricky beating me up. Things I couldn't control. But now – now I have control. Not only over my own life, but over other people's too.

And that's what makes me a good counsellor. I can empower people to do what they need to do, however frightening.

Thirty One

My mother's birthday happened to fall on a Sunday. Last year's birthday had been low-key and rather dismal, because it was her first after she'd been widowed. This year I wanted to make it a bit more special. I considered the options. We could have our normal Sunday lunch together, but I would take a cake with candles, and chocolates, and a present, and try to give her some quality time. Or, as she doesn't drive, I could pick her up and take her for a meal in Norwich, just the two of us. Or I could do the same thing, only ask Justin to join us. It was time they got to know each other. Or I could ask Justin to cook something special, and invite her for a meal at our house.

And then I had a brainwave. I could invite her to our house, to have lunch with me and Justin, and – in view of her budding friendship with Philippa – we could invite Philippa and Brian to join us. There were a number of pluses to this. Firstly, if it worked out, it would seem more like a party. Secondly, it would give everybody a chance to get to know each other better, and for my mother to see Justin on his own territory, doing something he was good at, so that she might stop thinking he was a waste of space. Thirdly, it might help to smooth waters between Philippa and me, after the Boxing Day fiasco, and, with a bit of luck, maybe help me to see her as a person rather than a monster. To dispel the nightmares.

There was a practical and, for me, selfish advantage too. Brian and Philippa would be able to pick up my mother and drive her home again, leaving me free to relax and to drink as much wine as I felt like drinking.

Finally – I had a hidden agenda. My detective work, as Justin had called it, was incomplete. I believed there were truths still buried in dark corners,

207

and that this just might be an opportunity to unearth them, in a gentle way. I promised myself that, whatever happened, I wasn't going to do or say anything to upset Philippa. This needed to be a time for repairing damage. A time to be circumspect.

***

Once I'd talked through the pros and cons with Justin he was more than happy to cooperate, welcoming the opportunity to show off his cooking skills – the one area where he seemed immune to self-doubt.

As for me, I approached the occasion with as much anxiety as I would if we'd been on one of those television contests, even though I wasn't doing the actual cooking. Luckily there were no vegetarians or vegans in our little family circle, and Justin and I ate more or less anything, but we had to take into account that Philippa didn't like aubergine or courgette and that my mother didn't like anything too hot-spicy. In the end, we decided on an Italian dish: chicken pieces marinated in white wine and herbs, cooked in passata, and served with mixed fried mushrooms and bruschetta. This to be followed by fruit stewed in wine and cinnamon and left to cool, and finally the birthday cake, which I ordered from Waitrose.

I left Justin to work his magic in the kitchen, while I looked after the decorative side of things. I'd bought a white tablecloth especially for the occasion, and serviettes, and a candle. While waiting for the three parents to arrive, I drank two half glasses of wine. I wanted to be relaxed but in control. A difficult balance to achieve, of course, and I hate to be pushed in the direction of responsibility. I briefly wished there'd been four parents coming. I still missed my father, that calm and quiet presence in the background, unobtrusive but somehow always there, keeping an eye on everyone.

***

My mother and Philippa were both laughing about something as they came to the door. That seemed a good sign. I said 'happy birthday' and we all went through the kissing and greeting routine. I tried not to cringe when Philippa kissed me on the cheek. I left them with a glass of wine in the front room, and joined Justin in the kitchen. The doors were open, and I could hear the two women chatting away as though they'd known each other for years, not months. Maybe this new best-friendship wasn't quite the disaster I'd been thinking it was. Come to think of it, although my mother had always known hundreds of people, she'd never really had any special friends. Maybe Philippa was meeting a need.

***

We arranged ourselves around the table, my mother at one end, Justin at the other, me at one side, and Philippa and Brian next to each other on the other side, with Philippa nearest to my mother and Brian nearest to Justin. Although we'd had a drink, some of us more than one, we all seemed suddenly a bit tense and on our best behaviour, like children at the beginning of a party in someone's house they don't normally go to.

Then Justin cut through the awkwardness by turning to Brian and asking him what gigs he'd been to lately. Brian, apparently, was passionate about live jazz, and Justin knew a bit about all sorts of music, except perhaps opera, so they easily found something to talk about. Philippa took this as a cue to resume her conversation with my mother, featuring people I didn't know, books I hadn't read, garden plants I wasn't the least bit interested in. I hadn't planned the seating arrangements, but somehow they were exactly right. My head was turning one way and then another, my ears tuning in and out of the two parallel dialogues. On any other occasion I'd have felt excluded, but I was happy to see everybody starting to relax, and to wait my turn.

When the chicken dish seemed to be emptied, I piled up the plates and took them to the kitchen. I scraped the residues into the pedal-bin, rinsed the plates and left them in the sink. I could hear the table chat continuing, my mother's and Philippa's voices in particular. Carrying the fruit dessert, I returned to the party. Everybody seemed to be getting along so well that I felt reluctant to break the flow. But I'd set myself a task. As the dish was being passed around the table, and there was a lull in the conversation, I turned to my mother. 'Remember all those birthday parties we had in the old house,' I said, and watched her eyes light up nostalgically.

'We had some good times.'

I was aware that our little exchange had become centre stage, which was what I'd wanted. 'I know. Remember that fancy dress one, when Joshua dressed up as Doctor Who, and I was the Companion, and Jake was a Dalek. And then the one when we had someone come and do magic tricks. I think that was Jake's party. I remember he felt cheated that there wasn't a headless woman.' My mother laughed at the memory. 'And then there was that one of mine when we decided we were all going to perform something, and I did a belly dance with a tambourine, and Josh and Jake did a sort of Morecambe and Wise act. And Jake's friend, what was his name, pretended to be Michael Jackson.'

210

She was beaming at the memories. I didn't want to break the spell, but I was driven to continue. 'And then there was that one, much later, when it was lovely hot weather and we had a barbecue, wasn't it a joint party, for me and my friend? My friend Sarah. Sarah Bannister.' I made sure I said the name, loud and clear. 'Her birthday was a couple of weeks after mine, and I don't think her parents ever let her have any birthday parties.' I was turned towards my mother, but at the same time I was watching Philippa, surreptitiously. I was wondering whether to mention the suicide, but decided not to. No sad stuff, not on this day, at this little party.

I saw a flicker of suspicion in Philippa's eyes. She looked across at me, then down at the table. She must have guessed I knew something. But what I wasn't prepared for was my mother's reaction. The smile disappeared from her face, and so did the colour.

I could see nothing in what I'd been saying that might have upset her, and I started to wonder if maybe she was allergic to something in the meal, or it was the onset of food poisoning, and any minute now the rest of us would be doubling up with it. I saw her resolutely grip the edges of the table, and gradually, blotch by blotch, the colour started to return to her cheeks.

Meanwhile I had to carry on talking. 'I don't think we were friends for long after that. I suppose we both grew up and moved on. That's what happens, isn't it?' I couldn't think of anything else to say.

It was Brian who rescued me. 'They're funny things, memories. You talking about your hot summer. Summers were always hot, weren't they, when we were young?'

Philippa said, 'Maybe we were better at make-believe. We all get a bit cynical as we grow older.' If

211

she'd been at all disconcerted by hearing Sarah's name, she'd quickly recovered.

'Justin, that was a wonderful meal. Thank you.' My mother was starting to look more like herself again. If anybody else had noticed the onset of whatever had affected her, they'd pretended not to, as I had.

'I told you he was a brilliant cook.'

'So what are *your* hidden talents?' That was Philippa, turning to me.

'I haven't really got any. What about you?' I was rather hoping she'd say she was a good therapist, so I could have probed a bit further.

'Same as you, I suppose. I think I'm quite good at just being me.'

I asked if anyone wanted coffee, and when everybody said yes, I went to the kitchen. While the kettle was boiling, I brought in the cake. 'Before anyone asks, I didn't make it. But I think Waitrose made a much better job than I'd have done. Happy birthday.'

With a little flourish, I placed the cake in front of my mother, and gave her a kiss. She blew out the candles in one go, and we all sang to her, out of time and out of tune. She seemed happy again. That was all I wanted for now.

***

It was later, sometime that night, when I woke with a slippery sliver of a memory. That party for me and Sarah. It was just finishing. Everybody had gone home. It was still light outside, and the patio was cluttered with the table and chairs and barbecue paraphernalia. The smell of burned hamburger lingered in the air. Polystyrene cups littered the lawn. I must have only had a cup or two of cider, but I felt slightly drunk and unreal. I had a sense that everything was about to change, that I was suddenly older, that soon I'd be leaving school and having all sorts of new experiences. And my mother put her arm around my shoulder and said to me, 'Did you enjoy the party?' And I said yes. And then she said, 'I think it's best if Sarah doesn't come round here again.' And I had no idea why she said it, because all our friends – Joshua's and Jake's and mine – had always been welcome at our house, whenever they felt like turning up. But I thought maybe she'd seen what a good time I'd been having with Sam and the other girls we'd invited, and she was giving me permission to break off my friendship with Sarah. Perhaps it was her way of saying to me that Sarah was holding me back, that I didn't have to spend the rest of my life feeling responsible for her.

And it might have been the next day, or very soon afterwards, that I decided not to call for Sarah on my way to school, and that our friendship ended.

Thirty Two

SARAH'S DIARY

25ᵗʰ April 2012

I feel dreadful. I feel like a book with all the pages ripped out and shredded. There's just the cover, with nothing in the middle of it to hold it together.

All these weeks, months, I've been turning myself inside out for Philippa. I've lived only for that hour a week when I've sat with her in her little blue room. I've shared my darkest, most secret fears and anxieties. All that childhood unhappiness of not being loved and cared about. I thought she would understand because of what happened in her own life. Nobody has seen me cry and be vulnerable except Philippa. I wanted my body and soul to melt into hers. To be a part of her. So we could share each other's pain and suffering. I thought I could trust her.

There was one story I still hadn't told her. I'd never told anyone. I'd tried to forget about it, but I couldn't, and things had happened that reminded me. I'd thought that, if I shared it with Philippa, she would cleanse me. She would give me words to say that would make it better. I was going to tell her today.

I dressed for the occasion. I wore my favourite vintage dress that Oliver liked so much, the one I wore in his portrait of me. The navy blue one, with little red flowers. A lovely gathered skirt. Tiny grey buttons down the front of the bodice, and two sweet little pockets on the chest. I think I look better in that dress than I do in anything else. 'It's absolutely *you*,' Oliver said to me, once.

How I saw things unfold, I would tell her the story. I would be brave. I would cry a bit but not too much. And then, when I'd finished telling it, she would see me sitting there, demure and – dare I say it – beautiful in that dress. And she'd stand and take my hands, and pull me towards her, and at last we'd embrace and hug one another, and feel each other's love, and she'd tell me I was a strong, brave, beautiful person.

But that wasn't the scenario. Because today, she wasn't the Philippa that I loved and trusted.

Just as I was about to begin my story, she yawned. A ghastly big gaping yawn, she didn't even try and hide it. I wanted to shrivel up, this wasn't how it was meant to be, but I asked her if she was bored with me. So she rubbed her forehead and said she wasn't feeling too good, she had a splitting headache.

So then I felt really bad, because all I'd been thinking about was me. Well, I know within our professional relationship that's legitimate, she's meant to focus on me, not the other way around. But even so, I should have been sensitive enough to realise that she wasn't just a listening machine, she had her problems too. And I wished I was able to make *her* feel better. I loved her so much. And I thought maybe my story could wait till another time. So I asked her if she wanted me to leave.

And then she said, all matter of fact, 'Let's finish the job now you're here.' And I felt as if I'd been kicked in the stomach. But I tried to keep my composure, and I asked her if that was all this meant to her. Just a job. And she didn't say anything. She sat there looking at me, with what seemed like contempt, and I started to suspect that maybe she didn't even like me, let alone love me. And I didn't want to start crying, not with Philippa feeling rough herself, but it was hard not to. And then she said, 'You're not going to start crying again, are you?' She looked at me as if she was really fed up and angry with me, the way my mother used to. And I told her not to be so beastly.

215

And I thought of those affirmations she'd taught me. *I am not a nuisance. I have a right to ask for what I need.* So I stood up and said them. And she looked pleased at first. I started to think that maybe she'd had a strategy, that she'd been testing me. And I still hoped that we could help each other, love each other even, so I said, 'I need us to give each other a hug.'

And that was when she told me to leave.

I was cast out into the void.

It was just like that other time, just like my story. The story I'd wanted to share with her.

And I thought I heard her say, 'If things are really that bad, there's always suicide.' But I must have imagined it. No therapist would ever say that to a client.

Thirty Three

It had been a busy day. There were student assessments approaching, and all the paperwork involved with that, and, in addition, I was sorting out the arrangements for a group visit to New York. One of the Graphic Design students had pulled out because of personal problems, which meant that, unless I could find a replacement, all the others might have to pay extra to cover the cost. Finally I managed to recruit a student from the Fine Art course, and we then had to clear it with her department.

I'd only just put down the phone, when I had a call from my mother. She almost never phones me at work. I've made it clear to her that not only is it unprofessional to be sitting in the office chatting on the phone about family matters, but I simply don't have the time.

But she sounded rather desperate, and I knew I had no choice but to hear her out.

'I had to ring you. It's something . . . I really don't know what to do about it. I'm so worried, I really don't know what to do.'

'OK, do you want to tell me what it is you're so worried about?'

'The thing is, I'm not supposed to know about it. I promised Philippa.'

Bloody Philippa again. That woman was starting to control our lives. And just when I thought the birthday party, only a few days ago, had helped to normalise things. I waited for her to continue.

'Mellie, I'm worried about her.' She hadn't called me Mellie since I was a child. When I was about fourteen I asked her to stop, and she did. She must have forgotten, regressed. 'I'm really worried,' she said again. 'I don't know what to do.'

The conversation wasn't going very far. My mother was worried. We'd established that. But it was out of character for her to sound so helpless.

'What do you want me to do about it? I mean, if you can't tell me what the problem is.'

'Not over the phone, I can't. It's too risky. Someone might be listening, you know how it is these days, all that hacking that goes on.'

'Do you want me to come over?'

'Could you? Tonight?' I could almost hear a little catch in her throat.

I had no plans. Justin had arranged to have a jam session with Ellie's husband Paul, who played keyboard. It felt like progress in our relationship, that he was starting to share my friends. To meet independently. 'OK, sure. I'll come straight from work.'

'I'll have a casserole in the oven. I know you'll be hungry. You're an angel.'

'I know I am.' It wasn't like her to be quite so appreciative either. Given that she'd spent most of her life looking out for other people, she expected everyone else to do the same. It rather shocked her that this didn't always happen.

***

We ate first. No wine. My mother didn't drink alcohol except on Sundays and special occasions. She rather frowned on people like me, who drank routinely. We didn't talk much over the table. I think we both wanted to get the eating out of the way so we could proceed to whatever it was she'd wanted me for. She must have realised that, if we hadn't eaten first, I wouldn't have had a stomach for eating.

'Leave the dishes. I'll sort it all out in the morning.' That was another first. 'I've got something to show you.'

'Can I just make a coffee.' I was gasping for one, and I thought whatever it was she had to show me could wait another couple of minutes. Micky, the spaniel, was blinking, as if puzzled to see me there midweek, and he kept sniffing around my legs. His nose started wriggling upwards towards my knickers. I was still in the skirt and tights I'd worn to work. I pushed him away.

My mother had declined coffee, but said she'd like a glass of water. I took her glass and my coffee mug into the living room. She was holding a brown envelope. There appeared to be nothing written on it, no address. It had obviously been sealed and then torn open.

'It's about Philippa,' she began. Well I already knew it was. She'd told me over the phone. 'She came round this morning, and I could tell immediately she wasn't quite her usual self, not as, what's the word, ebullient? You know how you can always tell when people are a bit down. I shut poor Micky in the kitchen, she can't stand dogs, and we sat down and had a coffee. I hadn't been expecting her this morning, and to be honest I'd had other plans. And then, just as we were drinking our coffee, Brenda came and knocked on the door, and Philippa said, "Oh god, not that awful woman again." I must admit she does have a point about Brenda, she does have a habit of popping up, bless her, whether she's wanted or not. But what with all her mobility problems she doesn't have a lot of excitement in her life, though she does have a lovely big family, children, grandchildren, great grandchildren. Well I didn't have the heart to shut the door on Brenda, so she came in and joined us, and I made her a coffee, and she drank it, and then Philippa said to her, rather rudely I thought, "I hope you don't mind, only I wanted a little private chat with Joyce." And so Brenda took the hint, only I could see she was a bit put out about it. She went out looking a bit huffy. I'll have to go and have a chat with her tomorrow, won't I, try and make amends.'

For somebody who'd wanted me round there so urgently, she did seem to be taking her time. But you can't rush my mother, she has to tell a story at her own pace.

'Anyhow, after Brenda had gone and left us on our own again, Philippa said, "I've got something I want to leave with you. Only I want you to promise me that you won't open it. I want you to keep it safe, and if anything happens to me, if I have an accident or a heart attack or something, anything can happen can't it, I'd like you to open it and read what's in there. I'm giving it to you because I know I can trust you." So I took it from her. And she said, "Do you promise?" And so I promised. And she said, "You've been a good friend." And then she said something rather strange. Whispered it really. She said, "There's always a way out, you might want to follow me." And off she went. And I put the envelope in that drawer in the sideboard, where I keep all my bills and receipts and bits and pieces – I'm afraid I don't like that paper-free stuff on the computer, even though it's supposed to be better for the environment, I suppose I'm a bit old-fashioned about this but I do like to have everything written down in black and white, and filed away. And by that time it was much too late to go where I'd been intending to go. As a matter of fact, I'd been thinking of joining a new reading group that's just started, a couple of people I know go there, I mentioned it to Philippa last week but she didn't seem interested. And maybe she's right, I do overcrowd my time, maybe I should try to relax a bit

220

more, spend time just being myself, instead of whizzing around like a blue-arsed fly, as if I'm trying to escape from whatever it is I am. Well that's what Philippa's said I do.

'But anyhow it was too late for the reading group, I'd missed it now, so I went out and did a bit of shopping. And I had my lunch. And then I started thinking about Philippa, and about that envelope she'd given me, and I knew I'd promised not to open it, but promises are easier to make than keep, aren't they, and I thought maybe it wouldn't hurt if I just took a little peep to see what was in it. She'd said I could open it if she had an accident or a heart attack or something, so I thought probably she was making a few arrangements for after her death, like people do. Like where she kept her will, or how she wanted her funeral to be, that sort of thing. Though really she should be telling all that to Brian, shouldn't she? But anyhow, I told myself I'd just take a peep, I wouldn't actually read it, and then I'd put it straight back in the drawer, and she'd never know.'

She was twiddling the lobe of her right ear, like I often do myself when I'm feeling unsure about something. Maybe it's a habit I picked up from her. She seemed to expect some sort of comment from me, something like 'Don't worry, no harm in having a peep, as you say she'll never know.' But I said nothing. I was impatient for her to reach the point.

'So I did. I only meant to have a quick glance, as I said, but I found myself reading it, and I couldn't stop, and anyhow,' she slowly took some handwritten pages, torn from a spiral notebook, out of the envelope, 'I can't possibly keep this to myself. It's put me in a moral dilemma. I wish to god I hadn't opened it.' She stood up suddenly, and seemed, now that she had the preamble out of the way, to be a bit more like her usual fidgety self. 'So that's why I rang you. I need you to read it and tell me what you think I should do. I'm going to make a cup of tea, do you want one?'

'I wouldn't mind another coffee.' I took the pages, and flicked through them. They were all written in the same blue ballpoint ink, so had apparently been completed in one or two sittings. To begin with, the writing was rounded and careful, like a child's. As it went on, it became spidery, and almost undecipherable. There were lots of underlinings and capitalisations. There was a red wine stain on one of the pages. I started to read.

Thirty Four

PHILIPPA'S CONFESSION

19th March 2013

I'm addressing this to you, Joyce. Because, in the short time we've known each other, you've become my best friend. The person I trust.

Before I die, I have something to confess. I need absolution, and I hope that by writing this down, by taking responsibility for my actions, I can set myself free. I spent the first part of my life blaming everybody but myself. Sandra, Lizzie, Ricky, Justin. It was only when I stopped blaming, and took responsibility for my life, that I achieved some sort of equilibrium. And I wanted to help other people do the same. That was my mission.

But things happened that I didn't plan for.

A name was mentioned at your birthday party, two days ago. The name of one of my clients. Sarah Bannister. Apparently she used to be Melanie's friend. And I have a feeling that Melanie knows more than she's saying. She had, after all, been looking at my diary. She'll snoop till she finds out what she thinks is the truth. Sadly, that's the sort of person she is. I know she's your daughter, but we can't help what we bring into the world.

The truth, of course, is much more complicated than anything she might find out about me. I'm not a bad person. I didn't want Sarah to die. I've often thought of death myself. I've thought of it as freedom, a wonderful release from all that angst we carry around inside ourselves. Sarah was full of angst. She was choking on it. But she couldn't let go of it. She wouldn't let me help her. She just wanted me to feel sorry for her. And I remember thinking to myself, if everything was so dreadful, why didn't she just kill herself and put an end to it all. But I wouldn't have said that to her. My only crime was not to give her one hundred per cent attention that last time we met. I know I should have done, I should have fulfilled my obligations as her therapist, but I had other things on my mind. And if she chose death, then that was her choice. It must have been what she was wanting all along.

But as for Lizzie, I wanted her to die.

I say in my video, the one I put on my website, that I didn't actually dislike Lizzie, I just thought she was weird. That's a lie. I hated her. I despised her, from the bottom of my heart.

Lizzie wasn't like Sarah. She was a different kettle of fish altogether. She had no intention of dying. She was a stubborn old bird. I'm mixing metaphors. Clichés. But, when it comes down to it, life and death are one big cliché. Whatever fancy language we use, it all comes down to the same thing.

And so, THE HATE. It started when she first moved in with us. I thought she was over-endowed with self-esteem. More than that, she had a superiority complex. She used to look at me as if I was the dog's dinner. Just because I was fat, and hadn't learned how to make the best of myself. Once she even had the cheek to start telling me what to do with my hair. Well, I wasn't having it. So I found a way to retaliate. I used to give her what I called MY LOOK. If looks could have killed. It was that sort of look, and I meant it. I perfected it.

And if that wasn't enough, there was AN INCIDENT. I can't say any more about that. It was all hush-hushed, swept under the carpet. I've sworn secrecy, and I do at least respect my promises.

224

Well things moved on. I was grateful to Lizzie for looking after Justin, that I do admit. If she hadn't, I'd never have been able to have a job and make my own way in life. And Justin, frankly, was a pain in the ass. I could never have spent much time at home with him. So yes, she had her uses.

But then, things moved on again, and changed. I grew older, of course, and I became a therapist. I found my purpose in life. I wasn't as useless as people thought I was. I didn't have to spend the rest of my life doing shit jobs for hardly any money. As a qualified therapist, I was worth at least £30 an hour. That was what I charged. Cheap at the price. But you can't really put a price on therapy. How much do you owe someone who changes your life for you? And that's what I did. Even for those people who came for just one session, the supposedly first session that I didn't even charge for. They didn't need any more. They went off into the world, heads high in the air. Just a single hour with me and their life was changed.

So back to Lizzie. When Peter left her, I tried to help her. I thought, now she knows what it feels like to be rejected and abandoned. And she was getting older. She was losing whatever it was she'd had that men seemed to find attractive, not that I could ever see what all the fuss was about. So I used to say to her, 'Of course you can meet someone else, you're a good-looking woman, you still have the rest of your life, you don't need to spend it on your own.' But she rebuffed me. She didn't seem to want my help, or maybe she was just being pig-headed. She said she was perfectly happy on her own. She said she had her art. That's exactly what she said. 'I have MY ART to keep me company.'

Well, you can't have a good fuck with art, can you? And I'm pretty sure that was what she really needed. I don't think she had a lot of it with my dad. That's why that other business happened. Our family secret. And that's why she got up to all sorts of perverted nonsense with Justin. That's why she tried to seduce my Brian. I think that was the last straw for me. What had happened before was happening again.

When I learned that Sarah had killed herself, I realised that, although it wasn't what I really wanted to happen, I actually had power over people. I had power over other people's life and death. If I hadn't given her the courage to realise her own needs, she would never have taken her own life. And that was what she wanted, deep down. She wanted to end it all.

But like I said, Lizzie was a stubborn old bird. It wasn't going to be easy. I had to give her a few pushes along the way.

Hypnosis wasn't part of my training, but I'd thought it might be a useful tool, and I'd read quite a bit about it. It's used in sales techniques, of course, to persuade people they can't live without something they can't really afford. Well, if people can be persuaded to part with their money, why can't they be persuaded to part with their life?

So that was my hypothesis, and I used Lizzie as my guinea pig. The fact that I'd wished her dead so many times must have helped, of course.

One of Lizzie's favourite songs used to be Forever Young, by Bob Dylan. I said to her, 'Don't you want to be forever young, like in that song you were always listening to? Wouldn't you like to die before you get old? Really old.' I was perceptive, you see. I knew Lizzie feared growing old more than death itself. In fact, she may have said this to me once. We'd had so many chats together since Peter had left her. I continued with this theme. 'If you die before you're too old, people will remember you as a young,

226

attractive person. You know you're still an attractive woman, but you won't be soon. All people will see when they look at you is an ugly old has-been.' I kept on repeating those words, embedding them into the conversation, every time I went round and had coffee with her. Then one time I went and the stupid cow was all excited because Kate was pregnant. Kate, her precious little daughter, who was. Only now she doesn't want to know about her mother, and I can't say I blame her. So Lizzie was going to be a grandmother. I said to her, 'That's good news for Kate. It's not such good news for you, though, is it, having a grandchild you'll never get to see. How often does Kate come here and see you? She'll come even less when she has a young child to worry about.' And I reminded her, once again, that soon she was going to be old and ugly and lonely if she stayed alive. And I said, 'All that art stuff you keep doing, you know nobody wants it don't you? At the end of the day, it's all going to have to go into landfill. Cluttering up the environment. You're not doing the world any favours.'

And then, that Friday in September, I decided it was time to implement what I'd been working towards. I chose that particular Friday because I knew Justin was away in London for the weekend. So I raided Brian's supply of morphine that he takes for his back troubles. He doesn't take it regularly, like he's supposed to, he stockpiles it for when the pain gets really bad. So I knew he wouldn't miss a few tablets. Besides, I was going to say that Lizzie must have taken them, one of the times she'd used the bathroom. I read on the internet that fourteen 15mg tablets would do the trick, so I took sixteen of them for luck. And I popped them in one of those little money bags you get from the bank, and put it in my handbag.

***

I rang Lizzie's doorbell, and she came to the door and said, 'Come in.' She always said that. Giving me permission. How dare she! As if I hadn't lived in that house before she did. So I went in, and I sat at the kitchen table, as I always did, while she fixed the coffee. There was a plate on the table, with crumbs on it, she must have used it for her breakfast toast. And so I tipped the tablets on to the plate. And I said to her, 'Can you get a glass of water.' She thought it was for me, and put it in front of me, but I said, 'No, that's for you', and obligingly she took it back. I said, 'You'll need that for the tablets.' She said, 'What tablets?' So I said, 'Remember what we've been saying. About how you want to die before you get any older.' And I carried on talking, on and on, in circles, repeating myself. I said, 'That song you like, Forever Young, that's how you want it to be for you don't you.' And she nodded. And I said, 'Now make it happen. Swallow the tablets.' And she did, one after another, without stopping. And it wasn't long before she started to look woozy. I told her to go and lie down on her bed. And then I spotted a little pile of plastic shopping bags on the floor. She was such a slut, she never tidied stuff away. And I said to her, 'Take one of those plastic bags up with you and put it over your head before you go to sleep. Only wait until you're on your bed. We don't want you falling over, do we?' And she said 'no' and she went upstairs like a little lamb. And that was the last I saw of her before she died.

I waited a while to make sure she'd settled down, and everything went quiet so I knew she must have done as I'd told her. I couldn't go up to check, of course, I didn't want to leave a trail. There were no fingerprints to incriminate me, only in the kitchen, and

I never hid the fact that I'd been there for our usual coffee and chat on the day she'd died.

***

Strange, I actually felt quite sad as I left the house and got into my little car to drive home. I suppose it was because she'd been part of my life for such a long time.

But lately, things have been playing on my mind. It's as if I've started to develop a conscience. I never set out to be a bad person, but sometimes I wonder if that's how people perceive me. Melanie, for instance. The way she looks at me. She doesn't look at me like Lizzie used to look at me, as if I'm shit. She looks at me as if I'm scary.

The truth is, I've lost my sense of mission. I no longer feel it's my destiny to heal people's lives, empower them, help them to be the people they really are. I suppose I've got that out of my system. I don't have a destiny any more. I think that's the worst thing, that emptiness. I think that's how Lizzie would have felt, without her art. I'm wondering now if that wasn't the worst thing I could have said to her, that nobody wanted her art, that it would all end up in landfill. She must have already known that, deep down, but probably nobody had ever said it to her before. But it needed to be said. She needed to accept the way things were.

And so there it is. The boring truth of the matter is that, just like Lizzie needed her art, and you, Joyce, need to fill up your life with all your good deeds and your causes, I needed my sense of destiny as a therapist. I needed to believe I could change people. That's gone now, and I have nothing else. Brian and I tick along, but I don't kid myself he loves me, and I certainly don't love him. I haven't loved anybody

229

since Ricky, and that was probably just an adolescent crush that went on longer than it should have done. I have sufficient money and a home. Whatever I need to keep me alive, I have. But I have nothing to look forward to, to live for. And that's no life.

And so, it's time to shed this mortal coil. This is rather a long suicide note, but I never did do things by half.

I've made my will, and all that I own – little as it is – will go to Brian. I may not love him, but he's the only person who's stood by me all these years.

He also knows the songs I want played at my funeral. Just three. I don't need to be greedy. And maybe a tribute or two, but that's for other people to decide. Lizzie had a beautiful funeral. I don't expect as much. I don't kid myself that people are fond of me, or even have a great deal of respect.

In my life, I've done some things wrong and some things right, and I take responsibility for all those things. What I'm about to do will be my final act. My final choice.

And so this long note is for you, Joyce. We all need someone to confide in. Do what you want with it.

Your friend,
Philippa

Thirty Five

By the time I'd finished reading, I felt as if I was upside down on a big wheel fairground ride that had stuck mid-cycle. I put the notepaper down on the coffee table, beside the coffee that had gone cold. 'You need to go to the police.'

'Would they be able to stop her?'

'From killing anybody else? Hopefully, yes, if you show them this.'

'But can they stop *her*? From killing *herself*.' By some huge effort of will, she'd forced herself to keep still and quiet while I was reading. Now she was pacing and jigging about.

I didn't give a shit about stopping Philippa kill herself. I just wanted to stop her doing any more harm to anybody else, such as my mother. She said she was her friend, but I didn't trust her. I didn't trust the way she was trying to change the way she lived her life. And look how the façade of friendship with Lizzie had ended up. My mother had been doing fine without Philippa's so-called friendship. And how were we to know she was serious about her final act, as she called it? It could be just histrionics. The mood of the moment. We'd all experienced her mood swings.

'She needs to be charged. She killed Lizzie. It's all there, written down.'

'Lizzie's dead. Nobody needs to know how or why, not now. That's over. She can't be brought back to life. It's Philippa I'm worried about. Only how can I stop her when I'm not supposed to have read what she's written?'

'Philippa's sick, and dangerous. We need to remember that. You rang me because you wanted my advice. I'm going to have to go to the police, if you're not.'

As I spoke, I couldn't help worrying how this would affect Justin, and consequently, of course, our relationship. Already it seemed blighted. But I'd never felt a sense of responsibility more clearly or keenly. I wanted Philippa locked away, unable to do more harm. I wanted to tell someone now, this very minute. Not next week, or the week after.

***

But, as it happened, even as we spoke, it was already too late.

***

This is what happened, though Justin's garbled phone message to me that evening made little sense, and I had to piece the picture together from the local TV news and newspaper reports.

There's a place not far from the B1150 from North Walsham to Norwich, where, if you stray, you might end up in one of the hundreds of narrow lanes, little more than tracks, that criss-cross the landscape of Norfolk like an old person's wrinkles. This particular lane is crossed by the train line that runs from Norwich to Sheringham, and back from Sheringham to Norwich. Few car drivers take this route, so there is no level crossing, no lights, simply a gate that can be opened and closed manually, and a phone from which anybody driving a vehicle can call and ask how long there is before a train is due, and whether it's safe to cross.

It was here, on 20th March 2013 at approximately 18.22, that a large middle-aged woman, wearing leggings, black boots and a black cape, parked her car, opened the gate, and walked into the path of an oncoming train. The car, a Renault Clio, was recorded to be owned by a Mrs Philippa Johnson.

Apart from the driver of the train, who was in a state of shock, and the passengers, whose journey was of course delayed, Brian was the first person to know of the death, and Justin the second. Brian identified what remained of his wife's body.

***

I can't pretend I was upset about Philippa. She'd deserved what she got, or rather what she'd chosen. That would have been *her* word. Chosen. And she had, of course, quite deliberately.

But I was concerned for Justin, and how he was going to cope with another suicide in his close family.

And now, of course, there was no question of going to the police, digging up dust that had settled, and upsetting Justin even more. We would have to destroy Philippa's confession. Now wasn't the time to be worrying about the truth, about what really happened. Whatever Sarah's ghost might have told me, and possibly Lizzie's too, the truth only mattered if it was helpful or necessary.

Besides, I was also concerned for my mother. Philippa must have walked into that train while we were drinking coffee, arguing about what to do with the notes she'd thrust into my mother's hand. Now she'd probably spend the rest of her life thinking she could and should have tried to stop her, as soon as she'd read the notes. Rather than phoning me, waiting for me to arrive, eating, talking, dithering. Even though Philippa had expressly told her not to open the envelope before she was dead.

***

I went with Justin to the funeral. It was a dry day, but cold and unspringlike. I expected it to be a small, subdued affair, but there were more people there than I'd expected. Some of them no doubt regarded it all as some weird sort of spectator sport. There'd been a fair bit of coverage of the suicide in the local media, and this had encouraged some ghoulish fascination with the other suicide in the family such a short while before.

Justin had been withdrawn and unapproachable at home. There was nothing I could say, all I could do was be there with him, try to show him I cared. He was wearing his only suit, and looked awkward in it, like a teenager going for his first interview. I couldn't stop myself from thinking that a dark dress would have suited him better.

The three songs Philippa had chosen were California Dreaming sung by the Beach Boys, Another Train by Pete Morton, and My Way sung by Nina Simone. The one about the train seemed a bizarre choice, given the way Philippa had chosen to end her life, but Brian, in his tribute, said it was a song she sometimes played to her clients, when she wanted to give them hope, and that she'd always said she wanted it played at her funeral. The words kept promising that the next train may be yours. I thought how Justin had become my own 'another train'. The right one, after all those wrong ones. I suppose I had Philippa to thank for that, at least. I held his hand, and he didn't resist.

The only member of the family not at the funeral was Kate, whose baby – a girl, Rosie – was only a few weeks old. I'd seen the photos on Facebook. She'd felt it was too far to drive Rosie all the way from Brighton, and she didn't want to leave her when she was still breastfeeding. She was probably glad of an excuse. There wouldn't have been all that much closeness between her and Philippa. I told myself that soon I'd have to contact Kate and ask her what she wanted to do about Lizzie's paintings, still taking up all that space in my mother's garage. Perhaps we could go and visit. I was curious to meet Lizzie's daughter, and besides I rather fancied a trip to Brighton.

***

However, it was Kate who made contact with us first. A couple of weeks after the funeral, she sent an envelope, by special delivery, addressed to Justin at our address. She'd emailed Justin the day before to say she was sending it, and that it was something he needed to know about Lizzie. Something she'd written, and given to Kate for safekeeping. She warned him that it might be something of a shock. I asked Justin whether he guessed what it might be, and he shrugged and said he had no idea.

We were both out at work and unable to sign at the time of delivery, so I went to the sorting office on my way home from work and picked it up. I was torn between curiosity and apprehension. I felt there'd been enough family confessions, although Justin still didn't know about Philippa's, and now, if I had anything to do with it, he never would.

I left Kate's envelope on the dining-room table, where I always put Justin's post if I picked it up first. When he came home, I poured him a glass of wine, and then I hovered in the kitchen, pretending to be busy at the sink, while he sat at the table reading it. The door was open between the kitchen and dining room, and I was watching him. He took a long while, and then he put it down and he just sat there, and his expression was inscrutable. All these family matters were driving a wedge between us. I was beginning to wonder whether we'd ever return to how we were before. Eating, drinking, having sex, enjoying each other. I couldn't stay in the kitchen forever, so I went into the dining room. 'Do you want to tell me what it's all about?'

He shrugged, and stood up. 'Read it if you want.' His voice sounded strangled. The pages were lying on the table, he hadn't bothered to put them back in the envelope. Head down, he left the room and charged upstairs. I waited a minute or two. I could hear him strumming chords on his guitar. Loud, angry ones. He hadn't even finished his glass of wine.

He'd given me permission to read it, and of course I needed to share this with him, whatever it was.

I sat at the table, where Justin had been sitting. The seat of the chair was still warm. The pages had been torn from an A4 loose-leaf pad, one of those with holes at the side for filing. I'd seen Lizzie's handwriting before, in her sketchbook. It was very different from Philippa's schizophrenic scrawl. It was bold, cursive, almost decorative, and punctuated by little squiggles and doodles. The first page was headed LIZZIE'S STORY, and a frame of wavy lines was drawn around the heading.

I started to read.

Thirty Six

LIZZIE'S STORY

And now I'm finally reaching the point of what my story was all about. I'm writing this for Justin. Sometime in the future, when Philippa and I are both dead, however old he might be by then, there's something I want him to know. It might be difficult for him, but I think he has a right.

But before I come to this, I want to record how delighted and excited I was when Kate rang the other day and told me she was expecting a baby. The next morning, I caught a train into Norwich. I went into Jarrolds, and spent ages looking at baby clothes and baby toys. I never had money to spend when Kate was a baby, everything she had was hand-me-down. Not that she minded, she was too young to know the difference. But I have money now – not a lot, but enough, a few small inheritances – and I wanted to spend, to celebrate. Only there was so much stuff, and I couldn't make up my mind what to buy, and then I thought maybe it was too early, that I shouldn't tempt fate, and that maybe I should wait a few months until we were sure everything was going to be alright.

So, instead, I went into Lacy Daze, and bought the most beautiful dress. I bought it for Justin. The girl who sold it to me had a French accent, she was very attractive. She was looking at me a bit curiously, so I said the dress was for my daughter. She said if it didn't fit I could bring it back. But I knew it would fit. I know Justin so well.

So this is my story. And Justin's. And it involves Philippa too. It's a hard one to tell.

Not long after Peter and I were married, when Kate was still a child, and Philippa was a moody teenager with a boyfriend called Ricky, Peter drove Philippa to see her mother, Sandra, who was living with her partner, Marianne. Philippa didn't want to go. It was a Saturday, and she'd rather have spent it with Ricky. So rather grumpily she followed Peter out of the house. She was wearing platform shoes that were supposed to be fashionable at the time, that she could hardly walk in, and she turned round and glared at me. After they'd gone, I took Kate to play with her friend across the close, a little girl called Joanne. Her mother Jean and I used to take turns looking after each other's daughters so we could have some time on our own. I was happy to have the house to myself. I wasn't in the mood for doing housework, I'd just started on an embroidery, a sort of Japanese design of birds and cherry blossom, and I was itching to get on with it. It was rather ambitious and I don't think I ever finished it. I never really enjoyed embroidery as much as painting, but it was easier to pick up and put down when a young child was around. Anyhow, I was working on this, and listening to my favourite Joan Baez record, I remember, when the doorbell rang. My first thought was that it was Jean come to bring Kate back already, because she'd hurt herself or something. A mother is always alert to something going wrong, to accidents of one sort or another. But it was Ricky.

I told him, 'Philippa's not here, she's gone to see her mother.'

He said, 'I know.' And then he said, 'Are you going to ask me in?'

Well, I didn't really have a choice. He was always in and out of our house, part of the family almost, whether I liked him or not.

He saw my embroidery and asked me what I was up to. I asked him if he wanted coffee, and he said yes, so I made us each a mug of coffee. He'd sat down in the armchair he usually shared with Philippa, and I sat in another one, and we didn't really talk. I was waiting for him to tell me what he'd come for. And then he said, 'You know I fancy you, don't you.'

Well, it felt a bit unreal. He was only about twenty years old. I was in my thirties, for god's sake. It felt a bit like The Graduate, only much less sexy. So I just ignored him.

But the next thing I knew, he was on top of me, his dick poking out of his jeans, and his tongue was in my mouth, and he had his hand up my skirt and inside my knickers. I wriggled a bit, and I expect if I'd struggled and screamed and kicked out he would perhaps have realised that I seriously didn't want whatever was happening, and it wouldn't have happened. But the thing was, I didn't feel particularly violated or anything like that because, after all, I'd been giving away so-called free love for most of my twenties. The truth was, I didn't really care one way or the other. And, if I'm honest, there may have been a part of me that wanted to feel attractive to someone. Peter and I, as I wrote earlier, had abandoned the sexual element of our relationship by a sort of mutual consent.

So this thing happened, and it never happened again. The next time I saw Ricky, he was back in the armchair intertwined with Philippa. The incident would have been over and pretty much forgotten if – and you can probably guess now where this is leading – I hadn't become pregnant.

There was no way I could pretend to Peter that the child was his. There was no way I was prepared to have an abortion, either. I'm not one of those anti-abortion people, I believe in a woman's right to choose, but for me it wasn't an option. There was another new life beginning inside me, and I believed that it should take its course. But the situation was complicated, with Ricky being Philippa's boyfriend, and Peter, when I told him I was pregnant, made it absolutely clear he wasn't prepared to father another child that wasn't his. So we decided I would complete the pregnancy, have the child adopted, and pretend to everyone who knew us that it had been stillborn.

But by some freakish coincidence, Philippa fell pregnant at roughly the same time. Ricky's sperm must have been having a laugh. The following months were, I think, the worst of my life. Philippa was happy, things had been a bit up and down between her and Ricky just lately, but she believed he wouldn't leave her now she was having his child, she'd got him where she wanted him. Peter was unhappy about both of us, Philippa because she was still a teenager and unmarried, and me because I was his wife and carrying a child that wasn't his. As for me, I just kept mood-swinging. I remembered how excited and fulfilled I'd felt when pregnant with Kate. I wanted to feel the same way with this second pregnancy, but how could I when I knew my child would be going out into the world without me.

You'd think all that was as bizarre as things could get, but Philippa and I ended up in hospital having our babies only hours apart. Mine was a week or so late, Philippa's slightly early.

And the most ironic twist of all was it was Philippa's child who was stillborn, not mine.

She was devastated. She lay in bed crying and howling. The nurses had to curtain her off, because she was upsetting all the other women. I suspected that it was not just the loss of the baby that had affected her, but also the fear of what might happen to her relationship with Ricky.

Meanwhile, my own child was born. A boy, just as Philippa's had been. I touched his little fingers and toes, I smelt the peachiness of his skin, and I fell in love with him, just as I had with Kate. I couldn't bear to part with him. And suddenly I realised I didn't have to.

And the rest – you've probably guessed by now.

Things were less rigid in those days. I don't think this could happen now, with everything computerised. But I talked to one of the nurses, and she saw my point of view. She fiddled the paperwork, and suddenly the stillborn child was mine – as Peter and I had planned – and my child became Philippa's. Philippa chose his name: Justin. She and Ricky registered his birth.

But of course, I always knew, and felt, he was my own. And as it happened, I had plenty of opportunity to bond with Justin. I watched him growing up, while Philippa was out all day at work. And now of course we're living in the same house. We like the same music. We sometimes share a joint. We talk to each other. He has nothing in common with Philippa. I know he feels he was a disappointment to her. But I believe in him. I think he'll make his way in life as a good person. And I may not have been a mother to him in the eyes of the law, but I've been a mother in every other way.

As I said at the beginning, I'm not a writer, and I may not have told this story as well as I should have done. But it's the story I needed to tell. I hope that, when Justin eventually reads it, he will understand. That he'll forgive me.

Thirty Seven

I put Lizzie's story back in the envelope. I realised I was crying. For Lizzie and Justin. Even for Philippa. And for myself. With each new revelation, the abyss between Justin and me seemed to be increasing. I thought of how disturbed I'd felt when I'd first discovered his transvestism. How, initially, that had felt like the end of our relationship. Now, with the ground beneath our feet constantly shifting, each day bringing further chaos and instability, Justin's cross-dressing just seemed like a minor blip, already absorbed into the routine of our lives. But these new discoveries were much more fundamental. I was just an ordinary person, from an ordinary and mostly happy home. I wasn't equipped for all this complexity.

One evening, when Justin had been out, I'd played one of Lizzie's old CDs, The Time Has Come, by Anne Briggs. I hadn't come across her before. According to the sleeve notes, it had first been recorded as an album in the 1970s. The singer's beautiful guitar playing and gentle, haunting voice had echoed in my head long after the CD had ended. There was one particular track, called Tangled Man, that seemed to encapsulate my relationship with Justin. The words came into my head, as I sat there, thinking about Lizzie and Philippa and Justin. Tangled he might be, but I wanted to be tangled with him, now more than ever. Somehow I would have to find the strength for this. Whatever had happened to him in the past, I wanted us to be part of each other's future.

***

I went upstairs and knocked on his door. Unlike me, he still had his own private space. I knew how he needed this, for a whole range of reasons.

He ignored me at first, and went on strumming his guitar. I just stood there, and he must have realised I wasn't going to go away, because everything went quiet, and he said 'OK', though I could hardly hear him through the door.

He was sitting on the floor, and he looked very pale, and angry rather than upset.

'I've read it.'

He nodded. He didn't turn to me, just continued looking down at the carpet, lower lip stuck out like a child in a strop.

I sat down beside him, keeping a small space between us. I said, 'When you're ready to talk about it, you know I'm ready to listen.'

'There's nothing to say.'

We went on sitting there like that, I don't know how long, and eventually he said, 'You want to know how I feel?' I didn't prompt him. We shared another few seconds of silence, that horrible, eternal silence, and then he said, 'Apart from feeling deceived, I feel disgusted. With Lizzie. With myself. That closeness I had with Lizzie, thinking she was my *step* grandmother, that we weren't even blood-related. That modelling I did, with the clothes. Do you imagine I would have done that, if I'd known she was my mother? It all seems incestuous. As if the boundaries were all wrong. And Lizzie must have known that, she shouldn't have let it happen. That's what's going through my mind right now, if you want to know.'

I sat there, and I didn't know how to respond. And then I said, 'I hear what you're saying, but actually I have a different take on this.' I chose my words carefully, more carefully than I've ever chosen any

243

words before in my whole life. 'That stuff with the clothes and the modelling. The fact she bought those dresses for you. You might think it's incestuous, but the way I see it, it's about love. I think she loved you, like a mother's supposed to do, unconditionally. I think that buying the dresses for you, and doing those amazing drawings she did of you wearing them, that was her way of saying that everything was fine with you. Like you said to me before, she was cool about it. She wasn't going to flip just because you liked to wear dresses. Not the way Philippa did. The way I did.'

He didn't answer, but I could tell at least he'd listened to what I'd said, even if he wasn't ready to believe me. And we just sat there, side by side, not saying anything, until, feeling awkward, I stood, and left him sitting, and went back downstairs.

Thirty Eight

I emailed Kate. With Justin's permission, of course. Following his outburst about Lizzie, he hadn't wanted to talk about the matter further, and I didn't want to pressurise him. But I imagined Kate worrying that she hadn't heard back from us, wondering whether she'd done the right thing, sending Lizzie's story to Justin so soon after Philippa's death.

So I emailed, thanking her for sending it, saying that it had of course been a shock but that it was good to have everything out in the open. I said that it would be good to meet sometime, maybe in the summer. Especially now we knew that she and Justin were sister and brother. And I asked her advice about Lizzie's paintings. She didn't seem to know that my mother still had them in her garage.

And she replied.

Hi Melanie

So good of you to get back to me. I knew it would be traumatic for Justin, reading what Lizzie had written. Though selfishly, I was relieved to share it. It felt such a burden, knowing this thing that had been a family secret for so long, and not being able to divulge it to the person who really needed to know. My mother always had a soft spot for Justin, and I think they grew really close as time went on. She loved it that he was into music. She was always a bit disappointed in me for not being more creative. She couldn't understand that I wasn't particularly talented artistically, and that I wanted to have a different sort of career. I actually admired my mother. She always seemed such a strong person, such an individual. I still find it hard – almost impossible – to think of her ending her life like that.

Particularly when she'd seemed so delighted when I told her I was expecting. I feel quite sad that she never had a chance to meet Rosie. I agree, it would be nice for us all to get together sometime soon, and for Justin to see his little niece.

Regarding my mother's paintings, please just dispose of them however you want. I'm sure the charity shops will take them, if only for the frames. I know some of them were rather good, and in fact we have a couple of her landscapes on our walls. There is just one painting I'd like you to save for me, if you come across it. I don't think my mother ever quite finished it, but it's a portrait of me when I was about eleven. She made my hair look orange, and I'm wearing a blue T-shirt that's way too big for me, so my arms look like matchsticks. For some reason I always liked that portrait.

She did far too much stuff, of course, and she never tried to sell it. She could have been quite successful, probably, but sadly it's too late now.

I'm attaching a photo of me with Justin, when I was about six years old and he was a baby. I wish I'd known he was my brother.

I look forward to meeting you both soon.

Love,

Kate

***

I printed out the photo she'd attached. Baby Justin was grinning toothlessly. Kate was smiling and frowning at the same time. Smiling for the camera and frowning because of whatever was going on in her mind. I put the photo in a frame, and stood it next to one that had been taken of me with Joshua and Jake when we were children, sitting on the lawn in our lovely old garden.

The portrait Kate had mentioned happened to be the one I'd brought home with me. The one that Oliver had said reminded him of paintings by Alice Neel. Kate had said they had a couple of Lizzie's landscapes on their wall, and I thought it would be good to have the two that I'd taken from Lizzie's house hanging in our front room. So I hung them there, rather guiltily removing two of my father's wildlife photos, which I banished to the back bedroom with the shoes and the exercise bike and Lizzie's portfolios.

I thought of how I'd felt looking at Kate's teenage bedroom in Willowherb Close, embarrassingly like my own. I realised we must be about the same age, though perhaps she was a year older than me. We might even have gone to the same school, without knowing each other. You seldom have much to do with anyone in the years above or below you.

Thirty Nine

SARAH'S DIARY

1st May 2012

This is the story I've never told. The one I'd wanted to share with Philippa, only she'd been too beastly to listen to me.

It happened at a birthday party that I shared with Melanie. Our joint sixteenth.

I was never allowed to have parties at home, because of the way things were, with my mother's depression. Only once, I invited Melanie to have tea with us, when we were first friends, and I was so anxious and embarrassed I don't think I spoke a word the whole teatime.

But I was always in and out of Melanie's house. That big old house they lived in. At first, I found her family a bit overwhelming – everybody talking at once across the table, and her brothers charging around the house, always boisterous and noisy. But then we all grew a bit older, and when I was about fifteen I started to fancy Jake. Well no, I didn't 'fancy' him, that's what the other girls would have said. I started to fall in love with him. There's a big difference. I think he was seventeen at the time, and he was past that scruffy, spotty teenage-boy stage, and he was quite good looking. In retrospect, of course, I was more in love with the idea of being in love with someone. Jake just happened to be the love object. Anyhow, I convinced myself I was in love, and every night when I was home in bed I used to agonise about him, in that way you do when you're adolescent and you know nothing about relationships and sex, you just need someone to agonise over. I didn't tell Melanie, or anybody else. Before that, the only person I'd been in love with was my

French teacher, a woman. Nobody knew about that either of course.

I always thought Melanie's mum felt a bit sorry for me. She must have known a bit about my parents, because they used to go to the dentists, where she worked. Whenever I was around in their house, she always used to chat to me, whatever came into her head. The weather, the curtains she was making, the price of groceries, anything. I don't know whether she just chatted like that to anyone and everyone, or whether she was trying to make me feel at ease. I don't think I responded much. I was always a bit scared of grown-ups. Melanie's dad never had a lot to say, but he used to smile at me, and sort of nod.

I'm not sure whose idea it was to have this party, but the summer was lovely that year, as I recall, and somehow it was decided to have a barbecue in Melanie's garden. Her family had this big garden, wild and rambling, with a patio that led from the French windows.

I was so excited and full of hope. I'd never really talked to Jake, not one-to-one, but I'd dreamed that this was the day he'd realise he loved me. He would look at me, and our eyes would meet, and he'd have this flash of recognition, and somehow we'd find our way into each other's arms. Melanie'd already had her birthday, and her mother had taken her to a show at the Theatre Royal for a treat, and she'd had some new clothes. My birthday was two weeks after hers, and we had the party on a Saturday between the two dates.

I was going to wear my best dress, in fact my only dress apart from school uniform, but Melanie said come in your jeans, it's going to be a barbecue. So I persuaded my mother to give me some money for a new top to wear with the jeans, in advance of my birthday. It was pink, with lace edging.

I spent ages putting on make-up so that it didn't really look like make-up. Even so, I was the first person to turn up at the house. There was a table on the patio, with plates of crisps and nuts, and a birthday cake with sixteen candles, made by Melanie's mum. She said we were going to have to blow them out together, eight candles each. I was a bit worried that I'd get it wrong, and blow out more than my share, so I made up my mind that Melanie would have to have the first blow. Her father was preparing the barbecue. Melanie was fidgety, picking at the crisps. And then other people started to arrive. Melanie had asked some of our friends at school. They were more her friends than mine, I didn't really know them, and I always had the feeling they didn't like me. Sam and Debbie and Francesca, their names were. Others, I can't remember. We hadn't asked any boys of our own age, but we knew Joshua and Jake would be inviting some of their mates. Melanie had been out with one of Jake's friends a few times, but she told me she didn't really fancy him, it was just someone to go out with. Jake wasn't there at first, and I kept looking around for him.

And then he arrived, and he was with a girl. She had long dark hair and tanned skin, and must have been about eighteen. I'd never seen her before. I asked Melanie who she was, and she said it was his new girlfriend, Lucy. She said he was really serious about her.

Well, all my hopes and dreams came crashing earthwards, and I tried desperately not to cry. I was skilled at not crying. I had to be at home, because the only person allowed to cry was my mother. Suddenly the party I'd looked forward to so much became a nightmare, and I longed for it to be over.

Joshua poured cider into a Styrofoam beaker and handed it to me. I drank it quickly. I thought it might make me feel a bit better, or at least help me to pretend I was having a good time. Joshua didn't have a girlfriend, not just then, and he was helping his father with the barbecue. We all scuttled around with our paper plates. I felt rather sick, not hungry at all, but someone dumped a hamburger and a couple of chicken wings on my plate, and I forced myself to eat them. My hands were greasy, and I wiped them on my jeans that I'd so carefully washed and ironed. Melanie sloshed some more cider into my beaker, and then her own, and I remember her mother said, 'Be careful how much you drink, Melanie.' Everybody was talking and laughing, but as far as I was concerned it could have been another language, everything was blurring, none of it was making sense.

And then I started feeling really sick. There was a downstairs loo, but I didn't want anyone to know I was being sick, so I ran upstairs to the bathroom. I knelt on the floor, retching and heaving into the toilet. I've never drunk cider since then. At last I thought I was emptied out, but I still felt dreadful. I washed my face and dried it on one of the bath towels. There was sick in my hair, and I wiped it off with the same towel. And then I put my nose to the towel to see whether it smelt, and it did, so I bunched it up and left it on the floor, so that Melanie's mother would put it in the wash.

I suddenly remembered that we still hadn't blown out the candles on the cake. I couldn't possibly do it now. I couldn't face going back down to the barbecue. I could hear people laughing and talking, and there was music, probably dancing. I just wanted to disappear, and wake up in my own bed, at home.

I went into Melanie's bedroom, where I'd sat with her many times, talking about school and make-up and music and boys. I closed the door behind me, and lay down, on top of the quilt on her single bed. I buried my face in her pillow. I could smell her shampoo, mixed with the smell of sick in my own hair. And that was when I started crying. I'd never cried like that before, and I couldn't stop. Not even when the door opened and someone came in.

It was Melanie's dad. He sat on the bed and put his arm around my shoulders. I was still shaking and sobbing, I couldn't stop myself. He said, 'Now, now, what's all this about?'

And I managed to stop sobbing for long enough to blurt out, 'I was in love with Jake.'

And he said, 'Come on now, you don't want to shed all those tears for him. He's not worth it. You're a beautiful young girl.'

I thought he was just being kind to me. Nobody'd ever been kind to me like that before. I could still taste sick, and I swallowed, hard, and tried to stop crying.

And then suddenly I saw that his jeans were unzipped, and his thing was out, and it was huge, I couldn't believe how big it was. It was shiny, as if he'd been polishing it. He said, 'Stroke it.' And I just lay there, terrified. And he said, 'Come on, it won't bite.' And I was the sort of girl who always did as I was told, so I touched it, tentatively, with one finger, as if it was a snake. And he took my hand and placed it around it, so I was holding it. I just felt like a ragdoll, as if I didn't have a mind or will of my own. He took my arm and gave it a little shake.

And then he rolled me around, on to my back. And the next thing was he had his hand inside my new pink top, he'd moved my bra out of the way, and put his hand on my right breast, that still hadn't grown. He pinched it, hard. He was hurting me, and I tried not to call out. He unbuttoned my jeans and lifted up my bottom so he could pull them down, they were around my knees, and he was on top of me, his pants and jeans

252

around his ankles, and his legs were white and hairy, and his thing was between my legs, and I knew he was about to put it inside me.

The door opened, and Melanie's mum was there, and she looked absolutely wild, I'd never seen her look like that, but wild in a quiet way.

And she said, 'You'd better get dressed. The two of you.'

And we both did. Neither of us spoke.

Melanie's dad went first, I'm not sure where he went. There was a stickiness on the inside of my thighs. I pulled up my jeans and rearranged my bra. I waited as long as possible after he'd gone, but I knew I'd have to go downstairs. I went into the garden, and there was still the smell of burned hamburgers, and I could see Melanie having a laugh with Sam. Other people seemed to be drifting around the garden, or sitting in the conservatory. Francesca, who always used to look at me as if I was a waste of space, the way Sam did, was snogging with someone I didn't know. She glanced at me, over his shoulder. I couldn't see Jake and his girlfriend, nor Joshua. I don't know what happened to the birthday cake.

Melanie's mum put her arm around me and said, 'I think that's enough for today. I think you'd better leave.' And then she said, 'It's probably best if you don't come round here anymore.'

I went home, and crept upstairs, so I wouldn't have to talk to my parents.

That was Saturday.

On the Monday, I wasn't sure what would happen, whether Melanie would call for me as usual. I thought I'd better wait and see. I stood at the gate. I kept looking at my watch. My mother came to the front door and said, 'You're going to be late for school.' She was still in her dressing gown. I didn't know what to do. She said, 'If she comes, I'll tell her it was getting late, you've gone on ahead. You don't need her to hold your hand, do you?'

When I walked into the classroom, the register had been taken. The teacher looked at me and sighed, but didn't say anything. I could see Melanie was already there. Sam was sitting next to her, where I usually sat. I found a spare place and sat down. Melanie was pretending not to notice me, but I could tell she was watching me out of the corner of her eye. We never spoke to each other again. Not then. Not until we happened to meet all those years later, at work.

***

So that's the story I wanted to tell Philippa. The story I'd never told.

And now it never will be told. But at least I've written it. The writing of it was a sort of closure. I shall shred this diary, and nobody will ever see what I've written. But they say writing stuff down can be a form of therapy, and I think that's true.

I wonder how it would have been, to actually tell the story to Philippa. That's something I'll never know.

But I did learn something from her. I learned how to say, 'I have a right to ask for what I need. I need us to give each other a hug.'

Even though it never happened.

Even though she said, 'I think you'd better leave.' Just as Melanie's mother had done.

But, come to think of it, maybe I was right to trust her after all. She knew what I really wanted. Those words I thought I heard her say at the end. She knew what I wanted was an end to all the pretence. All the posturing and impostoring. She knew what I really wanted was oblivion.

And, when I do what I've decided to do, I shall think of her holding my hand, her fingernail digging into my palm, as I slip away.

Forty

Tomorrow's Sunday. I shall be having lunch with my mother, as usual. She said there was something she wanted to tell me. She said it was something that happened a long time ago, something she'd tried to put out of her mind, that she'd always been too busy to think about, but for some reason, lately, it had been bugging her.

It can't be anything too bad. She's always been a bit of a worrier, and lately she seems to dwell on things.

And I have something to tell her, in exchange. Something much more important. Some good news, for a change.

Justin and I are going to be married. After all that weird stuff that's been happening around us, I want us to try and make everything normal and good. Well, as normal as it's possible to be, being married to a transvestite. I want my life to feel like it used to be, when I was growing up. Our happy family life in that lovely old house, where people were always welcome. When one day followed another, and there were no horrible surprises.

***

There's never a right time in a relationship to start talking about marriage. But I found myself doing it. Today. A lovely Saturday afternoon, late June, that I know I'll remember. And it just happened. I just happened to broach the subject, without really thinking about it overmuch.

It had been a dreary spring, but today the weather was warm and sunny for a change. Just a breeze, and a scattering of clouds. Justin didn't seem to feel the pull to keep going back to North Walsham and meet his friends in the pub any more, at least not every weekend, and we'd decided to start attacking the wilderness that was the garden. We thought we'd tidy up the back-yard, which was littered with junk, and make it into a little patio with a table and chairs, and potted flowers and herbs. We'd dig up all the weeds, and put some turf down for a lawn, and then there'd be a trellis, and beyond it, at the bottom of the garden, we'd grow vegetables and maybe have an apple tree. My mother had found a book about small gardens in one of the charity shops, and given it to me, and I kept looking at the pictures and imagining how our own would look. We could ask our friends round for barbecue suppers or evening drinks.

So we'd bought a garden fork and a spade, and Justin was stripped to the waist, digging up the weeds, and I'd gathered up all the junk – empty wine bottles and beer cans and a broken bird table and a twisted old bicycle wheel – and loaded it into a rusty old wheelbarrow someone had left there that was still useable, and I'd wheeled it round the back alley and stashed the junk in the boot of my car, ready to drive to recycling. I didn't even know where the nearest recycling tip was.

I was going to throw some water and detergent around the yard, but I needed a rest. I carried a couple of dining chairs out to the back-yard that was soon to be a patio, and then I went to the fridge and took out a couple of cans, and we sat there, not really talking, each in our own space.

And then I said, 'Can we get married sometime?' As if it was just a casual everyday thing, like saying, 'Shall we have a takeaway tonight?'

And Justin looked a bit surprised.

And I said, 'I know we don't need to. I just think it would be a nice thing to do. Nothing big and expensive. No stag parties and hen parties. Just family and close friends. Maybe a bit of a honeymoon. It's not about having a wedding, all that silly stuff, it's just about us. Being married.'

And he shrugged, and he smiled with his eyes the way he does, and he said, 'OK, why not?'

And we left it at that.

And I felt something lift and flutter inside me, a sort of excitement, a looking forward.

Lightning Source UK Ltd.
Milton Keynes UK
UKOW04f2346130214

226470UK00002B/118/P